The Tamar Black Saga – Book Seven

BY NICOLA RHODES

IBSN: 978-0-9561495-7-2

In the same series

Djinnx'd
Reality Bites
Tempus Fugitive
The Day Before Tomorrow
Faerie Tale
Anything But Ordinary
Rise of the Nephilim
Pantheon

~ Chapter One ~

ON ONE OF THOSE late summer days, the kind that seems hotter than ever, if only because you were expecting it to be cooler by now, a girl of the teenage persuasion, very much so, in fact, extremely teenage – you know what I mean, stomped down the back steps of her magnificent home and dropped unceremoniously onto the bottom step with a look of deep chagrin on her face.

She was dressed almost entirely in black, as becomes the disaffected youth of any era. She may have been pretty, or even beautiful, it was hard to tell underneath the thick layers of makeup, which she wore like protective armour. "Keep away", her whole appearance and demeanour seemed to say. "I bite."

Nevertheless, a boy about two or three years older than herself (around eighteen years, not quite a man, but no longer a child) with jet black hair like her own and a gentle expression dared her wrath and sat down beside her giving her an enquiring look.

'*Parents*!' she huffed expressively, rolling her eyes. This was a standard beginning for a fifteen year old diatribe. 'If they aren't going off to save the world from pixies or dragons or some such shit, then they're grounding you for turning the library into an indoor swimming pool.'

This was a less standard continuation of the diatribe, but the boy never batted an eyelid. He was used to this sort of thing. He suppressed a smile as she continued.

'I mean it's not like I did it on *purpose!*' wailed the girl, giving her companion a sly sideways glance to see if he was following her. He raised his eyebrows at her sceptically.

'Oh, all *right,*' she conceded. 'But I was going to turn it back. I mean what's the big deal anyway?'

'Your Dad's mad keen on all those old books Iffie, you know that.'

Iphigenia Black turned her father's soulful blue eyes, ringed heavily in black kohl pencil, on her companion. 'I think mum thought it was quite funny actually,' she said. 'But they always stick together. – *Parents!*' she reiterated, waving enough rings to knock out a buffalo.

Iphigenia was going through what Tamar, who had read every book on child rearing printed since 1902, referred to as a "phase". This "phase" consisted mainly of her dressing like a fugitive from a crypt – cobwebs and all (in fact most of her clothes seemed to be spun directly from this material) wearing enough metal to make up a suit of armour and listening to the kind of music that made your ears bleed. Denny, rather predictably, saw all this rather differently from Tamar. He thought his daughter was cool.

Despite taking her mother's name – Black being so much cooler than Sanger.* Iffie, as she was usually called, adored her father. He was, she thought, the coolest, bravest, strongest and yet the gentlest, sweetest man in the world. The feeling was mutual. Her mother was more remote, the disciplinarian. And yet Iffie knew, deep down, that her mother's love for her was

---

* It had been suggested by Jack - Finvarra's boy, who had been a mere three year old curly mop when she was born and whom she had grown up with, that Iffie combine these names but the results - "Sack", "Slack" or possibly "Banger" had not been encouraging. – Double barrelling i.e. – "Sanger Black" or "Black Sanger" had not even been considered, which was probably just as well. Black Sanger, Denny said, sounded like a species of monkey.

fierce and protective. For her daughter's sake, as Iffie knew well, Tamar would scheme and kill.

Jack rubbed his head thoughtfully; these conversations were getting more difficult as Iffie grew older. He himself, being not human, but, in fact, a genuine Faerie Prince (although that is not as romantic as it sounds) had never really suffered from teenage angst which is a purely human complaint. And yet she always turned to him to moan at as if he would understand. He did not. All he could do was listen with his habitual courtesy and try to restrain some of her wilder notions. Perhaps this was the best thing he could have done after all.

'I don't think Dad's actually *keen* on all those old books,' she said now. 'He just thinks they're important or something.'

'Then perhaps they are,' said Jack mildly. He had a profound respect for Denny as did most people who lived in close proximity to him.

'Whatever,' said Iffie, signalling that she was fed up with this subject now.

'Still, it was a pretty impressive spell,' said Jack placatingly. 'I bet they were impressed underneath.'

Iffie shrugged. She had been born without powers since neither Tamar nor Denny had been born with their powers and they were unable to pass them on genetically. The only thing, Tamar had said, that we may have passed on is a predisposition to acquire power from some haphazard event – like we did.

But, rather than trust to fickle fate, Hecaté the goddess of witches had taken a hand, and from the age of three Iffie had been trained by her as a witch. Twelve years of intense training from the goddess of witchcraft herself had made Iphigenia Black, at only fifteen years of age, the most accomplished witch who had ever lived.

And, although she had no actual native powers, she did have a strange immunity to the powers of others that she had no doubt acquired before she was even born, simply to shield her from her mother's fiery spirit that could destroy, at a touch, an ordinary human. Somehow, nature had found a way.

This also meant that no kind of magical powers were of any use against her. No spells could be cast on her that would work. They simply bounced off her.

Jack thought Iffie was lucky. He had never really known his mother, and his stepmother, Cindy, whom he had thought of as his mother far more than the unknown real mother that he could not remember, had walked out on his father taking her own son with her fifteen years earlier, leaving his father heartbroken, and himself devastated. She had not been seen or heard from since then. It was something that was never spoken of.

He often wondered about that stepbrother who had looked exactly like him and had even borne the same name. Did he still look exactly like him, or had the long separation wrought differences in their appearance?* Where was he now? Did he ever wonder about *him*?

He spoke only to Iffie about these feelings. No one else wanted to talk about it, least of all his father, who had been a broken man from the day she had left.

Iffie gave him a shrewd look. All witches have exceptional intuition and Iffie's was so well developed as to be almost akin to telepathy. 'You're wondering about your stepbrother again aren't you?' she said sympathetically.

Jack nodded. 'I wonder where he is all the time,' he confessed. 'How could she just take him away like that?' he burst out suddenly in an uncharacteristic display of anger. 'Why did she leave anyway? Families are supposed to stick together.'

Iffie nodded understandingly. If her own mother or father were to desert her, she felt, she might never recover from it.

She took his hand and squeezed it gently. 'You'll always have me,' she assured him.

* * *

---

* Jack, being a Faerie changeling, had had to more or less extrapolate his own face based on the face he had taken as a child; his stepbrother may have grown up looking very different.

Ashtoreth came and knelt before his mother in the huge and shining circular throne room, built of honey coloured stone; the floor paved in golden streaked marble. Behind her, several pillars rose up, through which could be seen a glittering stretch of ocean beneath a cloudless blue sky. She was sitting on the throne itself; a large square affair built in the same stone as the walls and pillars, but intricately carved and gilded.

This ritual was repeated every day at the same time, but Ashtoreth did not resent it. Indeed, these days, it was one of the only occasions when he got to see her.

She was dazzling, wonderful, like a pure light – a golden goddess truly.

He remembered little about his early life, before she had taken him away from the evil man who had stolen him from her and tried to foist an impostor upon her. When she had discovered his treacherous deception, he and his cohorts had taken her prisoner and forced her to live with him in seeming amity, but she had escaped and rescued him. Brought him here to this shining palace by the sea and here they had remained hidden and safe until it was time for them to defeat the evil ones who had tyrannised over the world long enough.

He was to do this, he understood. The son of an angel, he and only he, had the power to defeat such evil.

But sometimes, early memories would intrude. Memories of a happy home full of laughter and people. Nice people, or so they had seemed. A gentle father a small brother, who was like looking into a mirror and others, including a woman with dark hair and flashing eyes who, had it not been the basest treachery to think so, he would perhaps have thought had been more beautiful even than his mother. And a man with scruffy blond hair who, he thought, had sometimes made his mother cry. He hated that man.

He looked up at his mother who threw back her hood and revealed her face to him, a daily treat; it was such a beautiful face. Then his eyes narrowed, *he* was there again, lounging on the arm of the throne. He had aged though, Ashtoreth thought with satisfaction. Not like his mother who was as young and beautiful as she had always been. In time, he would grow old and die, or his mother would tire of him as he became an old man. And then it would just be the two of them, forever. But first, there was the great task. He was almost ready; he felt it. He was growing strong in his righteousness. He chafed to begin the battle against evil, was he not eighteen years old now? – A man.

'My son,' said Cindy. 'You are looking well this morning.'

'Mornin' Ash,' added her companion insolently.

Ashtoreth snarled silently, but his mother only smiled – *why did she like that man so much? Why did she allow him such liberties?*

'I *feel* well mother,' he said choosing to ignore the interloper.

Cindy turned to Slick who had still not revealed his true name to her, and to Ashtoreth's pleasure said. 'Why don't you leave us alone?' It was an order, as both Ashtoreth and Slick knew very well.

Slick made a sulky face, but he left with alacrity. Cindy's wrath was not something any sane man would want to incur.

'Why do we have to have that man around mother?' said Ashtoreth sulkily.

'I know you don't like him darling,' said Cindy. 'Why?'

'He's not good enough for you mother.'

Cindy laughed. 'No dear, he is not. But he is our only ally. And you wouldn't want your mother to be lonely would you?'

'We don't need him,' said Ashtoreth. 'And you wouldn't be lonely mother, you'll always have me.'

In many ways, due to his sheltered upbringing, Ashtoreth was completely innocent.

'It's not quite the same darling,' said Cindy, thinking that perhaps she should have explained a few things to him at some point – it had just never occurred to her to do so. Ashtoreth was not a son to her – he was a weapon, a highly trained extremely powerful weapon that she intended, when the time was right, to use in her revenge against Denny and Tamar. If he died in the execution of that revenge, she would not care at all, as long as *they* did too.

She found his complete devotion to her an embarrassment if anything; and if he was going to start being jealous of her company, it would become even more difficult to curb her irritation.

It was a fine line she was walking here; she had allowed him no friends and certainly no girlfriends. His absolute loyalty to her must not be divided. And yet, *had* there been a girlfriend, at least they would not be having this embarrassing conversation.

Cindy had never heard of Oedipus, but she had a dim idea of what was happening here. Her son was a normal healthy eighteen year old with all the usual drives latent within him. Of course, she had no desire to awaken those desires personally, but neither must anyone else. Much better that he channel these feelings into a passion for his mission.

'*I* don't matter, darling,' she said now. 'Nothing matters except what must be done. The battle against evil. Oh my son, you must be ready when the time comes. Do not think about me, or about anything but your great task. Do you understand me?'

'*That ought to do it*,' she thought.

'Yes, mother,' Ashtoreth bowed his head reverently. She was so wise, his mother, so selfless and dedicated.

But when he had left her, the doubts began to resurface, faint memories of another life. Apart from the thin man with the blue eyes, whose face he could still see so clearly – making his mother cry – the people he remembered did not seem evil in his memory. They seemed kind, and he thought there had been love in that place. Love for him. But of course, he was foolish, his mother, who was so much wiser than he was, had told him that they were bad. And so they must be. They had pretended love, pretended kindness. He had only been child, how would he have known the difference? His mother was a goddess and his father an angel. How could his cause be anything other than righteous? He was good, and if he was to defeat them, then they must be bad. They *must* be.

* * *

Denny was feeling contrite about his outburst at his daughter about the swimming pool incident. He had woken up again that morning bathed in sweat after yet another horrific nightmare – the third in as many nights and it had been going on intermittently for some time before that too – and had been in a bad temper all day. Funny how little frightened him in real life, yet a nightmare could still terrify. In the nightmare, he was helpless. Not just his special powers, but even ordinary human strength seemed to have deserted him. And then *she* appeared. A horrible crone, hardly human, with skinny claws, she pinned him to the bed and ravished him thoroughly – God it was disgusting – all the while saying. 'Love me, love me, love me.' She would not leave until he said it.

He had not told Tamar about the nightmare. Given the nature of it – despite how revolting it really was – he was not sure she would understand.

He caught sight of himself in the hall mirror; it never ceased to amaze him. Not a wrinkle, not a grey hair. He looked no older than he had twenty years ago. Of course, he knew the reason. The Athame. As long as he had it in his possession, he would grow no older, not a day older, not even in a hundred years or more. But it was still a strange thing to witness.

'I thought I was the one with the vanity,' said Tamar coming up behind him.

'What?'

'Admiring your boyish looks,' she gestured to the mirror.

'Would you still love me if I was an old fart?' he asked her.

'You *are* an old fart,' she said. 'You just don't look like one.'

'I'm forty six,' he said. 'If I'm an old fart what does that make you?'

'Amazingly well preserved,' she said.

'Forever young,' he mused. 'I wonder how it's going to feel when I get to a hundred.'

'Trust me,' she said. 'When you get to a hundred, you start to *feel* young again. I think that's when it actually hits you. You know, that you've got forever.'

'It's funny how forty six sounds so old, but five thousand years doesn't sound nearly so bad.'

'That's because it doesn't sound real,' she told him.

'Anyway,' he said. 'I might *not* have forever, like you. If Iffie needs it, I shall pass the Athame on to her one day. No parent should outlive their child.'

Tamar said nothing to this. Although she approved of the sentiment, she had already made up her mind that it was not going to come to that. She had no intention of losing *either* of them.

'Where is the little devil anyway?' she said instead.

'Not so little anymore,' he said. 'Now that *does* make me feel old,' he added.

'Not me,' said Tamar twirling her hair. 'People think we're sisters.'

'Yeah, and it really annoys her, you know.'

'She'll grow out of it,' said Tamar complacently.

'Yeah, around about the time she makes you a grandma. How will you like *that*?' Denny teased.

'Fabulous,' said Tamar. 'A dynasty. In another thousand years there could be a hundred of us.'

Denny shook his head. She really was unquenchable.

'An unbeatable, evil-fighting, clan,' he said. 'I quite like the sound of that.'

'We're going to need a bigger house,' said Tamar.

* * *

Someone else in the house was looking in a mirror, but it was not at herself. Hecaté was scrying. Not something a goddess usually had to bother with, remote vision being a standard godly power. But she had tried everything else to find Cindy and, so far, nothing had worked. Of course, Cindy was now a goddess too. Or rather, she had the power of the gods – thanks to the power of the stolen Rheingold – which was close enough. In any event, Hecaté could no longer sense her. But perhaps the scrying would work. A sort of low tech back door method of location that Cindy might not have considered it necessary to guard against.

She heard the door open behind her and immediately picked up a hairbrush and began to brush her hair, clearing the mirror's cloudy appearance to reveal, standing behind her, her husband Jack Stiles.

She felt a little tug at the heart at the sight of him. He had aged well considering, but … a little more white at the temples, a few more lines about the eyes. He could not live forever. It made her sad because she would have to – without him.

However, he still had the old spring in his step, the same shark-like grin and the same sharp mind that he had always had. This last was brought home to her by his first words to her.

'Scrying?' he asked. There was no possible way he could have known this. How had he surmised it?

Of course, he had not. He was simply employing his interrogative technique of letting you think he knew what he really did not know and daring you to deny it.

However, there was no point in denying it.

'Yes,' she said. 'I will not bother asking how you knew it. I do not suppose that you would tell me anyway.'

'Still trying to find Cindy?' he asked, not bothering to point out that he had never, in nearly twenty years, seen her sit at a mirror merely to brush her hair. 'It's not your responsibility you know,' he added, knowing that it was a waste of his breath.

'She was my charge,' said Hecaté. 'I failed her somehow.'

'*She* failed *you*,' asserted Stiles. 'She was a grown woman and a human being with free will. She *chose* to do what she did. And in doing so, *she* broke faith with *you*. She promised to serve you in good faith then ran away when it became too hard. She failed in her devotion, and it's not your fault.'

'You speak of her as if she were dead,' said Hecaté.

'It's easier that way,' he said sombrely. 'The Cindy we knew *is* dead, for all intents and purposes. Let it be.' he used these last words deliberately to see if she would remember and understand.

She did. 'Let it be,' she repeated. 'Oh Jack. You are right,' she said. 'Perhaps there are some things that cannot be altered – cannot be undone. Let it be.'

The search for Cindy had been underway for fifteen years. During that time, she had been looked for by Tamar, Denny, Stiles, Hecaté and the worldwide network of spies employed by a mysterious Agency for the investigation of supernatural phenomenon, all to no avail. Wherever she was, she had apparently fallen off the map entirely. No one could find her.

But Tamar had predicted that she would return to wreak her vengeance one day, and it was with this in mind that the search continued. No one wanted to be caught off guard.

* * *

The man known only as "Slick", a nickname given to him by Tamar in reference to his winning ways as a con man and lothario, had yet to regret his decision to join Cindy, as Hecaté had once predicted he would. He accepted his position as a substitute lover with good grace. He had a nice life here. Cindy was gorgeous, passionate and made no claims on his emotional life, nor did she demand exclusive rights to his person. There had been others that she had found out about, and had done nothing but laugh about. He could do what he wanted, she implied. She did not care enough about him to want him to herself.

The only fly in the ointment was Ashtoreth. But Slick did not mind him really; he even felt sorry for the poor kid. He had a rotten life really. His resentment was understandable; after all, who did the poor kid have but his mother? Oh, the place was full of what Cindy referred to (incorrectly) as "minions" – they were really only servants – she even paid them well. But Ashtoreth was not allowed to talk to them.

The really sad part, as far as Slick could see, was that the kid had no idea that he had a rotten life. Had he shown even the slightest sign of friendliness Slick would have taken him in hand, shown him around the town a little. Maybe taught him a few of the ways of the world. What that kid needed, in Slick's opinion, was to tear it up a little, let off some steam. But he was kept at a firm distance and besides, Cindy would have hit the roof. No point rocking the boat.

He did not see himself as a kept man. It was an arrangement that suited them both. If anything he was a *free* man. She kept him around for a reason, and he knew it. It was *her* weakness, not his. As long as he was around, she would not give in to that weakness. And the closer she came to the fulfilment of her long held desires, the less she could afford to risk giving in.

In reality, be believed he held the power in this relationship, however it might appear. If he left her, she would be stranded and forced to face up to what she had been denying for fifteen years. It was a game they were playing. A game called "Cindy is not in love with Denny". For the fact was, the power of the Rheingold was a destructive force to those who wielded it without having forsaken love. And Cindy wanted that power. It was what she had chosen instead of a broken heart. Not realising that a broken heart can be mended but an empty heart can never be filled.

No, he had no reason to regret his decision as yet. But the day was coming.

To Slick's clear-sighted perception, the true motive behind Cindy's playing of this game was effortlessly transparent. Yet he was totally blind to – had never even thought to look at – the true reason behind his *own* participation; the reason why he *did not*, in fact, just get up, go, and leave her to it. Yet the reason was simple.

This game they were playing together, and he did not yet understand this, could also be described as "Slick is not in love with Cindy".

Of course, there was also the possibility that Ashtoreth's self-control might break, and he would kill Slick in a fit of jealous fury. That would be a good reason to regret his decision too.

Cindy, who had never been as stupid as she seemed, was nevertheless, unaware of this. It never occurred to her to wonder *why* he had stayed so long in what would be regarded by most men as an impossible situation. He accepted the insulting way that her son treated him without demur. In fact, Cindy herself found his treatment of Slick more annoying than Slick himself seemed to.

She considered him weak. Very different, in that respect, from the man that she refused to admit he was replacing. But weak was how she wanted him. A strong man who might have tried to assert himself was of no use to her. Then again, *he* would be of no use to her either shortly. Very soon, her power would be consolidated. Her enemies, particularly that one who most threatened her security, would all be dead.

She would never admit the thought openly to her conscious mind – it was too dangerous – but deep down, on some unacknowledged level, she was aware that until Denny was dead, she would never be completely safe. Should he stir even the slightest emotion within her, it was finished. This was the unadmitted but true reason why he had to die. A sacrifice in her quest for power.

On a more practical level (and this was the acknowledged reason) Denny and Tamar and their little conclave, represented a formidable barrier in their own right, to the ambitions of any power hungry evil genius bent on world domination.

And once Denny was dead, and her power and her heart secure forever, what would she need Slick for? Nothing. (Not that she was able to admit that she needed Slick for anything *now*. That would be to admit that other dangerous truth; the truth about *why* she needed him.) He was ultimately expendable. He always had been. Perhaps she would let Ashtoreth kill him. A little treat for a good boy.

And it was time, at last, to make her opening move in the carefully planned campaign that she had been patiently constructing for so many years. No bold frontal assault that was sure to end in disaster. No one could go up against Tamar head to head and hope to win. Subtlety was what was needed here. Everything she knew about them, and all that she had learned *from* them was to her advantage. That and the fact that they would never see it coming. They would never even suspect that it was she who was behind it. Not until it was too late anyway. Of course, some things may have changed in the intervening years. The one disadvantage of her well chosen hiding place was that it worked both ways. In order to keep them from finding her, she had been unable to keep an eye on them. But she did not believe that anything fundamental had changed. There was no reason why it would have.

She sent for her son. He had been waiting for this day almost as long she had.

But was he ready? Well there was only one way to find out? The first test.

~ Chapter Two ~

IPHIGENIA BLACK was sneaking out of the house. There was no valid reason for this, since no one was in anyway, except Jack and, of course, his ailing father who did not count since he never left his room anyway. Sneaking out of the house is just something teenagers do, even when they can teleport if they want to.

'And where do you think you're going?'

'Jesus Jack! You nearly gave me a heart attack. You sounded just like Dad.'

'Sorry, I thought it'd be funny. And it was too. You should see the look on your face.'

'Ha, ha. That's being a changeling, is it? Using your incredible powers of mimicry to make me fall out of the window?'

'You didn't fall out of the window, stop exaggerating. Where *are* you going anyway?'

'Ali's house.'

'Is that a euphemism for Griff's?'

Griff's was short for "The Grifters Arms", an all night bar that played loud music at all hours of the day and night and encouraged all patrons regardless of age, sex, culture, subculture, or sanity.

'Ali's going to be there,' she said, which was as good as an admission.

'I don't know what you see in that dump,' said Jack.

'It's the coolest place in *this* one horse town,' she told him.

He waved her away, 'Go on then,' he said. 'I'll see you later. Don't turn anyone into a toad.'

'I never …'

'Or a bacon sandwich,' he added.

'I was *five*,' she said indignantly. 'It was an accident.'

'You were ten,' he corrected her, 'and you said it was because she stole your poster of that weird looking singer. You know – the one with the hair.'

'A good memory is a treacherous weapon,' said Iffie resignedly, and she hopped off the sill.

* * *

Finvarra was a sick man. (Well, a sick Faerie anyway – but no amount of clapping children were going to make *him* better). He was not sick of the body, but of the mind. He kept to his room seeing his son only on rare occasions, and seeing no one else at all. Jack had been raised by the combined efforts of Stiles and Hecaté mainly – with interference from Tamar and support from Denny.

The room was dark, but the familiar figure was instantly recognisable even in the gloom.

'Jack? That you my boy?'

The light snapped on brutally. Finvarra shielded his eyes from the unaccustomed brightness, then peered out from between his fingers.

'I waited till everyone had gone out,' said his visitor. 'Like my mother told me to.'

'Jack – Jacky?' Finvarra sat up abruptly. It was his son and yet not his son. Unless his son had cut his long hair off into a severe crew cut and taken to wearing a suit instead of baggy pants and T-shirts. Perhaps he had a girlfriend. Women could do that to a man. But he knew it was not Jack. The hatred in the eyes could never have belonged to his son. 'Jacky?' he said. Not knowing what else to call him.

'My name is Ashtoreth,' said the boy coldly.

'Ah!' said Finvarra nodding. 'I see. Of course, my boy.'

'I'm not *your* boy!' Ashtoreth spat at him. 'You *stole* me from my mother – she told me.'

'It wasn't like that,' said Finvarra feebly.

'So it *is* true?' said Ashtoreth. 'You admit it? You stole me and put an impostor in my place. I know you did. Didn't you? *Didn't* you?' He brought his face menacingly close to Finvarra's.

Finvarra shrugged. 'Yes I did,' he admitted. 'But it wasn't how you think – if you let me explain …'

'No more lies!' shouted Ashtoreth. 'I don't want to hear it.'

'It is your mother who has lied to you,' said Finvarra unwisely.

'No!' she told me the truth. You've admitted it. I used to wonder if – if maybe she had made a mistake. But it's all true.

'Oh mother, I am sorry that I doubted you. I am unworthy. I have been tainted by the evil of this man, and not all your great care has been able to shrive it from my soul. But now I see the truth. This old sinner must die, as you have always said. They must all die.'

Finvarra put out a shaking hand to the boy – there was love and understanding shining through the tears in his eyes. 'One day,' he said. 'You will understand what you have done. On that day, I want you to remember this – just this. You were not to blame. Forgive yourself as I forgive you now. I am ready to die. Perhaps it is a mercy you do me now. I have lived long enough without her. It is fitting that it is by her hand – by proxy – that I perish. I always knew that she would be the death of me. I forgive you my son. My son that I love …'

Ashtoreth spread great white wings that burst from his back. They filled the room with menacing shadows that enveloped all the light.

He turned slowly away. First blood had been shed, and it had not been the divine experience he had expected. The old man's last words had shaken him. Robbed him, in the end, of the satisfaction of vengeance.

It would not be so the next time.

* * *

Iffie had gone outside, ostensibly for some air, but really to escape from Josh Whathisname, who was a semi-friend of a friend who tended to get a bit sentimental after a drink or ten. Better to get out of his way before he did anything really embarrassing. He would thank her later.

Iffie had a talent – one that she had inherited from her mother, and, like her mother, she often employed that talent unconsciously. She was, although she did not know it, about to employ that talent now.

Something fundamental *had* changed in the household that Cindy had laid such meticulous plans against. That "something" was a teenager with her mother's uncanny ability to throw a spanner right into the workings of the best laid plans.

Completely unaware of any imminent spanner hurling, Iffie looked up at a familiar figure striding down the street toward her and curled her lip.

'You *followed* me?' she sniped. 'What am I, a baby?'

The figure stopped and looked down at her in bewilderment. 'What?' he said.

'And what's with the dorky suit and that stupid square haircut?' Iffie continued. 'Have you joined The Agency in the space of the last two hours? And … you're not Jack, are you?'

'Who are *you*?' he said.

'Gosh, you look just like him – *really*. Well not *just* like him 'cause… the hair and everything but – wow! I mean it's you isn't it? You're him?'

'Who *are* you?'

'Oh. Name's Iffie, forget everything I just said, I ramble sometimes,' she added. The look on his face was rather worrying, and Iffie did not have a witch's intuition for nothing.

'What's *your* name?' she asked.

'Ashtoreth,' said Ashtoreth, utterly fascinated by this little person with the enormous eyes and the big gestures, she would have someone's eye out with those rings one day. He had never imagined anyone so energetic.

'Really? What a dorky name. Can I call you Ash? That sounds much cooler. It would suit you much better.' she added slyly – the honey within the sting.

There was an insult if you liked, but delivered in such a charming manner that it was robbed of all offence. He was certainly learning a lot today. Especially about the power of words.

But Ash? That was what the loathed interloper called him; he detested it. But somehow, he did not mind it from her.

'I don't mind,' he said. 'What's wrong with my name?'

'It's just dorky that's all. I can't explain why. Sounds like a Bible name or something. Utterly grim.' And she waved her arms about and pulled a gargoyle face at him. 'Yuk!' she exclaimed expressively.

Ash was completely enchanted.

'Why don't you come in?' she suggested, throwing a wide arm in the direction of the bar. 'Have a drink, have a dance, let your hair … loosen up a bit. Do you good, I should think.' She looked critically at him. 'You look like you need unbuttoning a bit.'

Again she had insulted him. He should have been angry at such an affront to his dignity, but he was not. There was a refreshing lack of malice in her attack. When the despised Slick said these sorts of things to him, he felt the fury building up behind the levees of his patience. But she was different; she clearly meant no harm at all. She was teasing him. As if … as if … they were friends. As if she *liked* him. The thought gave him a strange warm feeling inside.

'Come on,' she urged. 'It's retro tonight – they're playing all really old stuff like Madonna. Should be right up your alley,' she added with a slight sneer.

'I-I really shouldn't,' he said reluctantly. 'I have to get back. My mother …'

'Huh, *parents*!' Iffie rolled her eyes. 'If you do what *they* want all the time, what's the point of living?'

Ashtoreth was startled by this philosophy. It was so alien to what he had been brought up to believe.

'Come on!' she wheedled. 'We're young, we're gorgeous,' she yelled waving her arms about like a crazed windmill. 'Live a little, the olds never have to know. And what they don't know won't hurt them.'

'You love your parents don't you?' he asked anxiously.

'Of course, stupid. Like millions and millions. They're great. My Dad's the greatest man in the world (probably literally)' she added *sotto voce*. 'But we're young you know, it's practically our *job* to rebel.'

'It is?'

'Of course it is, don't you know anything?'

'Apparently not,' muttered Ash following her in.

'That's right, "Angel face",' said Iffie with a touch of wicked humour. 'Have some fun. It won't kill you.'

They wandered into the club to the strains of an old Madonna song. The words of which rather appropriately ran: # *You're an angel in disguise. I can see it in your eyes.*

'At least they aren't playing "Like a Virgin",' said Iffie cruelly.

* * *

While Iffie was buying the murderer a drink, Jack was discovering his father's body.

'Father? Father? *Father*?' he shook the inert body futilely. There was no response.

'Tamar! Denny!' he yelled. 'Help! Help us!'

Both appeared in the room instantly. Tamar had some rather mysterious goop in her hair and Denny's face was streaked with something unmentionable looking. Both also looked rather charred. None of this was unusual enough for Jack to comment on, or, in his distressed state, even notice.

Tamar ran to the body while Denny held Jack in a fiercely protective grip, turning his body away from the sight on the bed. 'Oh no,' she breathed. She turned to them and shook her head sadly.

'He's gone?' croaked Jack. He bit back tears. 'I know he wasn't much of a Father, not after … but he was all the Father I had.'

'You've still got us,' said Denny.

Tamar came over and put her arms around them both. 'You'll always have us,' she affirmed.

'Oh, I know I've been luckier than most,' he said. 'But it still feels bad.'

'It's supposed to, I'm afraid.' said Denny, who had not shed a single tear when his parents had died.

'What … How did it happen?'

'Looks as if it was natural,' said Tamar. 'I think he just gave up. How long can a broken heart keep beating?'

'At least the angels took him,' said Jack picking up a large white feather that had fluttered to the floor. He did not mean it, literally. Faeries were not visited by angels, nor were they taken to heaven. He was referring to an old superstition that says when you find a white feather, it means the angels have visited.

Tamar stared at it.

Denny hustled Jack from the sombre room; this was no place for a child – this horrible chamber of death. As he left his father, he placed the feather reverently on his bed. But, unobserved by him, Tamar picked it up and gazed curiously at it for a long time after they had gone.

* * *

Cindy paced the throne room impatiently. Where was he? He should have been back hours ago. Had he been overwhelmed by the task before him? Was he cowering somewhere, working up the courage to do what she had told him must be done? Had he lost his nerve? Had he been *caught*?' Disaster!

'You'll wear a groove in that floor,' said Slick. King of original thought.

Cindy gave him a look. 'Are you *trying* to be annoying?' she said.

'Don't you realise what this means? If he's failed ... fallen at the first hurdle, it's over. If he can't even do *this* right, what hope that he can face the greater challenge?'

'You *are* asking him to commit a murder. It's a big deal. 'Specially the first time.'

'Not for him,' she retorted. 'Or at least it shouldn't be. What has he been trained for, if not for this?'

'The theory can be a little different from the practice,' said Slick. 'Anyway we don't know that he *has* failed.'

'Then where the hell is he?'

* * *

#'Holiday! Do, do, doo. Shelebrate! ' Ashtoreth was drunk. Very, very drunk. Iffie was beginning to wonder, for the first time in her life, if she might not have gone too far this time. She was half carrying him as they lurched together down the street. 'Wanna see my wings?' slurred Ash. 'They're really... *cool*!' he dredged up the unfamiliar word with a triumphant grin. Then his face fell.

'Of course I haven't really got wings,' he said, remembering where he was. 'I wash jush kidding.'

'Where's home?' said Iffie desperate to get him off her hands. 'Boy when you loosen up, you *really* loosen up,' she muttered and suddenly felt terribly guilty. 'Perhaps we'd better sober you up a bit first though,' she said. 'Your mum'll kill you if you come in like this.'

'Mother? Hmmm,' said Ash. 'Oh God! Oops mustn't blash... bals ... blaspheme.'

'Right!' said Iffie distractedly.

But he took this as concurrence. 'You're good,' he said. 'I can tell.'

'Look Ash, we've just *got* to get you sobered up somehow.'

'Or my mother will kill me,' he affirmed.

'Probably. Is she a bit of a dragon?'

'Dragon?'

'I mean, you know, kind of bossy, always telling you what to do, never letting you have any fun, that sort of thing,' she explained, realising that he probably had pretty literal turn of mind.

'Oh, yes,' he said happily. Then he giggled. 'Dragon lady,'

'Yeah, well we don't want her getting upset then, do we?'

'Right no, we don't want that,' he agreed.

'Okay, well then we should probably lie low tonight until you're back to full function mode. We'll get out stories straight in the morning, okay?'

'You mean tell *lies*?' he was shocked. 'To my *mother*?'

'It's better than getting into trouble ... I mean it's better than upsetting her,' she amended.

'Right, don't want to upset the dragon.' he said. 'She might breathe fire on me, burn my wings – that I haven't got,' he added hurriedly.

Iffie sighed. The sooner he passed out the better. At least he was not an amorous drunk. It could have been worse.

'You *are* a good person,' he said to her now. 'I can tell. I'm glad you're good y'know. 'Cause I like you. I wouldn't want to have to kill you.'

Iffie went cold all over. It was a joke. It had to be. Only... it had not *sounded* like a joke.

'You have to kill people who aren't good?' she asked nervously.

'Not *all* of them,' he said. 'Not yet, anyway. Later maybe ...' He trailed off smiling, he was thinking, although Iffie could have no way of knowing this, about Slick. He would enjoy killing him.

Iffie started to shake all over – he was a monster. She dropped him in the gutter and took to her heels.

* * *

Cindy was furious. No, *more* than furious. She was a towering tempest of wrath.

'Drunk!' she shrieked at Slick, 'He was *drunk*. Not injured, not ill – *drunk*. I know that look. He was so unfocussed that he didn't know who I was.'

'What are you yelling at *me* for?' asked Slick mildly.

'Because *he's* lying in his bed passed out and oblivious.'

'Well, I don't know what you expected,' said Slick. 'You keep him locked up here for fifteen years and then you let him out on his own into the real world for the first time. You should think yourself lucky that getting drunk was *all* he did.'

'He said he met a *girl*.'

'*Did* he?' Slick's eyebrows went up. 'Good for him.'

'Oh, I don't think anything of that nature went on, he was far too drunk.'

'Maybe they got drunk *after*,' said Slick wickedly.

'He kept saying she was iffy,' she said, ignoring this feeble attempt to bait her. 'What could he have meant by that?'

'Well, you can't hit the jackpot the every time,' said Slick philosophically.

'Don't be crude,' she snapped.

'From now on, *you* are to go with him,' she ordered. 'He clearly can't be trusted on his own.'

'He hates me,' protested Slick.

'That's your problem.'

'All right, all right, I'll go along – keep him in line or whatever. But he isn't going to like it.'

'And I want that girl found – whoever she is – and killed.'

'Hold on, that's a bit strong. He's a good looking boy, he met a girl and they had a drink. She didn't do anything wrong you know. And neither did he, for that matter. Ease up off his back, why don't you? Poor bastard.'

'I'll deal with my son as *I* see fit,' she said.

'Okay, fair enough, but no random girls are getting killed Cindy. I'm not sticking around for that. See?'

'I see,' she said sourly. 'Very well, I don't suppose she's relevant really.'

'That's right. So he met a girl, what can it matter?'

'He's probably forgotten her already,' said Cindy.

The truth was, Cindy was afraid. The second part of her plan was, in many ways, the most important, the most vital. The beginning of the end. If it failed then it had all been for nothing. Nothing must go wrong – nothing.

It would be difficult; it relied on timing and subtlety. Was her oaf of a son really ready for this? Was his loyalty to be depended on? Was he capable? He had proved that he could be easily distracted – after all her training too. If he allowed himself to be distracted now, it could prove fatal to all her plans.

Slick was shrewdly aware of her thoughts.

'Don't worry,' he said. 'I'll keep an eye on him.'

~ Chapter Three ~

WHEN IFFIE SNUCK back into her room shortly after three a.m. she was shocked to see her dad sitting on the bed waiting for her.

'Dad?'

'Good night?' asked Denny amiably.

'Not really.'

'We've been waiting for you to come in,' he told her. 'Bit of a family meeting. Everyone's downstairs.'

'I haven't done anything – honestly,' she said automatically

'It's all right. You aren't in any trouble

'Not even for coming in so late?' she asked.

'We've got bigger problems at the moment. And if *you* can't look after yourself, who can?'

'What problems? What's going on Dad?'

Iffie walked into her dad's study with a nervous smile on her face. It was a slight relief to see Jack sitting there – clearly it was not going to be a telling off. But Jack looked strange, as if he had been crying. Suddenly Iffie was afraid. She grasped at her dad's hand as she had done as a small child. He squeezed it reassuringly.

Then Iffie saw something even worse. Her mother had clearly been crying too. This was like the end of the world or something – it had to be. (Of course, Iffie did not know that

Tamar had faced the end of the world more than once and never cried about it either. It would take worse than that to shake her. This was worse.)

Who died?' she said in a shaky attempt at levity.

'My father,' said Jack.

Iffie's hand flew to her mouth. She had seen all the people in the room that she had expected to see appropriate to her dad's description of "everyone". Finvarra had not even entered her thoughts; no one ever saw him anyway. 'Oh God, I'm sorry,' she blurted out.

'You didn't know,' said Jack dully.

So, this clearly was not the time to tell Jack that she had found his stepbrother. She had been having doubts about that anyway, but now those doubts were, for the moment anyway, resolved. Ash was clearly crazy – a real bedbug, in fact. Jack did not need any more trauma at the moment.

She went over to him and put her arms around him, and they sat together in unabashed companionship and silence. Then Jack began to sob, as if her unspoken sympathy had split open the dam that had held back his grief.

Tamar went over to Denny, who put his arm around her, and she laid her head on his shoulder.

Stiles and Hecaté sat in silence too, her head in his lap as he stroked her hair.

And safely enclosed within the love and silent sympathy that surrounded him, secure and unashamed, Jack's sobs grew louder and louder.

* * *

Crack! Ash gritted his teeth obstinately as the whip whistled down on his back. *Crack! Crack! Crack!*

He would not cry or flinch. He had never cried in his whole life, and he was not about to start now. He would not give this muscle-bound minion the satisfaction.

'Enough,' said Cindy. And that was the part that really hurt. Not that she had ordered this punishment, it was not his first beating by a long way, but that she could stand there and watch its execution without so much as a flicker of emotion. Even the man Slick had flinched and left the room radiating speechless disapproval. At one time, Ash would have taken this as a sign of contemptible weakness. But now he wondered.

Was it really a weakness to despise violence? Even *necessary* violence. For Ash had no reason to believe that he did not deserve his beating. He had behaved abominably, he might have risked everything. But the problem was, despite the beating, he still wanted to do it again.

But that was wrong, he was weak himself, weak and polluted by evil. One day out in the world of sinners – just *one* day, and he had allowed himself to fall. Become a sinner himself. His father would be so ashamed.

His mother was only punishing him for his own good. For the good of the cause. She was strong, strong enough to witness his pain for his own sake. But, instead of his mother's face, which he had always pictured in the past to distract him from the pain, this time, he saw only the girl.

She was smiling at him. 'Poor thing,' he heard her say. 'Let me make it better for you.' As his mother had used to say. He wanted her now, wanted her to comfort him. Wanted … He did not know what he wanted. But he knew he wanted her.

He despised himself for being so weak.

He fell on his knees as he was unstrapped and his mother dismissed the minion with a curt nod.

'Get up,' said Cindy coldly. 'We have work to do. Fortunately, your little adventure has caused no real harm to our plan … this time. But it must not happen again. Who knows what might happen the next time.'

'Yes Mother.'

'Since you clearly cannot be trusted to behave yourself, I have decided to send Slick with you from now on.'

'Yes Mother.'

Cindy raised her eyebrows. She had been expecting more objections. He must be thoroughly chastened to have accepted this so easily. Good!'

She allowed herself a smile. Ash responded instantly with a tremulous smile of his own.

'Well, it's time for the next part of our plan. The rest of them will not be so easy to deal with, as I have told you. The one with the demon spirit, Tamar, has stolen powers that are a formidable challenge, even for you. And the other one, he has a dagger that he stole from a demon. With it, he could take your power from you. You must be careful not to confront either of them directly.'

'The Athame mother.'

'I am glad to see you have been paying attention.'

Cindy had been lucky in as much as she had not had to tell lies as such, to her son, only twist the truth. Because of this, there was much literature available to back up her claims. Ash had read of the secrets of the demon Athames and the origin of the Djinn (demons). He had also read about witches and the severely distorted accounts of Hecaté in the Greek legends, where she is described, most unfairly, as an evil witch who lived in the underworld with Hades. Even had it all been true, people can change. There had not been much that even Cindy could say about Stiles. But after all, he had been a policeman. And it is not hard to malign the police. There was plenty of available literature that did just that.

As a result, Ash now viewed the household that he had once been a part of as a veritable den of iniquity.

'You must be very careful my son,' she said. 'These are dangerous people.'

'I am not afraid of the demon woman mother.' said Ash stoutly. 'Good must always triumph over evil.'

Cindy looked properly at her son, so eager for the fray, and decided he needed to be warned.

'It's not *her* I'm afraid of so much,' she said. 'It's *him*!'

'Him, Mother?'

'Denny.' She nearly choked on the word. 'He's far more ruthless than *she* is. Although he doesn't admit it, even to himself. I suppose it's because he *thinks* he is a good man.'

'Mother?'

'He would destroy us without a word, without a thought and without regret, if he felt he had to. But *she* – ha! She *knows* she has done some questionable things in her time, and she fears to judge, lest she be judged likewise.'

I see Mother. Then it is *he*, we should beware of?'

'Oh, I'd be bloody careful of all of them if I were you.'

'It behoves us to be cautious when dealing with the devil,' said Ash, as if he was quoting from somewhere.

'Indeed, which is why we cannot simply take the fight to them. We must use strategy. The *second* phase of our plan. Divide and conquer.'

* * *

Denny was reading a book by the light of a standard lamp. It was one of his old, musty books of power and magic, and it was so exceedingly tedious and written with such ignorant pomposity that Denny was wishing that, instead of his library, they had left the swimming pool. Perhaps it was because of this that, try as he might, he could not keep his mind on what he was reading. And that was when he realised, as his attention began to wander, that something was wrong. He felt a kind of creeping horror come over him slowly; the kind of horror that has nothing to do with monsters and demons and has everything to do with the familiar becoming the unfamiliar. They did not *have* a standard lamp. Denny was sure of this even though he had as little to do with home decor as possible. He rose nonchalantly from his chair and yawned. The feeling of horror crystallised around him, but he ignored it, and as he moved as if to switch off the lamp, he felt the room tense. He snaked out a hand and grabbed the lamp by the pole and shook it, feeling (and looking) like a considerable lunatic. 'All right,' he said. 'I've got you now, so let's have it, who are you?'

Tamar was wandering in the garden when she spotted it; an extraneous statue. She knew it was not one of theirs; it was far too ugly. Rather than confront the situation, as was her usual wont (Denny was the cautious one) she carefully disregarded it and wandered back into the house. '*Interesting,*' she thought, then burst out laughing.

Despite a complete lack of supernatural powers, Jack Stiles had learned to sense when things were not quite … normal. It just took practice, and he had had a lot of that over the years. It was a natural extension of the almost psychic ability to spot the criminal in the lineup up, that he had always had.

Anyway, a large house plant that was almost as tall as a man was a pretty noticeable addition to any room, particularly when someone had apparently been stupid enough to place it right in front of the hall closet, blocking off the door. And Stiles was pretty certain that it had not been there the day before. That coupled with the feeling that it was *looking* at him, combined to make it a *fairly* suspicious incident. Especially in view of what they now knew.

He heard a snort of suppressed laughter behind him and turned to see Tamar beckoning him over with one finger pressed to her lips.

* * *

They laid Finvarra to rest on a blustery November day. There were patches of frost on the ground, even a little snow in the air. Everyone was shivering; Denny had dark circles around his eyes. He had not slept well the night before. In fact, he was beginning to dread sleeping at all. Tamar looked at him in concern. When was he going to talk to her about it? She knew he was having nightmares; she recognized the symptoms, but it was unlike him to try to hide them from her. Well, if he did not say anything soon, she *would*.

It began to snow in earnest.

'Dad hated to be cold,' observed Jack wistfully. 'But I suppose he can't feel it now?' Iffie squeezed his hand. 'He can't feel anything now,' she said. 'Perhaps he's happier now. He suffered so much.'

'I know you're trying to help,' he said. 'But you can't understand how I feel. I hope you never do.'

And Iffie shivered again, not from the cold, but at the thought of how it would be if she ever lost *her* dad.

~ Chapter Four ~

THERE WAS AN awkward silence between the two men as they walked down the street.

'Fancy a drink?' said Slick. 'No sorry, bad joke.' he added, cursing his inappropriate sense of humour.

But Ash actually laughed. He was in quite a good mood anyway. This part of the plan appealed to him; it dealt with Denny – the hated one. 'Better not,' he said. 'Mother really *would* kill me this time.'

Slick let this sink in. 'Christ,' he thought. 'That must have been some night – or some girl.' The little stiff really seemed like a different boy. 'I must say, you're taking this a lot better than I expected you to,' he commented. 'You aren't planning to slip off somewhere are you? Or maybe you think this is the perfect opportunity to fit me for a pair of concrete boots.' He raised his eyebrows interrogatively.

'I don't know what that means,' said Ash. 'But I can guess. You don't have to worry.'

There was another long silence then suddenly Ash said. 'I heard you, you know. I heard you sticking up for me, after I got inebriated. I wasn't in my bed at all, I was behind the door. I don't know why you did it. I know you don't like me. But … anyway I …'

'You're welcome,' said Slick. 'And for the record, I don't dislike you at all. It's you that doesn't like me.'

'No,' agreed Ash. 'I don't much. But perhaps I don't really know you. You're not like I thought you were.'

'Who is?' said Slick. *'Bloody hell, it's the body-snatchers. This isn't the same kid. It can't be.'*

'You said you don't dislike me. I would if I were you,' Ash confessed.

'Well, I don't. I think you're all right really. No one's perfect.'

'No.'

'It's not time yet,' said Slick. 'Why don't you tell me about this girl you met?'

'I'm not supposed to talk about her,' said Ash defensively.

'Hey, I'm not trying to catch you out kid. I won't tell, I promise. You *want* to talk about her, don't you?'

Ash made a grunt that might have been an admission.

Slick took it that way anyway. 'Was she pretty?' he asked.

'Beautiful. At least, I couldn't see her face too well. She was all painted up – like a Jezebel, but she wasn't like that you see, she was good.'

'It's confusing isn't it?' said Slick sympathetically. 'But, you know, a bit of make-up isn't a sin.'

'I'm glad you said that, I was worried about her soul. Vanity is a sin you know. And she was adorned too.'

Slick had to think about this one for a second. 'You mean jewellery?'

'Rings and necklaces and earrings and a silver pole stuck right through her ...'

'Too much detail,' interrupted Slick hurriedly.

'Eyebrow,' finished Ash, to Slick's relief.

'Why would she do that?' asked Ash in a puzzled tone. It must have been painful. I didn't like to ask her. She was very scornful if I said anything – dorky.'

'Dorky?'

Yes, she kept saying I was dorky. My hair was dorky, my name was dorky. What's dorky? *Am* I dorky?'

'Oh, god, from hated nemesis, to father figure in one easy move. He meets one girl and suddenly he turns into a human being.'

'Not dorky, no.' said Slick thoughtfully. *'Not with that physique,'* he thought. 'Just a bit sheltered. And no one can help their name.'

'She called me Ash, like you do. She said it sounded … cooler.'

'Why do you think I do it?'

'I thought you did it to be annoying.'

'Well, that too,' thought Slick. 'Well, now you know,' he said.

'So you *can* choose your name. You chose yours didn't you. I mean I know you aren't really called Slick.'

'Your mother told you, did she? Well the truth is I didn't choose it. Someone else gave me the name and it kind of stuck.'

'Like *she* gave me the name Ash?'

'Just like that, yes.'

'Slick suits you.'

'That's what *she* said.'

'And *she* said that Ash suits me.'

'It does.'

'So they were right, the people who renamed us?'

'Let's just say they saw a different side to us from our mothers. Look, don't take it all so seriously kid. It's just a nickname. A name given out of affection. It doesn't have to define who you are, any more than your given name.'

'Ashtoreth is an angelic name, given to me to honour my father.'

'Precisely. Be yourself kid, it's easier.'

'What's your *real* name?' asked Ash suddenly.

'No way, kid. That goes with me to the grave.'

'I won't tell anyone,' Ash wheedled. 'I think you *want* to tell … well, if not me, then *someone*.'

'Touché, kid. I guess I walked into that one,' said Slick, and he laughed.

He considered for a minute. 'Just between you and me kid?' he demanded.

'I promise,' said Ash eagerly as if he were about to learn the secrets of the universe. It was touching in a way, Slick thought, the poor kid had never even had a secret shared with him. It was little enough to do for him after all.

'You can't tell anyone, not your mother, not even your little girlfriend, right?'

'I promise,' said Ash solemnly.

'It's Veritas,'

'That means truth doesn't it?'

'Yep, I don't know what my mother was thinking. I think she hoped it would make me an honest man.'

Ash started to laugh. '*Veritas*, oh dear,' he said. 'And she said *my* name was dorky.'

'Not a word, remember?'

'Oh I won't tell. Who would believe me anyway?'

Slick started to laugh too. A miracle! They were laughing together.

Ash wiped his eyes. 'Have I been an absolute swine?' he asked seriously.

'No worse than any other teenager,' said Slick. 'No worse than *I* was. I hated *my* mother's boyfriends too. Mind you, they were a right bunch of drunken losers. Most of them used to beat me up or similar.' He shrugged. 'I tried to keep out of your face as far as possible. I never expected you to like me. I wouldn't have, if I'd been you.'

Ash's face was a picture.

'Confusing isn't it kid?' said Slick. He looked at his watch. 'You're on kiddo, time to roll. I'll meet you back here.'

And Ashtoreth went off to put part two of his mother's plan into action. Divide and conquer.

* * *

Denny was beginning to be afraid to fall asleep. Every night she came to him now. Like the tales of alien abduction or the olden time stories of being ridden by witches in the night, it began with the sensation of waking in a paralysed state. Then, contrary to all expectation, even in the blackness of the room, it seemed that the shadows deepened.

As he tried vainly to move, the deeper shadows around the bed resolved into a figure. It was not just paralysis; it was a deep lassitude, a bone weariness that made it impossible to fight the invisible bonds transfixing his limbs.

The figure was skinny but strong, the raddled face and claw like fingers utterly repulsive. And she crept up the bed like a spider and pinned him by the shoulders bringing the distorted countenance close to his own. 'Love me.' she would whisper, but Denny was capable only of the rapid breaths of fear.

Her gestures at first were gentle, caressing and she would gaze at his – as far as he was concerned – very ordinary face, as if he were Adonis himself.

He tried to close his eyes but found that he had no control over his body at all. She had it all. 'Love me,' she said and, most unwillingly, he did. But even this did not satisfy her. He had to *say* it. Try as he might to stop himself, eventually the words formed and were torn from his mouth. He thought that if he could resist, it might break the spell – but he never could.

As soon as the words were out the figure dissolved into the shadows again with a sigh of satisfaction and his limbs were released. Then he woke sweating and shivering in horror and disgust.

He might have tried to explain this to Tamar, if he had not been so ashamed of it. He should have realised that Tamar, having been a slave for 5000 years, was uniquely qualified to understand the horrors of violation.

* * *

'Love me, love me, love me, love *meee*!' Denny woke up in a cold sweat. This was getting ridiculous. He was now certain that the dreams were prophetic. It had happened before to him. But what did it mean? Who was the hideous crone in his nightmare? And why did she … what did she *want*?

It did not *feel* like a dream or even a premonition. It felt rather too real for that. A pre-experience. Like a real life preview of what was to come, rather than just a dream of it.

The crone was a real thing; she just did not exist yet. But she would.

And it was getting closer, the experience becoming more vivid.

Denny reached over to turn the bedside lamp on and got the shock of his life. He was lying in a strange room, covered in blood. Someone *else's* blood. *Not* a cold sweat then.

Whoever it belonged to was obviously dead. No one could lose that much blood and survive. He was bathed in the stuff. Good God, it might even be the blood of several people. A massacre!

Denny had seen some horrible things, but nothing like this. The worst thing, was that the blood was still warm. Denny started to retch and shake convulsively all over. He leapt up off the bed and promptly fell over, he felt too weak to stand. *'Got to get out of here,'* he reached for the Athame – it was gone. *'Not now!'* He searched the room on his hands and knees for it. But to no avail. It was definitely gone. He sat in the middle of the room with his head in his hands, shivering and he stayed that way for a long time.

Eventually he realised that he could not stay here forever, wherever here was, and he did not remember how he had got here either. He took off his bloody shirt and wrapped it up in the bloody sheets. Then he dumped the lot in the corner of the room. He discovered that he was in a hotel room with adjoining bath. He took a shower. And then removed the bloody pile of laundry to the shower tray and ran the hot water on it.

He moved swiftly and calmly concentrating only on the details of what had to be done. He would have a nervous breakdown later.

Trying to contact Tamar for help had been a dead end. He could not find her telepathically without the Athame and his mobile phone was missing along with the Athame. But why was she not trying to contact him? She had telepathic powers too, and they were not dependent on his. Unless, some similar disaster had also happened to her. In which case they were all in really big trouble.

He checked his watch and was not terribly surprised to learn that it was Thursday. He was missing four days.

So what the hell had happened?

'Okay so keep calm,' he told himself. 'You've been in worse jams than this one.'

First, try to remember the last four days, try to piece together how you got here which leads to, secondly, try to find out where the hell you actually are.

When his clothes were more or less dry, he inspected them. Not too bad, they would pass all but a close F.B.I. inspection. His shirt still looked a bit grubby but nothing out of the ordinary.

A thought struck him, and he went to the mirror. Was the portrait out of the attic? He looked carefully at his own face. No, he had not changed. He still looked like a young man in his twenties. Still it did not prove anything. The Athame had prevented him from aging while he had it, but that did not necessarily mean that its loss would result in him being metaphorically "hit in the face" with the last twenty years all at once.

The key to the room was on the dresser. He picked it up, squared his shoulders, took a deep breath and went out to find out where in the world he was.

He checked out with no problems. The hotel was called the *Prima*. He had never heard of it. It seemed to be a resort hotel. There were sandy beaches and holidaying families. Not the sort of place, in other words, that he could ever imagine himself coming to voluntarily.

He walked along the beach feeling, despite the raucous family fun going on around him, like Robinson Crusoe. Truly lost.

Now that he was calmer and able to think straight, his experiences led him to look at his problem in a different way than other people might do.

First he had to consider the very definite possibility that he was not in a real place at all. It *looked* real, but that did not mean anything. He discounted the oceans of gore in the hotel room. He had a feeling now that it had been planted there to unnerve him. But even if that were not the case, it was low on his list of priorities right after getting the hell out of here and finding the Athame. Not necessarily in that order. After all, if he found the Athame he would get out of here in no time. On the other hand, perhaps he would not be able to find it *until* he got out of here.

First he tried the obvious. 'Close file,' he said. This should have worked in any case, should have taken him straight to mainframe. 'Close file,' if said with the right intent, *always* took you into mainframe, since the whole world is in a file somewhere. They had learned this handy shortcut some years ago when Denny had become one with the mainframe and, like all these things, it seemed obvious when you already knew about it.

However, it did *not* work, which proved that he had been right. He was not in the world. He was clearly not in a file of any kind. This was a little frightening. However, there *were* places that were not filed. He had been in Hell – it had been very like this in some ways – the heat, the noise, the screaming children – and Hell had an exit of a kind. He took heart, if there was a way in then there was a way out – *somewhere*.

But it did not make sense. Whoever had done this, clearly wanted him out of the way, but they had not just killed him. *Why?* He was evidently defenceless. They had managed to take the Athame from him, steal four days of his life and trap him in wonderland. They had obviously had complete control over him, so why had they left him alive?

If he could just get his memory back, he was sure it would all become clear, which was probably why it had been erased in the first place.

The last thing he remembered was a pretty routine natural disaster. A tidal wave. Then he woke up here. He did not even remember how it had been dealt with. That had been on Monday.

* * *

'Don't touch him,' said Ashtoreth. 'If you so much as breathe on him, he'll wake up and then we've had it.'

Slick looked down at Denny dispassionately. He had not had a problem with this part of the operation. He had never cared for Denny anyway, and it was not as if they had killed the guy. Privately he suspected that it would prove impossible, in the end, to do this. Even in this condition he was too dangerous to risk getting too close to. How could you kill a guy like that?

'Are we just going to leave him here like this?' he asked Ashtorteth

'Yes, for now. That's the plan. That's what mother said, and anyway there's nothing else we can do with him at the moment.'

'You said "wake up", but he isn't exactly asleep is he?'

'No, it's not sleep.'

'I don't pretend to understand what you did, it's all beyond me. But I do know that if he ever gets out of it – whatever it is – he's going to be royally pissed off. We should leave.'

'He *can't* get out of it,' said Ashtoreth. 'It's easy to get in but impossible to get out of where he is now.'

'I wouldn't underestimate him if I were you,' said Slick. 'I really wouldn't.'

Ashtorteth gave a slow, gloating smile that made Slick shiver (the boy was enjoying this far too much). 'Mother will be pleased,' he said.

~ Chapter Five ~

IT HAD BEEN a routine natural disaster. That was what Tamar could not get her head around. To think that something like *that* could be their Waterloo, it was unthinkable. She *could not* think it; it *was* impossible – ridiculous. But the fact was, she had seen Denny swept away by a tidal wave and she had not been able to contact him since.

And yet … *was* it so impossible? Was it not possible that they had dealt with so many far more dangerous things that they had become careless about the everyday, the supposedly "lesser" things, forgetting that they could be as dangerous as anything, if you were too blasé about them?

She refused to believe he could be dead. Just like that, so suddenly and finally. But she could not ignore the facts. If he had lost the Athame in the deep water, he would have died like anyone else. Oh but no, not *just* like anyone else, though. The power of the Athame was residual. It could last for hours, maybe days, after the actual loss, before his mortality reasserted itself. Surely long enough for him to save himself? But the fact remained, that if he *had* saved himself, he would be here. At the very least, supposing he had saved himself, just in time, before his power waned away, she should still have been able to find him.

She had not communicated her fears to Iffie, who was not yet unduly worried. She believed her father was indestructible. It was hardly surprising. She had, over the years, seen him stabbed, shot, drowned and hit by lighting, all to no ill effect.

And it was less than two weeks since they had lost Finvarra. Iffie had not been close to him, of course, but death affected everyone. And Iffie was still so young to have tragedy upon tragedy heaped upon her.

If he *was* dead (and Tamar, try as she might could not come up with any other explanation) she knew there were two things she could do to bring him back. And Denny would severely disapprove of both of them.

There were the history files. She could go back and change what happened. Get it right this time. And, no doubt, cause a hideous paradox that would probably trap them all forever, and maybe countless other innocent people too.

The other way… Well only *she* would get hurt. And Iffie would still have her father, after all.

No. She was a mother now; it was irresponsible in the extreme to even consider it. But … *if* she did it. Denny could save her. *Would* save her.

If she had not had a daughter to consider, she would not have thought twice about it.

'I am worried about Tamar,' said Hecaté. 'Denny has been missing for four days now. I fear she may do something … reckless.'

'First Finvarra and now Denny,' said Stiles grimly. 'I reckon there's a curse on this house.'

'Do not be so silly,' she replied, 'as if I would not sense such a thing.'

'I didn't mean it literally,' he told her. 'What do you think she will do?' he asked.

'What did she do the last time he died?' said Hecaté.

'We don't *know* that he's dead,' Stiles pointed out.

'I am sure that she thinks he is. What else would keep him away so long?'

'If we knew *that*, we'd have no problem.'

'You do not believe he is dead?'

'I *know* Denny. I reckon it'd take more than a tidal wave to finish him off. That's all I'm saying. I'm not saying he isn't in trouble – bad trouble maybe. There's definitely something fishy about this. But he *isn't* dead. I'd stake my life on it.'

'Then I believe I know what to say to Tamar,' said Hecaté.

'Are you *sure* you want to do this?' said Hecaté. 'There might yet be another way.'

'No,' said Tamar plonking a distinctive looking bottle on the floor between where they sat face to face. 'This is the only way.'

'My goodness. That looks just like …'

'There are a lot of them about,' said Tamar. 'It wasn't too hard to pick up another one.'

'It's a terrible risk,' said Hecaté. 'Are you …?'

Tamar grinned wryly. 'I'm certain,' she said. 'What I really need now is a dose of phenomenal cosmic power.'

Hecaté shook her head.

'I have to get him back, Hecaté,' said Tamar, clutching at her hand. 'I *have* to.'

'Whatever it takes?' asked Hecaté

'Whatever it takes,' said Tamar lifting the familiar bottle and clenching it in her fist. '*Whatever* it takes.'

* * *

'He is contained?' Cindy asked.

'As you desired mother. He fought me – he is strong. He does not look strong, but he is. It has to be the Devil's power he has in him. He will have nightmares because he fought. Blood and fire.' He looked pleased at the prospect.

'Fitting,' said Cindy. 'His own personal hell.'

'Yes Mother.'

'What a pity we cannot deal with her in the same manner,' said Cindy. 'She would certainly fight too.'

'It only works once,' said Ashtoreth.

'I am aware of that,' said Cindy. She surveyed her son with satisfaction. Such power. He was not aware of how much power he possessed. Her own paled by comparison. But no matter, all his power was at her disposal anyway. It was *her* power really. Angelic power, combined with a natural cruelty that was oh so very human. What he had done was nothing short of a miracle. And he did not even know it.

'Don't gloat,' said Slick. 'It's very unattractive.'

Cindy turned to him. 'You can always bugger off,' she said. 'See if I care.'

'He isn't dead yet, you know,' said Slick, breaking the rules of their game. 'Don't go getting ahead of yourself.'

Cindy glared at him and looked meaningfully at Ashtoreth, who was looking from one to the other with a puzzled expression.

'Next we deal with *her*,' said Cindy changing the subject. 'After that, the rest of them will be easy.'

'What shall I do with her mother?' asked Ashtoreth. 'You have not yet told me.'

'Ah, that's the beauty of it darling.' said Cindy with a smile. '*You* will not have to do *anything* to her. She will do it to herself. Divide and conquer. Take him away and she will destroy herself. It has already begun.' And she smiled cruelly.

'I might just bugger off actually,' said Slick, suddenly disgusted. 'I've had just about enough of all this shit.'

'Go then. No one will try to stop you,' she said.

Slick slouched and pulled his hair over his face, and suddenly, Ash saw it. He was much older, but he looked like … What had he looked like as a younger man?

Cindy caught her breath.

'Are you sure you want to risk it?' said Slick and stalked from the room.

* * *

Denny awoke bathed in sweat. That horrible dream again, this was getting ridiculous … He snapped the light on when he smelled the smoke. He sat up, horrified. He was in a strange room and, apparently, it was on fire.

That explained the sweating then.

The room was filled with fire and smoke and Denny suddenly realised, to his utter horror, that he was choking. He did not *choke* – or burn. He snatched his hand away from the superheated wall and wrung it painfully. *Ouch*! He tried to teleport and found the he could not. This was a problem.

'Okay. Don't panic. You're only in a strange place, without powers, burning to death. You've been in worse jams.'

And what the hell was that horrible smell? He forced himself to pay attention. He looked around to see if there was a viable way out of this furnace and noticed that, not only were the walls burning, they were running with blood. It was a nightmare. He ripped off his shirt and wrapped it around his face – ugh blood on his shirt too – and fell to his knees, without removing the bloody shirt, remembering vaguely that you were supposed to keep low and cover your face during a fire. He crawled to the door and sat facing it, kicking out hard with legs that were far weaker than he was used to. The door was rotten, though, and even his limited strength was enough to kick it open.

He crawled out into the relatively fresh air of the corridor. People were running past him and screaming. Denny ignored them as he collapsed onto his face and passed out.

Strong arms picked him up and carried him outside – he was dumped onto a gurney and left. Gradually he became aware of ambulances and fire engines. Everywhere around him there was pandemonium. He slipped off the gurney and walked swiftly away to find a nice quiet place to have a nervous breakdown. No one noticed him go.

Standing on the beach trying to clear his mind so he could figure out what had happened, he glanced at his watch – an automatic gesture, done without thinking, but then he did a double take. It was Friday – *Friday*? Somehow he had lost five days.

~ Chapter Six ~

IFFIE SWUNG LAZILY on the garden seat; Jack was lying face down on the grass.

'Jack?' she said. 'I need to talk to you about something.'

'Mmm?'

'What if there was something that you really wanted to know about, but it turned out that it wasn't really a good thing after all. Would you want someone to tell you about it anyway?'

'What?' Jack sat up, the better to wrestle with this unusual conundrum.

Iffie patiently repeated everything she had just said.

'*Is* there something?' he asked.

'Theoretically,' she temporised.

Jack sighed. 'You'd better just tell me,' he said.

'I think … I *know* I found your stepbrother, but … he … he isn't right in the head or something.'

'You *found* him? When? Where? Why didn't you tell me? Is he all right? Why didn't you tell me? Where is he?'

'Jack, *Jack*, slow down. I'm trying to tell you.'

'Sorry, it's just … okay, tell me then.'

'I don't know where he is now. I-I ran off. He scared me. I think he's … dangerous.'

'He *scared* you?'

'He was talking about killing people. I think he meant it. He isn't like *you* at all.'

'*Killing* people? Oh Iffie, he must have been joking.'

Iffie slipped of the seat and came to kneel in front of him; she took his face in her hands. 'He wasn't joking Jack,' she said seriously.

'He … he didn't hurt *you*, though?' stammered Jack.

'No. Not me, but I think he might have hurt someone else.'

'Who?'

'I don't know. It was just the way he was talking. Jack I think he needs help. I've been thinking about it, and I don't think he's a bad person. He was really nice in some ways. I think he's just messed up.'

'You liked him?'

'Yes, he was nice … until he said … all that stuff about bad and good and how he has to kill all the bad people.'

'He said that? Like a nutty religious serial killer. Oh my God!'

'I shouldn't have told you.'

'No, I'm glad you did. At least I know he's alive. But … what a fruitcake!'

'We don't know what his life has been like. I know he isn't *all* bad. He was so … well … He was kind of sweet really.'

'Ted Bundy,' said Jack laconically.

'Oh, shut up, *he* was a psychopath. I think Ash is just … messed up royally. We could help him maybe. We're his *family*.'

'*Ash*?'

'Ashtoreth. I mean anyone named *that* is *bound* to have severe psychological issues.'

'She re-named him then?'

'Well? So what? He's still your brother, whatever he's called.'

'Did he … does he still look like me?'

'How do you think I knew who he was? But he's way better looking than you … I'm *kidding*. He was kind of a dork actually. I don't think he gets out much.'

'No, just at night to go on a killing spree.'

'Don't!'

'I don't want you going near him again Iffie, do you hear me?'

'But ... I could ... we could ... if I could just *talk* to him maybe ...'

Jack took Iffie by the shoulders and shook her angrily. His face was dark, suffused with emotion. 'I said *no*, Iffie. Stay away from him. Just ... stay ... away.'

'All right, all right, I promise. *Jeez!*'

* * *

Jack lay on his bed pondering on what Iffie had told him. It was wonderful and yet terrible. His brother was alive, but a killer. He just did not know what to think. He had wanted to find him for so long, and to find him *now*, when it was too late for his father. And what exactly had she found anyway? A murderer? A possible murderer anyway. And Iffie had *liked* him. She was crazy that girl. He was as confused about his reaction to this as he was about any part of this. Why was he so angry about the fact that she clearly wanted to find him again? It was a noble sentiment, and one that he would have expected of her. Was he just worried about her safety, which would be understandable considering what she had told him, or was it something else? Was it that he was – ridiculous idea – jealous?'

Iffie was his. They had been as close as bugs in a rug from their earliest years. Now there was a chance that he might have to share her. And he did not want to – not even with a brother – perhaps *especially* with a brother.

Was it possible that all the love and companionship that he had built up with her over the years could be so easily transferred to another who just happened to look like him? Surely not. Or worse – *he* was a mere brother to her. What might this one become to her? More than that? The comfort of the familiar mixed with the tang of the unfamiliar. What might *that* conjure up? Horrible idea – disgusting. Why, in all the years that he had yearned for his brother, had he never considered this possibility?

He realised he was being ludicrous. Iffie was still a child for all her world weariness. Still sharp and cynical and cold, in the way that only the very young, who have not yet been bruised and battered by life, can be.

When she said she *liked* him, she meant just that and nothing more.

No more tender emotion had been awakened in her yet. No one knew it better than he. After all, when you got right down to it, *he* was not her brother either.

* * *

Iffie had no intention of keeping her promise to Jack. She had thought it over and decided that Ash was not a threat to her. Jack was just being overprotective. Probably because Dad was away from home.

She had a feeling that she would find him down at Griff's again. He was probably looking for her too.

She called a friend to go down with her, in case he was not there. After all, what kind of a loser hung around a bar on their own?

For some reason, she paid special attention to her appearance – the bedroom was strewn with clothes (all black) and she reapplied her face three times before she was satisfied.

She practised, in front of the mirror, what she would say if he showed up. A casual greeting, the carefully inviting brush off, a mere knowing smile.

It was important to get it right, she felt. Not because he was attractive. That would be silly. But because it was important to Jack. (Jack who looked exactly the same, but who was not attractive in the same way because he was only Jack.)

This time she would teleport out of the house. Just in case Jack was hanging around to catch her again.

She checked her watch; it was 2.30. Griff's would not even be open for another five hours. Oh, well, maybe she would change into the dark purple. It brought out her eyes better anyway.

What if he were not there, though? But he would be, of course he would be; it was Saturday night – hard rock night. *Everyone* would be there.

* * *

Cindy was pleased with herself. Denny was dying and Tamar had reacted exactly as predicted. She knew this because she had taken the chance of sending out spies – as she had always known she would have to do at this late stage. It was true that if her plan had *not* been working, then the spies could have been traced back to her, which was why she had never risked it before. But there could be no victory without some risk.

And victory was now within her grasp. Tamar's predictability, her reckless sacrifice, had made it certain.

And Denny was not going to be able to save her this time. He could not even save himself.

'Two down,' she thought. And with those two out of the way, there was no one left on earth who could stand up to her. She had no real grudge with either Stiles or Hecaté, but they would still have to die. Casualties of war, for even without the protection of Tamar, they would certainly try to stop her. And it was better that way anyway. They had not been a part of her humiliation, but they had witnessed it. She wanted no reminders.

She reviewed her plan from the beginning. The only pleasure available to her now, as she waited for the fruition of her plan. When her spies informed her that Denny was dead, then, and only then, would she risk returning to the world. There was no point in being precipitate, after so many years of careful patience.

So, first Finvarra had died to test her son's resolve and to throw the house into distress. A minor matter in itself but it had had the advantage of leaving Tamar questioning her own judgment when Denny had disappeared. Had she been distracted and misjudged the tidal wave? Was it her fault somehow? Had Denny been thrown off his game by the tragedy in the household? Cindy knew these thoughts had gone through Tamar's mind as surely as if she had been able to read them there. In this way, Denny's death by natural disaster would not seem such an impossible event as it might otherwise have done. The idea of a setup had not even occurred to them.

Cindy had seen Tamar stricken by grief and remorse before. Impetuous and thoughtless, she would risk everything to get him back. Without even stopping to consider the consequences, she would recklessly throw away her life or her freedom to save him; either would do. The only problem with that was that, *this* time, she did not know what she was trying to save him *from*. She would get it all wrong – never find him. She would make the deal to bring him back from the dead *before* he had even died. It was tragically funny to Cindy. And in the meantime, Cindy would take away her only chance of regaining her freedom by killing the only person left who was capable of freeing her. At least, the only one likely to do so.

Jack Stiles would die tonight at the hands of her son. That would leave only Hecaté, and Hecaté, for all her powers, was not a human being. She had not the power to save Tamar. Only a human could do that. Only a human being had the ability to make a wish.

As for the impostor (she must *not* keep forgetting him) well, *he* was not human either and would be easy to dispose of, at some point, if it became necessary.

* * *

'Hey, Ash!' Iffie spotted him across the street from Griff's and hailed him over. She had *known* he would be here.

Ash hesitated, and then crossed the street. He had plenty of time to fulfil his mission – all night, in fact. What could a few hours matter? As long as he was back home by dawn.

* * *

Fire and blood, blood and fire. It was Saturday. He was missing six days.

And on the seventh day…

~ Chapter Seven ~

AT EXACTLY 10.28 a.m. (real world time – B.S.T) Sunday morning, Cindy received the news that she had been waiting for. Denny had died. Died in his sleep, in fact. The last way anyone would have expected him to go. It was almost funny really. At least, it was to Cindy, who had certainly acquired a god's sense of humour.

She closed her eyes and breathed out slowly. *At last!* She was now safe – forever. All her years of careful planning had paid off beautifully. It had all been rather quick at the end.

She dismissed the minion with a nod. He had his instructions; he was to dispose of the body, throw it into the sea, or dig him a grave if he was sentimental, she did not care. She told him where it was. It was safe enough now. Up until now, her minions had been monitoring him from a safe distance. She had kept his actual location a secret from them; a moment's curiosity could ruin everything and they were only human after all. She wondered idly who had won the pool. She knew that bets had been placed on where he was actually being kept.

The minion left her with alacrity. None of them liked to be in her presence for too long.

By 10.30, she was back in the real world, breathing the real air. A moment to savour. She would have the old house torn down, and build a palace in its place, right over the time/space vortex. Her palace would move from place to place as the house had once done. But not in secret as before. Her power would be visible – tangible. People were going to bow down before her and tremble at her name.

But first things first, she would have to evict the remaining incumbents of the house first. Perhaps she would keep Tamar, though. She could have the bottle on her mantelpiece.[*] The thought made her laugh and laugh.

* * *

The house was just as she remembered it but emptier, of course. She found Hecaté on the veranda holding a very familiar bottle and looking grief stricken.

'As well she might,' thought Cindy. The only one left – apart from the impostor. 'I always forget about him.'

Hecaté looked up at Cindy with an expressionless face. 'So you have returned at last,' she said in a chilling monotone. 'We have been expecting you?'

Cindy looked contemptuously at the bottle that Hecaté could never be the one to open. And there *was* no one else. The grief on Hecaté's face told her that.

'We?' she said scornfully.

'Look behind you,' said Hecaté, standing up and letting the bottle crash to the ground.

With a cold chill, Cindy slowly turned.

'Hello Cindy,' said Denny. 'Miss me?' He touched her cheek softly.

Oh, it was not fair! He had not changed at all in all these years; he looked exactly the same as she remembered him. Her heart gave a treacherous lurch.

'Apparently,' said Tamar ironically.

---

[*] Years earlier Tamar had sacrificed her freedom and returned willingly to the slavery of the bottle in return for the power to bring Denny, Stiles and Cindy herself back from the dead. As he had before, Denny had managed to free her eventually by making a sacrifice of his own.

Cindy had not even seen her, nor had she noticed Stiles and Jack who had come out from the house, nor did she appear to hear Tamar's remark.

She was backing away from Denny with a look of desperation on her face. '*No, no*, you're *dead.*' she cried, and threw her hands up in front of her face, trying not to see him.

'Not for a lack of trying,' he said. He took her hands away from her face and held her gaze. 'Did you *really* think that we didn't know what you were doing, Cindy?' he said. 'We knew all the time, ever since Finvarra died. We knew that was *your* doing. Give it up Cindy. It's over. Think of your son. What is this doing to him? Don't you care at all?'

'My son?' she said blankly. She could not tear her gaze from his.

'Where is he Cindy? Where is your son?'

'I don't know,' she said truthfully. He had not come home the night before, and she had not cared sufficiently to wonder where he was. But her mind was elsewhere. '*No, no, no, no, no, no...*'

'Stop now, Cindy,' he said. 'It's time to stop all this. You've lost, but maybe that doesn't have to be a bad thing.'

He gave her a smile, a gentle, heartbreaking smile. The same smile that had stopped Tamar's heart the first time she had met him. Her gaze softened; all the fight seemed to suddenly drain out of her, and the cold light faded from her eyes. 'Oh Denny,' she said.

Then she pulled sharply away from him. '*No, no, no, no, no, no,*' she shrieked. She looked down at her hand in horror. The golden Ring was glowing like molten fire; smoke was rising from her finger.

Denny panicked as he realised what was happening. 'The Ring Cindy. Take off the Ring. Take it off. Take it off *now*! Oh *Christ*!'

But Cindy was muttering to herself. 'I don't love him, *don't* love him. Don't, *don't* ...' But it was too late.

Her face contorted as if she were in some terrible agony, and she threw back her head and gave out a high pitched banshee-like scream that went on and on and on.

Denny was knocked backwards by the sheer weight of the terrible noise. Even Tamar threw herself on the ground and covered her ears, and Stiles ran for cover. Then Cindy vanished, and the sound stopped abruptly like a radio being switched off.

Denny covered his face with his hands. 'What have I done?' he said. 'What have I done?

'What *have* you done?'

Everyone turned. Iffie was standing at the gate. But it was not she who had spoken.

'What *have* you done?' asked Ashtoreth in a cold voice.

'Dad!' Iffie ran to Denny and flung her arms around him. 'You're back.'

Denny patted her on the back distractedly. He kept his eyes on Ashtoreth. They all did.

A look of angry confusion came over Ashtoreth's face. 'This – *this* is your *father*?' he spluttered. 'But it – it *can't* be. You're *good*. I know you are. How can this evil man be your father?'

'Hey,' said Iffie indignantly. 'My Dad's not evil.'

'Shhh Iffie,' said Denny, putting a protective arm around her and drawing her away.

Ashtoreth was advancing on them with a look of ferocious wrath on his face. 'He destroyed my mother. I *saw* him.'

'No he didn't – did you Dad?'

'Go inside Iffie,' said Denny. Iffie stayed where she was.

'My mother was always afraid that you would destroy her with your evil and now you have.'

'Dad?'

'Murderer!' shrieked Ashtoreth.

'You can talk,' said Denny mildly. 'You tried to kill *me,* didn't you? If we hadn't known you were coming, you might have even succeeded too. I have to give you credit, it was a masterful plan.'

'Destroying evil isn't murder.'

Iffie gasped. *Oh God, it was true?*

Ashtoreth suddenly seemed to grow larger. Great white wings sprouted from his back, and he advanced on Denny who pushed Iffie behind him.

He held out a hand. 'Stay back son,' he said. 'I don't want to have to hurt you.'

Ashtoreth hesitated, and suddenly Jack, his own Faerie wings spread, leapt in between Ashtoreth and Denny. 'Go away,' he said menacingly. 'Leave us alone.'

They faced off, these estranged brothers, for a few moments and then Ashtoreth backed away, but it was clearly Denny he was afraid of, even though he had made no aggressive moves.

'Betrayed,' he said looking at Iffie. 'My mother murdered,' he spat at Denny. 'And as for you!' He turned to Jack. 'You who dare still, to wear my face … You have not seen the last of me,' he threatened. 'I will have my revenge.' And he vanished in a rather showy flash of light.

'Like mother like son,' said Stiles.

'I think he means it,' said Denny.

~ Chapter Eight ~

IT HAD BEEN Tamar (of course) who had figured it out. The large white feather in Finvarra's room had convinced her that a *real* angelic presence had been there. And they all knew about Cindy's son. It had suddenly become horribly clear to Tamar why Cindy had come back for him.

Not an angel, in fact, but the legendary Nephilim. Such a creature – the child of a fallen angel and a mortal woman – had not been born upon the earth since the beginning. Before even Tamar's time. Therefore, they had no idea what to expect. The powers of the Nephilim were not well known, and what little data was available seemed to consist mainly of wild stories of giant men who were sent by Satan to interrupt human development and corrupt the pure human bloodlines. A kind of early genetic experiment. Satan was contacted and denied it vehemently. Tamar, for one, believed him. He had never been that interested in the corruption of humans, despite the stories. Besides, they all knew how this particular Nephilim had come to be born.

However, knowing that Cindy had finally opened her war with them gave them an advantage. From that moment on, although it had been too late to save Finvarra, they were one step ahead of every move she made. Although she did not know it.

It would remain on open question whether or not Cindy's spy would have been spotted by them (hiding out in the form of a particularly ugly standard lamp) if they had not been half expecting him. But the fact was that he was, and when Denny got his hands on him, he turned on Cindy faster than a weathercock in a hurricane. From that moment on, he was working for them. The other spies that had been discovered within the house had been kept in careful ignorance of their discovery and allowed only to see what they were supposed to see.

When Denny was swept away by the tidal wave, Tamar was, at first, genuinely fooled. Her intention to enslave herself back in the Djinn bottle, in order to save him was only thwarted by the forceful urging of Stiles and Hecaté that he was still alive.

If that were truly the case, a simple wish should find him. Tamar had contacts – and she agreed to put off her decision until they had tried using them. An un-emancipated Djinn was procured (against Hecaté's better judgement – the Djinn were notorious tricksters as Tamar knew better than anyone. But as Tamar said, they had to try *something* to discover Denny's fate.) And when it was discovered that he *was* still alive, Cindy's turncoat spy was enlisted to release him at the right moment, i.e. right after he told Cindy (through an intermediary, whom he had enlisted on Tamar's behalf, since he was not allowed to go back to her palace himself after being out in the world) that Denny had died.

It was, the spy had assured them, the only way to get the location out of her. Even the Djinn had not been able to trace his whereabouts and Cindy had kept that information close to her chest.

* * *

It had been a damn close thing in the end. Had Cindy been given the news that Denny had died before she might reasonably expect to hear about it, she would probably have been suspicious and might even have checked on the information and, therefore, found out that she had been lied to and, from that, judge that she had been exposed, and she would undoubtedly have killed the minion too. But, had they left it too long, he might have really died before the spy could get to him.

Denny – his body at least – had been washed up on the shore of a small coral promontory in the middle of the Mediterranean, not even an island; it was certainly not on any map. But where his mind had been was anybody's guess.

'Somewhere far away,' said the minion, who only vaguely understood what had happened (and Tamar knew that this much at least was true, or else *she* would have been able to find him easily) but what he *was* sure of was that waking him would be easy. That was the reason, so he had heard, that Cindy allowed no one to go near him, or even to know where he was since, for as long as he was still alive, the slightest contact would revive him immediately. Cindy's minions, it appeared, had known a damn sight more about what was going on than she had ever guessed. Minions have ears too it seems (and feelings of being underappreciated – Denny really had not had to threaten him all that much to get him to switch sides.)

On the smallest events does the fate of men hang.

Had the feather never been shed in Finvarra's room, giving cause for doubt, not only about Finvarra's demise, but also any other suspicious circumstance that might occur (and to Stiles at least, *every* circumstance was suspicious) there could be no doubt that she would have won.

And Denny, even though he knew that the Nephilim was after them, still never saw him coming. Without the help of the spy in Cindy's ranks he would not have escaped the dreamscape. Ashtoreth had been right about that. Even the Djinn that Tamar had used could not do more than reveal Denny's fate. He did not even know for certain where Denny was only that he was alive – *somewhere*. Nor was he able, any more than anyone else, to locate Cindy's hiding place. That remained a mystery.

Cindy's fears that she could have been traced back to her hiding place through the capture of one of her spies had proved unfounded. Tamar had tried, but Cindy had covered her tracks better than she realised, even her own servants had no idea where she was. The irony of this was that she could have been spying on them in perfect security for years. Had she known about Iphigenia, things might have gone very differently for her.

A child is leverage; Cindy had had Tamar's child within her grasp and never known it. And, had she known about the existence of a child, she might not have anticipated Tamar's reaction to the loss of Denny so incorrectly. A more circumspect Tamar was a new development, a direct result of motherhood. Her uncharacteristic hesitation towards drastic action (thus giving Stiles time to convince her otherwise) had all been for Iffie's sake. And finally, it had been Iffie herself who had unwittingly saved the life of Stiles, by occupying Ashtoreth's attention on the night he was due to murder him.

Denny for one, and Tamar for another wanted an explanation about this.

'We we're just *talking* Dad, honestly,' said Iffie. She had been devastated to learn that the boy she had spent so much time with, had *liked*, had been the murderer of Jack's father, and worse, had tried to, and almost succeeded in, killing her *own* father.

Tamar was inclined to blame herself. Had Iffie and Jack known the story of Cindy's defection in the first place, maybe this would not have happened. However, as Denny pointed out, there was no excuse for going off secretly with young men – whoever they were, without telling anyone.

And why, when she learned his identity, did she tell no one about *that* either? They could have warned her, had they known.

Iffie agreed to it all. She had been wrong – foolish – arrogant. Here, Jack stepped up in her defence. He too had known, he said, and had also kept his mouth shut.

'He tried to stop me,' said Iffie. 'I wouldn't listen. I thought I could help him. We *can* help him right Dad? He's *family*, whatever he's done. He's messed up Dad, and now I think I know why. His mother's crazy.'

Tamar and Denny looked at each other.

'She's not crazy,' said Tamar. 'She's bitter and hurt and under the influence of a power that she was never meant to have.'

'It's my fault really,' said Denny.

'Dad?' Iffie was startled.

'A woman scorned,' said Tamar. 'This was about vengeance. Cindy's vengeance.'

'I never meant to hurt her,' said Denny.

'What are you saying?' said Jack, leaping to his feet angrily. 'Why did my father die? Why did my mother leave?' He turned on Denny viciously. 'What did you do to her? What did she want vengeance *for*? *Tell* me.' And he pounded Denny with his fists.

Tamar dragged him away. 'Don't hit him,' she said. 'He didn't do anything.'

'That's not true,' said Denny. 'I *did* do something.'

'I don't want to know,' said Tamar quickly. 'Ever.'

'Perhaps it's not as bad as you imagine,' said Denny.

'I *don't* imagine, I never do, and I don't want to hear it, please Denny don't.'

Jack and Iffie were now staring at them both in bewilderment. Like all teenagers do when it finally becomes apparent that their elders actually had lives before they were born.

'I knew she loved me,' said Denny softly, 'but I didn't want to face it. Perhaps if I had … You were gone, and I didn't know if you were ever coming back. I was lonely and hurting. I made a mistake. Not … not the big one, not that. But enough. Enough to hurt her. And then I just pretended like it had never happened. I didn't know what else to do. And she seemed okay. I thought …'

'Thought you'd got away with it?' said Tamar tersely.

'Yes, I suppose so. I know all this is my fault.'

'It's not you know,' said Jack surprisingly.

'No it isn't,' agreed Tamar. 'And I bet ... Oh I just bet she threw herself at you. Just when you were at your lowest ebb. You might just as well say it's *my* fault for leaving.'

'It's no one's fault,' said Jack. 'It's just a big mess as far as I can tell. My father loved her – she loved you – and you loved Tamar. Broken hearts all round. But nobody's *fault*. You can't pick who you love. Can you? She should have known better.'

'He's right you know,' said Tamar. 'And you were right too. What I imagined *was* worse than the truth. I wish I'd let you tell me years ago.

'Well, this is all very cathartic,' she said with a touch of her usual sharpness. 'Big group hugs and all that. But the fact is, the story doesn't end there. It's actually what Cindy did next, not what made her do it, that's important.'

'What *did* she do?' asked Iffie curiously.

'Do you know your Wagner?' asked Denny.

'Er, yes, you know you insisted on a classical education, but what ...?'

'Assume its all true,' said Tamar. 'Cindy stole the Rheingold. And that one was *my* fault.'

'Bloody hell!' said Jack.

'Language,' said Tamar automatically.

'She stole the Rheingold,' resumed Denny. 'You know what that means?'

'She had forsaken love for power,' said Iffie. *Thank God for a classical education.*

'Right,' said Denny. 'Great power. Not enough power, not against ours. But the Nephilim ... Well, its dicey that's all. He has a power that I doubt even he himself fully understands. And she has spent years corrupting him – priming him to destroy us. And now he's out there, furious and grieving. He saw all her lies apparently confirmed. He saw me destroy his mother. I swear I didn't mean to. I was trying to save her. God knows what he'll do now.'

'I'm not so sure she *was* destroyed,' said Iffie surprisingly. 'Not in the way you mean anyway. I mean I don't think she's dead.

'You see,' she continued, 'the ring is a *thing*, like a magical *thing*. Hecaté says a thing like that can't go against its basic nature or whatever. So as long as she's still wearing it, it'll still make her immortal and powerful and all of that. What's happened is that it's destroyed something inside her or something like that. Like her soul or whatever makes her – *her*. You know?'

'No, no,' said Jack impatiently. 'You've got the right idea, but according to the story. What the ring destroys isn't the self. It's whatever's most *important* to the self. But with Cindy already being a witch before all this. I reckon something even worse could happen.'

'What *was* most important to her?' asked Iffie.

'Her looks,' said Denny and Tamar without hesitation.

'So she could end up like a hideous old crone or something?' said Iffie.

All the colour suddenly drained from Denny's face.

* * *

It is not for nothing that Satan is called "The Prince of Lies". There are more descendants of the Nephilim on the Earth than anyone knows. Ashtoreth intended to find them all. He had seen what had happened to his mother when she tried to face the evil ones alone. But there was strength in numbers.

Denny's innocent and still slightly juvenile face was imprinted on his memory as the epitome of ultimate evil and degeneracy. He would peel the mask from him, he vowed. Expose his evil to the world and then slowly and painfully destroy him. He was really looking forward to it.

But first things first. Hiding here in the haven that his mother had created was not forwarding his plan. He was safe here, but in order to recruit his army, he *would* have to go out into the world.

She was out there. He found his thoughts wandering often to Iphigenia. She *was* the spawn of evil he told himself, yet he could not stop thinking about her. No doubt, he told himself, that was the idea. She had been sent to tempt him away from his cause. To pierce the armour of his righteousness and leave him weakened. And she had too, for a brief time. But there would be no more of such weakness. When the time came, she would die like the rest. It had to be so. And yet ... and yet ... she was young. Perhaps it was not too late for her. She was not deep in corruption like the others; there was good in her, he was sure of it. He might yet be able to save her. He would offer her a choice. If she chose evil then he would do what he had to. But he fervently hoped that it would not be necessary.

Perhaps even more than he wanted to kill her father, he wanted to save her. Although based on a flawed premise, this was, ultimately, an unselfish emotion. That Iffie did not *need* saving by the likes of him was a thought that never occurred to him. But the fact that he wanted to do it, was perhaps a sign that he was not completely lost.

He would have been amazed and outraged to discover that Iffie wanted to save *him*.

So he wandered through the empty halls thinking of the past and the future. Slick had left now, and he had been close to becoming the nearest thing Ashtoreth had ever had to a friend, but that was over now. His mother was dead, and the minions had been sent away before his mother's tragic foray into the world. He was alone. But not for long; he had plans.

* * *

It was not a dream this time, although Denny did not know this. It was still happening in his sleep. He awoke completely enervated – drained in a way that was totally unfamiliar to him. Even before the Athame, he never remembered feeling like this. It was still dark outside; Denny rose quietly so he would not disturb Tamar and staggered drunkenly into the bathroom where he threw up violently.

It was not normal to feel like this after a dream. The other times he had not felt like this, he had woken up agitated and unnerved but not strung out like this. He had felt recently as if the dream was getting – not worse exactly, but closer.

Definitely closer to being real, but he had put that down to being stuck in the dreamscape, where *all* his dreams had seemed real.

He had really been hoping that the dreams had been a part of Cindy's plot, something she had had Ashtoreth do to him to unnerve him. He had good reason to know that Ashtoreth was more than capable of this kind of subconscious manipulation. The fact that the dreams had continued to plague him, even in the dreamscape, seemed to support this idea. But it was time to face the fact that perhaps there was something else going on.

* * *

When Jack caught Iffie scrying in her bedroom mirror he hit the roof. 'You're looking for *him* again, aren't you?'

'I'm just practising,' she said defensively.

'Really?' said Jack sarcastically. 'What's with the feather?' He held up exhibit A with disdain.

'Oh, all *right*. But you needn't worry. I can't find him anyway. I've tried scrying, divining, locator spells. It's like he's just vanished off the face of the Earth.'

'Well, we *know* he has,' said Jack, 'or weren't you listening? They were trying to find Cindy for years. No one knows where she went, and she took him with her. What do you want to find him for anyway? He's *dangerous* Iffie. Let your mum and dad handle him.'

'I just wanted to help. I thought if I could *find* him … I wasn't going to go *near* him or anything.'

'Oh, come on Iffie, who do you think you're talking to? I *know* you. You're Jonesing. I can tell. What's so great about him anyway? He tried to kill your dad, Iffie. He *did* kill mine. And all you can think about is helping him get over his rotten childhood. What about a bit of family loyalty? If not to me then to your own father. How would you have felt about him if he *had* killed your dad, eh? Would you have been so hipped on helping him then? Or does your family mean so little to you, that, even then, you would still want this bastard in your life? – Oh God, I'm sorry. Don't cry Iffie, I didn't mean it.'

'He's coming after us Iffie,' he said, more gently, 'to kill us all. You heard him yourself. *I* didn't want it to turn out like this either. He was like my brother. But … it is what it is. If you keep this up you *are* going to get hurt. I don't want to lose you too. I've already lost enough.'

Iffie looked up into his eyes. Black eyes, like the eyes of a shark. The only outward sign that he was a Faerie and the only physical difference between him and Ashtoreth unless they unfolded their respective wings.

'He gave me something Jack, she said, and she produced, from somewhere among her clothing, a shining white orb filled with light.

'What is it?

'I don't know. He never said. I thought it might be some sort of communication device. You know, like giving out your phone number. But I can't see how it works. Do you think maybe Mum or Dad might be able to use it to find him?'

Jack shook his head. 'I don't know. It doesn't look like a communication device to me.'

'Oh, I don't know, it's kind of like a crystal ball don't you think?'

'Iffie you're a *witch*. You *know* that crystal balls are just … well *balls* basically.'

'Nice *double entendre*,' she said.

'Thank you,' he nodded his head in a mock bow.

'Oh, hell, maybe he got in a gift shop and it's just a paperweight,' she said.

'I'd be careful of it. It might be a booby trap.'

'No, it was a gift. He might want to kill me *now*. But he didn't when he gave it to me.'

'What …? began Jack, and then decided that he did not think he wanted to know.

'*What*, what?' she said.

'Nothing, never mind.'

'I didn't do anything stupid Jack,' she said. 'We just talked,' Jack did not believe her.

* * *

Everyone except Iffie and Jack could remember what it had been like after Cindy had left. The horrible sense of limbo, of knowing that disaster was going to strike and having no idea how long they might have to find a way to avert it. Two days, six months, a decade.

After a while though, when nothing happened. Life had settled back down into its regular chaos. No one can spend every moment on high alert, and there were lives to live and children to raise, people to save. But you never quite forget. It hangs like a bat in the back of your mind. One day, one day…

'Deleted files, parallel universes, the history files,' Jack ticked them off on his fingers. 'They looked everywhere for her hiding place. She wasn't inside the mainframe at all.'

'How is that possible?' said Iffie.

'There *are* places outside the mainframe, your dad says, and they tried all the ones they know of. The old Faerie realm, Hell, places like that.'

'But she had to have been *somewhere*!' pointed out Iffie reasonably.

'Your dad said she was cunning, maybe she was hiding in plain sight,' said Jack

'That's an Oxymoron,' said Iffie.

'*What* did you call me?' said Jack with mock indignation and he threw a cushion at her. She leapt on him immediately, and they wrestled like puppies for a few minutes before Jack put his hands up in surrender. 'Okay, okay, I give,' he said. 'Man, you're strong for a little one,' he added.

Iffie preened.

'The point is,' he said, resuming the subject. 'If *they* couldn't find her hiding place in fifteen years, what makes you think *we* can?'

'Young blood, a fresh approach, no previous assumptions, lateral thinking,' she said. 'Anyway it can't hurt to try can it? Like what you said about her hiding in plain sight. What did you mean by that?'

'It's like when you don't look for something because you already know where it is. You don't notice it because it's right under your nose.'

'That would put her squarely inside mainframe then,' said Iffie.

'*If* that's what she did. Personally I think it's a long shot.'

It'd be damn clever if she did, though, and she must have done something *pretty* clever or they'd have found her. *I* think it's worth looking into.'

'*Someone* found her though, didn't they?' said Jack. 'Your mum said that some bloke they all used to know went after her and never came back.'

'We don't know that he found her at all. If he never came back, he might have gone anywhere.'

'But what if he *did* find her … I think we need to find out about this guy. I mean maybe if we knew a bit about him, how he thinks …'

'We might be able to follow how he did it,' finished Iffie. 'Now that's what I call lateral thinking.'

* * *

Everyone was working towards this end with varying degrees of fervency. But with, unfortunately, equal degrees of success so far, i.e. none at all.

Iffie and Jack were working together now; both determined to be the ones to figure it out.

Iffie decided to contact The Agency and find out what she could about Slick who had been calling himself Tony something at the time.

Director Dawber had been pretty forthcoming with what information he had when he understood what it was about, but it was depressingly little. It didn't matter, Iffie maintained, that the secret lair that this Slick character (stupid name) had found was not the same one they were now looking for. It was, as she explained dramatically, the *principle* of the thing.

Jack did not even pretend to understand this view of the matter. He was more interested in the orb that Ashtoreth had given her. Even if it was not a communication device as such, it was that thing they had precious little of, a clue.

And he mulled over it for hours and hours but, whatever it was, it was not telling. It just sat there looking as glowy and shiny as an orb can, but it never *did* anything.

They considered the principle of "hiding in plain sight". The ideas that this generated went from the sublime to the ridiculous, but nothing remotely helpful. A disused Djinn bottle, known for its TARDIS like properties had been favourite for one exciting minute, until they discovered that you can get *in* to a Djinn bottle quite easily, but it is not so easy to get *out*. They were learning, as Tamar and Denny had before them, that the right answers can only be found after exhausting all the wrong ones. It was a disheartening process.

Jack had eventually handed the orb over to Denny – let him cudgel *his* brains over it for a while. Who knew, he had far more experience of this sort of thing than Jack had, he might find an answer.

He did. He knew what it was immediately. 'It's a nightlight,' he said. 'You and Ashtoreth both had them. It's filled with Faerie light. He passed a hand over it, and the light went out. 'See?' he said. 'Very pretty but ultimately useless – sorry.'

'But it was his for years might it not … can't we use it somehow to trace him?'

'What did you have in mind?' said Denny. It was easy to love him at times like this; he was being perfectly serious.

'I-I'm not sure really,' confessed Jack. 'I thought *you* might have an idea.'

'I'll give it some thought,' said Denny. He really meant it too; he really did.

Tamar and Denny were taking a different approach to the search. Scouring the mainframe – not for the actual hiding place, they had already exhausted this avenue of enquiry over the last fifteen years. But for information on the basic background of the Rheingold and its owner's powers and behaviour to see if there might be a clue in there about what

Cindy might have done. And for information about the Nephilim to see what they were going to be up against when or if they did find him – or he found them.

No one had even considered looking for Cindy… She was dead, wasn't she?

~ Chapter Nine ~

IFFIE AND JACK did not bother going through the mainframe files. They knew perfectly well that this had been done and done and done again. They both agreed that it was as Iffie had said. Finding Ashtoreth was going to take some lateral thinking.

Iffie liked Jack's idea of hiding in plain sight. Since he clearly was not hiding in any of the usual places then it seemed most likely that he was in a much more unexpected location and what could be a more unexpected hiding place than right in front of you?

They racked their brains over this idea for some time.

'We're looking for something that isn't what it seems to be,' said Jack. 'Like the hidden code within a seemingly normal looking communication,'

'Or something very well camouflaged as something else,' said Iffie. 'Or is that the same thing?'

'And don't forget, they couldn't find it in the mainframe,' said Jack.

'Maybe they didn't know what they were looking for?' said Iffie.

'*We* don't know what we're looking for!' said Jack and they both laughed.

'What I mean is, if it's disguised as something else ... oh my God.'

'What?'

'Well, it's not a deleted file, we know that. But there are a hell of a lot of un-deleted files. What I mean is, maybe he's exactly where you might expect him to be. Hidden in plain sight. Where do gods usually live? What sort of place? '

'Er, Valhalla, Olympus, various ideas of Heaven ... I don't know. You think that Cindy just went to live with a load of other gods?'

'It's somewhere we'd never look,' pointed out Iffie. 'Because we think we *know* who's there. It's a lot easier to hide in a crowd, isn't it? She could have built her own house or castle or fortress or whatever.'

'Well, Asgard's favorite I suppose. What with the Rheingold and all,' said Jack.

* * *

It turned out that most of the old gods were deleted files themselves and that meant their homes were most definitely *former*. And there were many pantheons of gods that had no fixed home at all.

But there were a few left. Asgard was one of them, Avalon another. The Duat, the home of the Egyptian gods, was deleted, as was the home of the Olympians although there was some dubiety about this last, since it had never had an official name – no record of the file, deleted or otherwise, could be found. Iffie thought this weird and rather suspicious and even thought it made it a prime candidate for Ashtoreth's hiding place.

But top of the list was Avalon. It was close by and the only other likely place. Asgard turned out, on further investigation, to be pretty damn unlikely since, for one thing, that was where Tamar and Denny had actually been whilst Cindy was busy making her new home. It was practically inconceivable that they would not have known if she had been there. And further, the Norse gods would probably not have tolerated her moving in after having stolen the Rhine Maidens gold. Besides which, Odin owed Tamar and Denny a favour. Cindy would certainly have been handed over long ago, had she even set foot in Asgard.

And there were other reasons too, not least of which included Odin's humanitarian tendencies, which would definitely preclude the idea of his putting up with Ashtoreth's murderous urges.

All this added up to only one conclusion. That if Cindy *had* built her safe haven among the gods somewhere, it was on Avalon.

* * *

Iffie was quite excited about the trip to Avalon. She had grown up hearing the stories of her parents' adventures in such places as the Faerie realm and Mainframe and Valhalla but had never been to any places like that herself.

For the first time since she had met him, Ashtoreth was the last thing on her mind, and this, in spite of the fact that he was the object of the journey in the first place.

'We have to remember that we don't have their powers,' said Jack. 'We'll have to be careful. We don't know what we might find.'

Iffie disregarded this advice. Her dad, at least, had been to some pretty dangerous spots before he had had any powers at all and he had managed to survive somehow. In fact, it had been as a prisoner in a vampire's dungeon that he had found the Athame in the first place.

According to the files, they could expect to meet the Celtic gods in Avalon. But they both knew they would not. Hecaté had taken care of them some years ago when they had tried to help Loki start the Ragnoroc rumble.

Other possible denizens included the personalities of the Arthurian legends.

It was also expected that there might be dragons.

The file took them to a misty lake apparently in the middle of nowhere. There was a boat. They untied the boat and got in. There were no oars, and whatever the motive power was, it was invisible to the passengers. The boat just seemed to float off on its own, into the mist.

They floated through the mist for a few minutes until it suddenly rolled back and parted like a pair of curtains (which is not a romantic simile but that is what it was like).

The scene it revealed was breathtaking. The isle of Avalon was perched high above them apparently floating in the air. From its shores, a vast waterfall fell steaming and hissing into the tranquil lake beneath. It was just possible, from their vantage point below, to see the cliffs of Avalon rising from the shores, and these cliffs had waterfalls of their own, falling from who knew what pools and lakes higher up.

There was a decision to make, and they had to make it fast. The boat showed no signs of stopping but seemed set to take them through the falls and out the other side, possibly right to the other side of the lake.

Jack acted quickly. He spread his wings – Faerie wings very unlike Ashtoreth's muscular, solid and heavily feathered wings. Thin and translucent with a myriad of rainbow colours shimmering through them. You would not have trusted them to hold up a puppy let alone a full grown man plus passenger. But Jack took hold of Iffie around the waist and rose easily and gracefully out of the boat and up the waterfall and further, high above the shores of Avalon to the summit of the cliffs where he landed softly and placed Iffie gently on the ground keeping his hands on her waist just a fraction longer than was strictly necessary – just to steady her of course.

Iffie barely noticed; she wriggled free and ran to the nearest lake to look in. Jack's arms dropped to his sides, and his head drooped for a second as he became conscious of a sense of disappointment that he did not really understand. But then Iffie ran to him like an excited child and took him by the hands and dragged him forward. 'Jack!' Jack, you've got to see this.' She tugged insistently at him.

The lake was absolutely choc full of gleaming swords.

'What do you think it means?' she asked.

Jack shrugged. 'Spares?' he said, and Iffie fell about laughing. She stopped abruptly as Jack, with a curiously intense look on his face, reached into the water to take one.

'*Don't!*' she screeched in a panic.

He turned and looked interrogatively at her. 'Why?' he said. 'It might come in handy.'

'It … just might not be a good idea that's all,' she said lamely. 'We don't know what will happen. It could be a test or a trap or something.' You could see that she had been paying attention to her bedtime stories over the years.

Jack took a reluctant step back from the lake. 'You're right,' he said, and forced himself to turn away.

But now it was Iffie who was staring in utter fascination at the lake. There was a good reason for this, however. Jack turned back to follow her gaze and saw a sword rising vertically from the lake, it was followed by a hand gripping the hilt, and that was followed by an arm.

The arm shook slightly, and a muffled, waterlogged voice suddenly said. 'Well, come on, are you going to take the damn thing or not. I can't do this all day you know. I'm not as young as I used to be.'

'God, it's just like dad always said it was,' said Iffie. 'Every magical maiden has an attitude on her like a fishwife.'

'Should I take it?' said Jack uncertainly.

Iffie nodded. 'It should be all right now that you've been offered it. It's not like stealing it. Take it, go on.'

'That's right,' said the voice, 'unless you want to fight the Black Knight without it. Just hurry up will you?'

Jack grabbed the sword. The arm disappeared.

'Black Knight?' he said.

'Oh, yeah,' said Iffie. 'I think I read about that somewhere. You have to prove yourself worthy to enter Avalon by defeating the Black Knight in combat.' She shrugged. 'Medieval code. Different moral values I guess.'

'But I *can't* sword fight,' said Jack.

'You can fly,' said Iffie. 'That should give you an advantage.'

'What am I, Peter Pan?' said Jack grumpily.

'Anyway, I don't think it works like that in this sort of place,' she added comfortingly. 'I mean dad beat up all those ninja dudes that time, and he'd never held a sword before either. Maybe you just have to have like a worthy heart or something. And I reckon if anyone has, it's you.'

'Will I have to kill him do you think?' he said. ''Cause I don't think ... Uh oh!'

'Time to see what you're made of,' said Iffie confidently.

Jack held up the sword tentatively as the black armour clad figure clanked heavily toward him.

The Black Knight slashed at him cutting his arm open, blood flowed down his sleeve, and Iffie gasped in horror as she suddenly realised this was real.

Jack staggered back and clutched at his bleeding arm. A sudden, rare anger filled him – he had never liked bullies, even though he had rarely been bothered by them himself, being tall and somewhat well built.

This guy was bigger. Not to mention well armed and protected, but well ... Iffie was right, he did not have wings.

Jack lifted off as the next stroke came at him – it went under his feet and Jack turned in the air and slashed downwards at the helmet knocking it right off. A chain mail hood still concealed the features of his opponent, but it offered far less in the way of protection than the helmet had. Iffie cheered.

Now the Black Knight was slashing futilely at the air – Jack was keeping just out of his reach seeking an opportunity to strike.

He drew back further and then, with a faint buzzing sound, which was the whirring of his wings, he bore down fast on the Knight and kicked out hard at the sword arm knocking the sword out of his hand. Then he landed behind the knight and held his own sword out at the side of the knight's throat.

'Forfeit!' he said coldly. The knight fell on his knees and held up his hands in a gesture of surrender. Jack kicked him hard in the back so that he fell on his face. Iffie watched in horror as he raised his sword in both hands and brought it down in a stabbing motion towards the inert figure. Then she breathed out again. He had only stabbed through the chain mail pinning the knight to the ground.

'That wasn't too bad,' said Jack. He sounded more relieved than triumphant.

'Oh, but your poor arm,' said Iffie. 'Are you all right?'

'Fine,' he said. And he meant it too. The adrenaline still rushing through him was overriding the pain, at least for the moment.

'You were really great,' said Iffie admiringly. 'I told you, you could do it.'

'If I hadn't had the wings, I don't think my "worthy heart" would have done me much good though,' he said wryly. 'So does this mean we get to go further in now. I was kind of expecting a welcoming party or something.'

'I think *he's* the welcoming party,' she said pointing to the knight. 'From now on we're on our own.'

'I don't have a problem with that,' said Jack. ''Specially if *that's* the kind of welcome we can expect.'

'But we don't know where we want to go,' said Iffie. 'Don't they have like a tour guide or something?'

'It's not Disneyland,' said Jack impatiently.

'I know, but ...'

Merlin's Citadel,' said Jack. 'If anyone can help us, I reckon it's him, don't you? It's supposed to be in the centre of Avalon so we should head sort of ... inland.'

'Well, why didn't you just say so?' she said.

It was not to be expected that Merlin's citadel would be unguarded, and it was not. In fact, despite the fact that the citadel itself was, like Avalon, floating free in the air above them, there was a whole city all around – or rather below – it. This then was where the inhabitants of Avalon were gathered. Human, elven (not to be confused with Faeries – elves are the messengers of the gods) the walkers of Weyland – not human, but they had been once, so the legends tell, and also ogres, goblins and dragons.

'We aren't safe here,' muttered Jack.

'No one is safe anywhere,' said a voice behind them. 'But there is no evil here.'

They turned to see a tall grim faced man in gleaming armour covered by a black velvet cloak and wearing a horned helmet reminiscent of the Norse style. He also carried a large horn as well as the obligatory sword. He was smiling at them. 'I am Gafael,' he said. 'The gatekeeper. I have come to bring you to Merlin.'

'Well, that's a relief anyway,' said Iffie.

'Is it?' said Gafael, with a strange smile. 'We shall see about that. Come with me.'

Merlin was pretty much as they had expected him to be – sort of Gandalf on steroids.

'You do not belong here,' he said. But not as if he was unduly disturbed by the fact.

'We're looking for someone,' said Jack boldly.

'Are you indeed? You know I think our lady of the lake took a bit of a shine to you,' he said confidentially. 'She sent word that I should see you, otherwise ... well I'm very busy you know. And you evidently are not evil or anything ... no evil gets in here you know. It all ends up ...' And he pointed downwards. 'So if you are "looking for someone", as you put it. You might have better luck in the nether realms below us. Go and see Necromon, he rules the netherworld.' He started to laugh at their horrified faces. 'No, no,' he chortled. 'A mere jest. I would not send you to *him*. Brave you are, but young yet. Not ready for that, not yet.'

'But if we are going to find Ashtoreth ...' began Jack.

'Ashtoreth eh? So that is his name, is it?'

'He's not here is he?' said Jack, looking downcast. 'He never was, was he? Well it *was* a bit of a long shot I suppose.'

'A very good idea though,' said Merlin encouragingly. 'You mustn't give up hope.

'Do *you* know where he is?' asked Iffie suddenly. 'You seem to know an awful lot about it.'

'No, no, I don't really. An old man's hubris, that's all you have heard. A little trick to make me seem wise. I have been out of the world for a long time now. But I do know all who come and go within my realm, and you two are the first visitors to Avalon for many a century.'

'Oh,' said Iffie. 'Uncle Jack does that too, I should have realised.

'Is he a sorcerer?'

'No, he's a policeman.'

'You expected to find gods here?' said Merlin, instead of replying to this.

'Not really,' explained Iffie. 'You see, we know what happened to the Tuatha de Danann ...'

'They were not the true gods,' said Merlin surprisingly. 'They took their form and their names, but before they came, there were the true gods of the Celts who were manifested in the same way as all gods are, through the sheer power of belief. Some of those gods still remain. Our lady of the lake is one.'

'And you?' asked Jack. 'What are you exactly?'

'A mere sorcerer,' said Merlin modestly.

'And if you believe that you'll believe anything,' said Iffie quietly, nudging Jack.

There was a silence.

'Before you go, 'said Merlin suddenly. 'Perhaps a little advice from an old man. You were on the right track. Your quarry is indeed "hidden in plain sight".' Suddenly he clapped his hands with a loud boom and they were back in Iffie's bedroom before they could reply.

'He knew' said Jack when he had got his breath back. 'You were right. He knew all about it. And I bet he knows where Ashtoreth is too. Damn it, *why* wouldn't he tell us?'

'Hidden in plain sight,' said Iffie. 'He said we were on the right track – oh stop sulking, it's obvious that he *couldn't* tell us for some reason. All that free will garbage probably. Now just think ... where else could he be hiding in plain sight?'

'And just where the hell have *you* been?'

They spun; Tamar and Denny were standing in the doorway. Tamar had her arms folded in that pose that tells you: "You're in trouble now".

'You met *Merlin*?' said Denny. 'I've got to admit, that's pretty cool, what was he like?'

'You shouldn't' have gone off without telling us,' said Tamar automatically.

'He was pretty much what you would expect,' said Iffie, ignoring her mother, who did not mean it anyway. 'You know long white beard, wizardly robes, talked a lot of mystical nonsense.'

Denny laughed. 'I can see we've turned you into a cynic,' he said. 'I'm not sure whether that's a good thing or not really.'

'That arm looks nasty,' said Tamar to Jack. 'What happened?'

'Oh, yeah,' Iffie answered for him. 'He had to fight the Black Knight. He was really great you know. It was amazing. He ...'

'Shut up Iffie,' said Jack turning red. 'It wasn't anything really.' Denny never boasted about his conquests and Jack did not want him to think he was getting above himself. He was forgetting that usually Denny did not *have* to boast because Tamar did it for him.

Denny merely raised an eyebrow. 'Impressed were you?' he asked Iffie.'

'Yes,' said Iffie, looking at Jack defiantly. 'Very.'

Tamar smiled. 'Well, I hope you aren't too macho now to let me heal that for you,' she said.

'Don't be silly Mum,' said Iffie, a little nettled. 'Jack isn't *macho*! He's got too much sense for that.'

'If you wouldn't mind,' said Jack holding his arm out. 'It does ache a bit,' he admitted.

'What did Merlin say?' asked Denny shrewdly, as Jack was having his arm healed. 'I know he must have said *something* about why you were there, was he any help?'

'Not really,' said Iffie. 'He just said that we were on the right track – sort of anyway. Said that he *was* hidden in plain sight, just like we thought.'

'And that's all?' said Denny, disappointed.

'Hey, it's all right Dad, we'll find him, don't you worry,' said Iffie patting his arm.

'Hidden in plain sight,' said Denny thoughtfully. 'That's quite clever really. I wish I'd thought of it.'

Iffie beamed with pride. She always flowered under her father's praise.

~ Chapter Ten ~

ASHTORETH HAD never dreamed, when he sent out the call, that so many would answer. The world was *full* of his brethren. Descendants of the Nephilim populated the earth in their millions. An army. An army of righteousness. All his to command. Their diluted blood made them less powerful than him, and they were easily bent to his will. It would be selfish to use them only for personal revenge. He saw his way clearly now.

God had taken his mother to show him the pain that evil caused in the world, and he had sent him an army to purge the world of that evil.

He would still have his revenge, but it could wait. Let them see first, what their evil had wrought. They would see their evil associates fall one by one and wait, trembling, for their turn.

* * *

Tamar had had an idea about finding Cindy's hiding place, where Ashtoreth might still be, but Denny was not buying it.

'But we *know* she wasn't hiding in a deleted file,' said Denny. 'Haven't we checked them all? And besides, it's a bit obvious, isn't it?'

'Okay, yes and yes,' said Tamar. 'But we don't know that he hasn't moved to a deleted file since then, but I doubt it …'

'And so do I.'

'... But it wasn't a deleted file, I was thinking of. It's more like a deleted *folder*.'

'Ah, I am intrigued, do tell.' said Denny steepling his fingers and looking mockingly over the top of them.

'Well, *you* ought to know,' she said. 'You were the one inside the mainframe.'

'I was a bit busy at the time.'

'Crash and override,' she said. 'I remember. So you must know that there are whole sections of the mainframe that are ... not exactly deleted files more like rewritten programs. Entire ages ... Look, I'm thinking of the mythological age.'

'They overwrote it to turn it into fiction. But the files it contained originally are still deleted files,' said Denny without hesitation. And the new files are just ordinary historical files such as anybody might get into. With the right access codes,' he amended, realising that it would be a pretty narrow definition of "anybody" that would fit his criteria. 'That's what they always do,' he added. 'All deleted files are created that way, filled with stuff that "never happened".'

'Yes, but when I said deleted files, that's not exactly what I meant ...' Tamar stumbled on. 'I can't explain what I mean. It doesn't make any sense, but *I* know what I mean ... damn ... just let me think a minute.'

'Look,' said Denny. 'We've looked thorough *all* the files, deleted or otherwise, it's taken us fifteen years. She wasn't there, and *he* isn't there now.'

'I *know*,' said Tamar impatiently. 'But ... she, and now he, has to be *somewhere*. Just let me think will you?'

Denny held his hands up in a gesture of surrender. 'Okay, okay, I'm sorry,' he said, and made a motion with his hand across his face as if zipping his mouth shut.

She leaned back and closed her eyes. Denny did not dare to do the same, he was afraid he might fall asleep.

'Okay,' she said. 'I've got it now. Where does all that stuff go, when it's been deleted?'

'Into people's heads,' said Denny.

'Into the realm of the imagination,' corrected Tamar. 'Redundant beliefs. And there's a file for that too, but it isn't in mainframe.'

Denny shuddered; he thought he could see where this was going.

'I'm not talking about the dreamscape,' she said. 'But answer me this, what sort of Being is good at accessing the belief of mortal minds?'

'A god!' said Denny snapping his fingers. 'But the belief isn't there anymore,' he added frowning. That's the point. Neither are the things that were the focus of that belief. In fact, that brings us back to the deleted files.' He sighed.

'That belief *is* still there,' said Tamar. 'Think! I know you can remember if you try.'

'People from the time, believed in the gods and so on,' said Denny. 'And they were real – at the time. People believed in them because they were real, and they were real because people believed in them – but they aren't now, and they never were because it was all deleted except ... It's a paradox,' he said. 'Redundant belief belongs in history.

'Right,' said Tamar. 'If you want access to that belief you have to go back to when it still existed. Even though the gods never existed *now* they did *then*. They may have all been tidied up into deleted files from our point of view, but there was a time, when they hadn't been. I know it's weird. It's like, how can they exist, even in the past, when they've been deleted from history altogether? But it's like – even mainframe exists as a part of time. The historical files are inside mainframe. But, put another way, mainframe also exists within the history files. You can access it from any point in time because it's *always* been there. Like you said – a paradox. That's what *all* of time really is.'

'I know,' he said. 'I saw it, but then, I sort of forgot. Too much information to handle, I suppose.'

'So, where is the belief?' she asked. 'Where is it now?'

'And I thought you knew everything.'

'I'm not the one who went into mainframe and saw everything. That was you.'

'It … lingers,' said Denny. 'Not everything that is believed in is real. But everything that is real is believed in by someone. It's not quantifiable. It can't be controlled. Not even by the gods. But sometimes seeing really is believing. So … the Hall Of Images … that's where belief resides. The pictures in people's minds. I'm sorry, that's not really helpful is it?'

'I don't know,' said Tamar thoughtfully. 'It might be.'

* * *

'Your dad's mad keen on all those old books Iffie,'

'I don't think Dad's actually keen on all those old books. He just thinks they're important or something.'

'Then maybe they are.'

Iffie decided that maybe Jack was right. Maybe they were.

There were books in that library that were unreadable. Not because of the ancient languages – that was another type of unreadable – these were … *magically* unreadable. The words themselves were in another dimension. Not a parallel universe, or a pocket universe, just another dimension like the astral plane, but not that simple. Of course, books take you to another world in a purely figurative sense anyway, but in this case, there was another side to it.

Iffie had, as a child, often cast spells which took her into the action of her favourite books. Just a tweak to the wording should take her into the action of one of *these* books even though the action was taking place in another dimension. It was a weird juxtaposition of the world of reality the world of fantasy and the strange realm in which the words were hidden.

And if a mere witch could do it, then a powerful god like Being should have had no trouble at all. And it made sense on another level. Cindy had been a witch too. Witches used books for a lot of things. Words had power; all witches knew this instinctively. And Cindy had lived here, in this house at one time, she would certainly have known about the strange intra-dimensional books in the library.

Now she just had to find the right book.

When she finally found it, it practically jumped out at her. This *had* to be it! If Cindy was going to hide in any book it was going to be one named "Gods and Monnsters". (This was the actual spelling, Monnsters with the double "n" – actually referring to all kinds of magical creatures not necessarily monstrous ones.)

Jack, when canvassed for his opinion, agreed with her.

It was, in fact, a pretty dry reference book written, as Iffie put it, about a million years ago (in fact it was only 700 years old) by an aging magician who had seen a thing or two. But it was not the words that were important in this case.

The spell involved getting into the dimension where the words could be read – luckily Denny knew how to do this and he had taught her, taught both of them; and actually, it was Jack who had taken to it easily, Iffie had had trouble learning. It was a cerebral connection; the body remained where it was. Once there, they could take the next step into the book itself. This part would be largely up to Iffie.

A dry and dreary landscape met them when they entered. But, and this was the important part, it *was* a part of the fantasy realm.

All books, even those that purport to be factual reference books rightly belong in the realm of fiction. All "facts" are coloured by the author's personal views to a greater or lesser extent and let's face it, so many "facts" are being proved daily as having been the merest fantasy after all, in the light of some exciting new "facts" that have emerged in their place. Historical data is particularly prone to this phenomenon. And scientific facts do not exist at all in any real sense. There are only scientific theories waiting to be torn down by the next generation. The word "science" refers not to a table of factual data but to a process which is ongoing. Add to this, the strange truth that most of humanity is simply stuffed full of random misinformation, and it is a wonder that anyone believes anything that they read or hear about at all.

Iffie was well aware of this, having been lectured on it, mostly by her mother, from an early age. Which was why, if someone had said to her that the sky was blue, she would probably have challenged them to prove it. If it had been a cloudy day, her arguments would have taken the other point of view apart.

Jack was one person who never allowed himself to be drawn into this endless loop of speculation about the nature of reality, but he was trapped now.

'Griffins,' said Iffie disparagingly as one hopped by. 'People will believe anything.'

'It's quite pretty, though,' said Jack mildly. 'In a deformed genetic experiment kind of way.'

'But it isn't *real*.'

Jack sighed. 'Nothing *is* here,' he pointed out. 'That's the point, isn't it?'

'Nothing?' she said looking around. 'You know I think, unfortunately, that you're right about that.'

'He isn't here?' asked Jack.

'Do *you* see anything?'

'Well, I don't really know how this works, I mean, maybe he's in another chapter or something.'

'That's not how it works,' she said. 'We came in at the beginning. From here we can see clear to the end. There's nothing here apart from what's supposed to be – if you don't count us that is.'

'There are plenty of other books ...'

'None that she would have picked. I checked them all. Huh! Another dead end.'

'Maybe she picked one at random, we shouldn't just give up.'

'I'm *not* giving up, but this isn't the way. Look out for the ogre,' she added.

If you're certain he's not here, maybe we should get out of here.'

'I'm certain. He's not here. I'm beginning to think he's not *anywhere*. Maybe he's just a figment of our imaginations.'

'That would be too much to hope for,' said Jack.

* * *

Okay. So there was *definitely* something else going on, Denny realised. The fact was, try as he might to hide it, he was getting steadily weaker after each of the horrible dreams. It was taking him longer and longer to recover from each attack – and he had to admit now that they *were* attacks, they were more than mere dreams anyway – and each time his recovery was a little less complete.

As had happened before, he was certain that he had read something about this sort of thing, but he could not remember where. The problem, this time, was that he was on his own. He had not told anyone else about the dreams, and he did not intend to. And how to explain what he was researching without telling them?

So why not just tell Tamar about it, and ask for help, as he would usually do? The truth was, he was horribly ashamed of the dream attacks; that was the thing. Ashamed and furious that he was apparently completely unable to stop it from happening. He *should* be able to stop it. The fact that he could not, made him feel unaccountably guilty, as if he somehow deserved it. He did not want anyone to know; he would sort it out for himself. He was sure he had read something somewhere … He fell asleep.

* * *

They had tried scrying with it, using it in a locator spell, crystal divination, and all the things that an intensely personal object can be used for to find a person. All the things that Iffie had used the feather for. The orb did not work any better, so Denny gave it back to Jack, who gave it back to Iffie, who had another idea.

Iffie owned a witch's Athame, a fairly innocuous item compared with Denny's demonic version. It stole no powers, and in Iffie's opinion, a kitchen knife would have been just as good. But it *was* prettier, she had to admit that.

She also had a bunch of candles and incense sticks, salt, crystals and the orb.

Many teenage girls spend time sitting in the centre of a pentagram surrounded by candles and incense and chanting incomprehensible nonsense.

Iffie had never done this, and she was not about to start now. There were easier ways to cast spells.

She took the paring knife from the kitchen drawer – there was no point in spoiling the Athame, which had been a present – and scored the candle three times and lit it on the stove. Then she filled the room with steam from the kettle to provide a cloudy medium in the air. The books recommended incense smoke, but Iffie did not like the smell and they always set off the smoke detectors anyway.

A pentagram was not necessary, but some sort of barrier to sit within was. A circle on the floor was drawn with a handy crayon, and she sat down and chanted – chanting, unfortunately, is a prerequisite of any spell, and it always made Iffie feel self-conscious, like she was talking to herself.

Anyone could be a witch with incense, a fancy Athame and pentagrams drawn carefully in sacred salt. It took real skill to be a witch with a potato peeler, a steaming kettle and a crayon.

And the orb. It looked by far the most magical object in use – but it really was not, it was merely the conduit.

Iffie opened the book on her knee. It was perfectly acceptable to read a spell out from a book. Only pretentious witches took the trouble to learn all their spells off by heart beforehand. Of course, some you used so often that you remembered them anyway.

"To summon an angel" she read.

Of course, technically Ash was not an angel he was only a half angel, but she was sure the principle was the same. The angelic part of him would *have* to respond.

She hoped.

* * *

'At midnight last night, in the Capital, a total of seven arson attacks took place apparently simultaneously. The targets of these co-ordinated attacks were all well known brothels. In each case, there were no survivors. Witnesses said that the

fires seemed to begin spontaneously and instantaneously, although, in two cases, a man wearing a black mask was seen fleeing the scene.

'The fires consumed the buildings so quickly that no one inside had time to escape before they were burned to a crisp. Due to the extensive damage to the bodies, none of the victims have as yet been identified.

The fire department's arson investigation team have deemed that a powerful accelerant must have been used to set the fires to have made them burn as hot and as fast as they did. However, no evidence of this has as yet been found.

'In a bizarre Hollywood twist, it was later discovered that at each scene the single word "LUST" had been scrawled on one of the remaining walls. In a manner reminiscent of the horror film "Se7en". Police have determined that the words were put there after the fires had been extinguished. But, despite a permanent police presence at each scene, no one was seen.'

This was the substance of a report on the *local* and *national* news in a total of eighteen different countries. The stories never made it to the international news circuit. No connection was ever made.

Many local and national newspapers all over the world carried the story of local streetwalking prostitutes being massacred on the same night. The word "LUST" left in each case somewhere on the body.

In this case, within national boundaries, the connection was made but never explained.

Denny and Tamar did not see the story until it was too late. The mortal realm was not their province. By the time they did see it, it was only as a macabre piece of a much larger picture.

* * *

As soon as she made contact, Iffie realised that she had not really been expecting this to work. Ash appeared in the steam like a remote vision – floating in and out as the steam moved and dispersed and re-coalesced. But he was most definitely there, and Iffie was suddenly tongue tied.

'Hi,' she said tentatively. What was she supposed to say? "Hello Mr. Murderer, feel like giving yourself up"? She really, really wished that she had thought this one through.

'You *summoned* me?' Ash said sounding both outraged and a little pleased.

'I'm sorry, I didn't know how else to get in touch with you,' she said nervously.

'I see,' he said. 'Well, I suppose it's all right. What do you want?'

'I just thought we could talk,'

'Hmmm,' Ash seemed suspicious.

'Best not to push it then,' Iffie thought. 'You know, talk,' she repeated. 'Like friends do.'

'*Are* we friends?' he asked almost eagerly.

'I'll always be *your* friend,' she said.

The floating face broke into a radiant smile. 'Oh, Iffie,' he said. 'I knew it, I knew you were good. I knew you would see the light. I'm so glad. I was so worried. But now it will be all right. I will save you, you'll see. But first I have much work to do. Can you wait? Will you be all right?'

'What work?' said Iffie.

'God's work,' he said a sly look coming over his face. 'I have to go now, but if you need help or guidance you can call on me again. Any time you like.' And the face vanished.

'He hung up on me,' thought Iffie. 'How do you like that?'

Still, she had made contact, it was a start. Next time, hopefully, it would go better.

* * *

At midnight, as Tamar, Denny, Stiles and Hecaté sat in the study, comparing notes, there was a sudden crash and a hundred armed men in black masks came smashing through the windows like the SAS, and attacked.

They were not exactly ordinary men – ordinary men are not known for their ability to throw fire from their hands – a strange pure white fire that burned cold like mercury. But they were still outmatched in this fight. It was enough to make you wonder why they had picked it.

'You know what this feels like,' said Denny, throwing a bolt of energy through three of them at once.

'What?' said Tamar, slicing off several heads at once with a large sword.

'A diversion,' said Denny.

Tamar dropped the sword and clapped her hands and time stopped for everyone except herself. She did not usually do this, it being dirty tactics, but it would not hurt them so to hell with it.

She released the others*and demanded of Denny: 'A diversion from what?'

'I don't know yet. Listen,' said Denny.

Tamar listened, they all listened. It was a moment frozen in time, but it was chillingly clear for all that.

'Oh, no,' breathed Tamar in horror.

Hecaté had gone white.

Normal sound needs time to travel through. But this was not normal sound; it hung around in the ether. It was the sound of a thousand witches crying out in terror.

'I'll get Iffie,' said Denny. 'Then we check the covens. If it's these same guys.' He gestured at the frozen men around the room, 'they shouldn't be too hard to take care of.'

'What do we do with *them*?' asked Stiles.

'A volcano somewhere should do it,' said Tamar, in all seriousness. 'Thaw them out nicely. But hang on to at least one of them. I have questions.'

Tamar left time frozen as it was and they went out to look for some trouble. Hecaté led the way, but they could all hear the cries, except Stiles.

And trouble was what they found too.

It was the same guys that had attacked the house, black masked figures caught mostly in the act of desecrating the

---

* To release someone from a time freeze one only has to move them. However, this is not as easy as it sounds, since time holds a person still with a strength that far surpasses the strength of the gravity pull within a black hole. But Tamar was unusually strong by anyone's standards.

shrines of Hecaté and killing any witches who tried to get in their way. And many who did not too. Strangely, not all of the world had remained frozen; some, in fact, quite a lot, of the mysterious warriors *appeared* to have beaten the time freeze and had to be fought off. Which was fine with Tamar at least, who liked a bit of mayhem when she could get it. The years had done little to soften Tamar's violent tendencies, but Denny could have done without it really at the moment. He was just too damn tired for this. Although from the way he was taking his share of the enemy apart, no one would have guessed this.

Appearances are not always what they seem, of course. It was to be much later on when they discovered what was really going on here.

Although they saved many thousands of witches that night, many hundreds died. For some, they were just too late. In each home or coven, the figure of Hecaté had been smashed, and the word "IDOLATRY" had been scrawled on the wall.

It was incomprehensible.

'What the hell are they?' said Stiles walking around the immobilized prisoner. They had had to fight quite a lot of them tonight and not only were they able to throw freezing fire, but they were unusually strong. 'They aren't human are they?'

'I'm not sure *what* they are,' said Tamar. 'They *look* human.'

'Why were they attacking witches?' said Stiles.

'That wasn't an attack,' said Denny. 'It was an extermination.'

'*Attempted* extermination,' said Tamar.

'Okay, why were they trying to *exterminate* witches?' Stiles insisted.

But no one had an answer.

'Let's ask *him*,' said Stiles. 'With extreme impoliteness,'

'You mean beat him up?' translated Denny.

Tamar unfroze the prisoner.

He collapsed to the floor – dead.

'What the hell?' Denny crouched to the floor and checked over the corpse. 'Cyanide pill,' he said. 'The bastard killed himself.'

Tamar touched the body gently with her foot, and then they all jumped back as it was enveloped in a bright white light and then vanished.

'Christ it nearly took your foot off.' said Denny. 'Are you all right?'

Tamar grinned. 'Never stop asking me that,' she said. 'Even if it is a superfluous question.'

'I guess that's put paid to those pertinent questions,' said Stiles, sounding disappointed.

'Why did you do that?' said Denny. 'They all exploded like that when they died.'

'I thought it was just us that made them do that,' she said.

'Persecution,' said Hecaté hollowly. 'That's what it was. I have seen it before but never like this, never on such a scale.'

'Bigots?' said Stiles. 'I don't think so. Bigots use guns. Perhaps it's the start of some kind of war. They see the witches as a threat, a rival power,' he theorised. 'These things *are* supernatural in some way. We saw that.'

'The witches were as clueless as us, though. They didn't know who they were either.' said Tamar.

'Do you think we got them all?' said Denny. 'Or are there more?'

'We'll soon find out,' said Tamar.

* * *

They were so busy for the next few days arranging sanctuary for thousands of terrified witches that they all missed this:-

'In the last twenty four hours an unprecedented series of what can only be described as terrorist attacks took place around the world. The targets apparently selected at random. Corporations and large businesses in London Paris, Rome, New York, Washington, Chicago, Los Angeles, Beijing, Hong Kong...

'The Attacks appear to have taken the form of nerve gas bombs but this is, as yet, unconfirmed as no signs usually associated with these types of attack were found on the bodies. Unconfirmed police reports state that the victims "Looked as if they might just be sleeping".

In each case the word "AVARICE" was written in red paint on the wall of the office of the company C.E.O.

The death toll is estimated to be in the hundreds of thousands. Authorities are said to be baffled ...

Ashtoreth waved a hand for the link to be broken. He had seen enough to satisfy him. 'So shall all sinners be cleansed,' he said. 'This is only The Beginning.'

When someone starts capitalising words at the *end* of a sentence you know you're in trouble.

* * *

'Ash? You there?'

'I am.'

'I can't see you too well, not enough steam.'

'You can see me well enough.'

'Couldn't you come through? There's nobody else here.'

'I cannot leave my sanctuary. It is not safe for me. Besides, I am weak. My powers have been – "diverted".'

'Diverted?'

'To a greater cause.'

'Oh Ash, what are you up to?'

'You will know in good time. For now ... Well I understand, you have ties, ties of family. You are not ready to know yet. I do not think, in your heart, that you *want* to know. And it speaks well of you. Loyalty is an admirable quality, but the time will come when you will have to choose to whom you really owe that loyalty. Your family or your own redemption.'

Iffie resented the lecturing tone he had adopted. Also, she thought he was talking a lot of specious bollocks. However, she hid her feelings quite well.

'Redemption?' she said in a fairly neutral tone. 'For what? I haven't really done anything.'

'You *were* sent to tempt me from my path,' he asserted.

'I don't think so,' she said. 'We met by accident. No one sent me.'

'There *are* no accidents. You must not be naïve. But then again, you are still so innocent of evil, perhaps it is not surprising. I do not want you lose that, of course, but you must be alert. For neither do I want you to be used for evil purposes without your knowledge.'

'So, now I'm stupid too?' snapped Iffie, unable to hide her annoyance.

'A pure mind is not a sign of stupidity,' said Ash placatingly. 'That is not what I meant.'

'Well, whatever,' she said agreeably, deciding there was no point antagonising him at this point. She wanted to find out what he meant by "a greater cause"

'You can tell me anything you know,' she tried. This was a bit weak and Ash made her feel it. He laughed.

'I said you are not ready,' he said. 'I have to go now anyway.' And he was gone.

'*Damn!*' said Iffie, in unconscious imitation of her mother.

* * *

It was cold and dark in the alley where Chris McBain, detective 2nd class lay on his side, huddled under a pile of newspapers and pretending to be dead drunk. There was a very good reason for this. He had been *ordered* to do it by the Chief. An amiable fellow by the name of Patrick Currens. Ha! *He* should lie in a freezing cold alley one night.

And why? To stake out a drug ring? To bust up a bank robbery? No. To find out which punks/louts/thugs/maniacs delete as applicable, had been setting the local vagrants on fire recently.

God he stank. Stank of booze that he had not drunk, stank of unnameable filth that the alley was piled up with. He wondered for a moment if he had not over done the filth. Surely no human being could smell this bad? He was making himself gag.

Still, homeless or not, the citizens of this great city had a right to protection from being set afire in the middle of the night. His hand tightened on his gun. That was why he was here. He was going to catch the bastards in the act this time.

He lay very still as he heard footsteps coming up the alley towards him. The other vagrants never stirred either but Chris never expected them to. Then suddenly, as the silence lengthened, Chris realised that something was screwy. He sat up and pulled his gun. Several men in black masks were standing in the alley, and somehow, three of the vagrants were already dead, burned to a crisp within seconds, and there had been no heat, no sound, and no cries of pain. Chris scrambled to his feet and backed away, just as a jet of white flame hit him in the chest. He did not even have time to cry out with the agony before he was dead.

~ Chapter Eleven ~

A FRANTIC HAMMERING on the door heralded another night of horrors.

Tamar opened the door to a bloodstained and weary centaur, who barged his way inside and then collapsed on the mat. 'Denn-eee!' Tamar yelled.

The news was grim. Hank was dead; the forest creatures were either dead or on the run like himself. They needed sanctuary. They needed help. That was why he had come to Tamar.

'Who did it?' snarled Tamar.

'I don't know who they were,' said the centaur, whose name was Rochen. 'They were a kind of creature I have never seen before. They called me an *abomination*,' he added indignantly. 'They said Hank was a false idol. I don't know what they meant by that, but they seemed to think it was pretty terrible. What *does* it mean?'

'Wait a minute,' said Denny. 'Did these creatures happen to look human, but with black masks over their faces and able to throw a sort of weird, cold fire from their hands?'

'Yes, that's them. How did you know?'

'Looks like Hecaté might have been right,' said Denny. 'Bigots.'

'Not necessarily,' said Tamar. 'Remember the Faeries. Could be a sub species that we never knew about.'

'Not very likely,' said Rochen. 'They killed all the brownies and gnomes because *they* are a sub species of Faerie. They hate Faeries too. They seem to hate *everyone*. There's a rumour that all the Djinn are vanishing too. But it might not be true. You never get to see those guys anyway.'

'Oh God, it's a bloodbath,' said Tamar.

'Just like the reign of the Faeries,' said Denny. 'They killed for fun, though. I don't get that feeling about whatever's going on here.'

'Just because they killed the brownies and gnomes, doesn't mean they *aren't* a kind of Faerie,' said Tamar. 'Humans kill other kinds of humans all the time. And Faeries will kill *anything*. '

'I just don't think it's Faeries,' said Denny.

'No, I don't either,' admitted Tamar. 'But it might be that they have the same MO.'

'Indiscriminate slaughter you mean?'

'I'm not so sure that it *is* indiscriminate,' said Tamar thoughtfully. 'There always seems to be *some* reason.'

'Or excuse,' said Denny tersely.

'Why do they need an excuse?' she said. 'So they can tell you "I'm going to kill you, but I do have a good reason."?'

'It'd help if we knew *what* they are.'

'Something new,' said Rochen.

'Or something very old,' said Tamar. 'Something that used to be powerful before all these other magical species even existed. Something that's only just come back from somewhere and wants to be back on top.'

'Now we're back to the Faeries,' said Denny.

'But they *aren't* all that powerful,' she said. 'We can take them out a dozen at a time.'

'They seem to have the numbers,' said Denny.

'I wonder just how many of them there are,' she said.

'Whatever they are,' said Rochen. 'You can catch a score of them in the forest right now if you hurry up.'

'Why didn't you *say* so?' said Denny.

'I thought I *did*,' said Rochen with an injured expression.

* * *

It *was* like the era of the Faeries, in as much as they had a houseful of refugees again. Only this time, the refugees were magical Beings rather than humans. There were far too many of them to all be housed at home this time. The overspill was secured away in a deleted file which Denny left open on the computer in order to keep an eye on them.

Iffie was in a kind of personal heaven. She loved magical creatures. The unicorns especially appealed to her. They were shy of most of the household, but they seemed to like both Iffie and Jack.

'Well, you know what they say about unicorns,' said Stiles in an uncharacteristically suggestive manner. (He was referring, of course, to the legend that a unicorn can only be captured by a virgin.)

Denny rolled his eyes. 'Well, I can pretty much vouch for Iffie,' he said. 'But I'm not so sure that Jack qualifies any more. He *is* eighteen.'

'Oh, well, maybe it's something else then,' said Stiles sounding unconvinced. But, as it happened, he was right.

* * *

Denny was sick of running into half-dressed witches in the hallways, of tripping up over gnomes on the stairs and of the smell of the centaurs in the garden.

'Good for the roses, though,' said Stiles.

But this was of small comfort to Denny. The quicker they got this sorted out the better.

He had other problems to worry about.

He had been covering pretty well, he thought. He was sure no one had guessed how he was feeling. Certainly he was getting thinner, but he had never been particularly well built to begin with so he did not think it was all that noticeable. And it was not as if he needed as much sleep as other men anyway thanks to the Athame, and staying awake was less tiring, these days, than the dream, so, for several nights in a row, he had stayed awake. Usually to work alone, in secret, on his research into the night-time phenomenon that was attacking him. He knew in his heart that if he asked them, either Tamar or Hecaté would probably have an answer for him. They had both been kicking around long enough to have seen just about everything. But, he told himself, they had enough to worry about what with mysterious black-masked warriors roaming about the place.

Denny did not usually resort to this kind of sophistry to explain his actions, but he was feeling desperate. *Anything* to avoid telling them the shameful truth. Getting a quick answer would be favourite right now. The trouble with that was, he did not have the first clue what he was looking for.

The Succubus had been a strong contender at one point, the behaviour, and his resultant symptoms all seemed to fit the profile. But all the sources agreed that the Succubus always appeared as a seductive and beautiful woman. Even though few women, if any, could compare to Tamar in the physical beauty stakes, Denny did not think he had been so completely spoiled by this as to mistake a gorgeous woman for an old hag.

Other contenders included the mare of the night – strangling men in their sleep. So, no to that then. He was totally knackered but so far completely un-asphyxiated.

The Hupia, who only attacked children. Denny still looked very young for his age, but the idea, especially considering the nature of the attacks, that he had been mistaken for a child was not only ridiculous but extremely disturbing. Besides, they sucked the breath, like cats were supposed to in old wives tales.

Houris, also good looking, definitely *not* old hags.

Denny was forgetting here, that he had met Houris before. *And* seen their true appearance, which was anything but attractive. There might have been a clue in this idea, had he only remembered that cheap glamours did not cloud his vision the way they did the eyes of ordinary men.

* * *

Jack was getting worried about Iffie. Well not worried more – concerned. She had abruptly seemed to lose all interest in the search for Ashtoreth. This could mean one of two things. One reason for her sudden disinterest was … quite encouraging really. The other was, frankly, not. He had tried tackling her about it, but the results were not helpful.

'What's the point,' she had said. '*We're* never going to find him, and anyway, he's a maniac.'

'All the more reason why we need to find him if we can,' Jack had argued.

'And do what?' she had said. 'You were right, there's nothing *we* can do. We should let Mum and Dad sort it out. They're good at that.'

This conversation had left Jack feeling uneasy. She was clearly hiding something from him. It just was not like Iffie to give up so easily. And she had been so determined … Now suddenly, she did not seem to care at all. So what had changed? And *where* did she keep disappearing off to? He could not be certain – Iffie had always been a free spirit vanishing for days on end for no apparent reason, concerts, parties, whatever – but he thought that just lately it had been happening more often.

* * *

Iffie gazed sternly at herself in the mirror. 'What do you think you are doing?' she asked herself. 'You know it's not right, so why are you doing it?'

Her reflection inclined its head. 'If you know it's wrong, then stop.' she said. 'And you know it is, because you're trying to hide it.'

'I think Jack's suspicious,'

'You're acting suspiciously.'

'Am I though? No one else seems to have noticed anything.'

'Dad would be really upset if he knew. You know he's a murdering maniac.'

'He's … troubled.'

'A murdering maniac, I said. You know it's the truth.'

'But I'm getting through. I know I am. He's … Maybe I can get him to tell me where he is and then …'

'You know he won't. He'll never tell you. He doesn't trust you. Or anyone.'

'But I'm getting there. He's definitely opening up to me a bit more.'

'He won't tell you where he is until it's far too late for anyone to do anything about it. Why don't you just leave him alone? How do you think Mum would feel if she found out? How do you think *Jack* would feel?'

'What do you know about it? You aren't me,' snarled Iffie, and stalked away from the mirror. Bloody conscience. It was coming to something when you could not even look in a mirror without being lectured on your shortcomings.

'Well *you* started it,' said the mirror – but Iffie was gone.

* * *

Calling the "gentleman's club" *Jezebels*, a reference not to the name of the owner but to the entertainment, was really asking for trouble, thought Lindy Lou Stevenson, as the latest police raid got underway.

The local sheriff, mindful of his voters, and the fact that most of the community were "good churchgoing folk" generally had the place raided about once a month.

However, in deference to the fact that he spent quite a few of his off hours enjoying the facilities, he usually gave them some warning before sending the boys in.

Clearly the message had not got through this time.

Lindy Lou sighed and tugged her feather boa over her modesty and prepared herself for arrest.

Mind you, these guys did not look like cops; they looked more like the SAS or something. Had some "community minded" citizen gone over the sheriff's head and called the Feds? That would be all she needed. She *needed* this job.

She was not going to need it for much longer.

* * *

The first thing to do then, was to try to find out exactly what this new threat was. This was a new problem. They had never before been up against an enemy without at least knowing what it was. It was not so much a name that mattered, and they knew its powers – which were limited. But they did not know where they were coming from or how many more to expect.

'They aren't a type of demon are they?' said Stiles. 'They seem like a type of demon.'

'Demon's don't have types,' said Tamar. 'Each one is different.'

'What about vampires?' argued Stiles. '*They* were a kind of demon.'

'They were a creation, it's not quite the same,' said Denny. 'But I see what you mean.'

'Did someone *create* these things then?' said Jack.

'If they did, it was in a vat,' said Denny. 'There're just too many of them for it to be a new species that developed from a single creation like the vampires. That sort of thing takes time.'

'They *are* sort of ... "Robotic",' said Tamar thoughtfully. 'But it's more like brain-washing.'

'We've seen magically created warriors before,' said Denny. 'But they weren't like this. They weren't real for one thing. These are *real*. And they have sentience, you can tell. They fight as if they can think for themselves, as if they want to survive. Some of them even ran away. Magic warriors *never* do that. They don't have the sense.'

'There aren't usually so many of them either.' said Tamar. 'Ten's about your usual limit on magical warriors. And magical warriors tend to fall apart at the slightest thing – and I mean that literally.'

'Okay, so that's great, we know what they *aren't*,' said Stiles.

'It's a start,' said Tamar.

'We need more to go on,' said Denny.

The phone rang. Everyone just stared at it.

'I didn't know we *had* a phone,' said Denny eventually.

'We don't,' said Tamar. 'Answer it anyway.'

'*You* answer it,' said Denny, looking at the ringing phone with deep suspicion.

It turned out to be Director Dawber of the Agency. 'You'd better get over here,' he said. 'We have a bit of a situation.'

* * *

That night there were attacks on temples and other places of worship associated with several different religious movements. Pagan, Wiccan, Voodoo, Hermetic, and Asatru (Norse and Germanic gods) temples were hit. All these religions use ritual magic as a part of their belief system.

On the walls of all these temples etc. the words "BLACK MAGIC" were scrawled and a man in a black mask was seen fleeing the scene of at least one of the temples involved. However, investigators found no boxes of chocolates at any of the scenes. But because of the high death toll and the terrible destruction to property involved it was assumed that this was an accusation rather than an IOU.

* * *

'We were investigating the mysterious disappearances of half the small gods in the area and these guys must have got on to us – unless it was a co-incidence. Now we're overrun with the buggers. Murder and mayhem all over the place. Say you can help.' was Dawber's breathless explanation of the "situation" he had mentioned.

'What're small gods?' asked Stiles.

'It's no co-incidence,' said Denny. 'Unless they were already planning to come after you too.'

'Gods of rivers and woods and so on,' said Tamar. 'Like Hank was. What small gods?' she asked Dawber.

'Quite a few. We have people monitoring the mainframe all the time. Some anomalies were noticed, and we looked into it. Pan is gone, and Silenus and many others – local river and woodland gods, like you said. I mean we could have put it down to deforestation and pollution and that sort of thing – happens all the time. But *Pan* disappearing was a bit odd. So we investigated and then these guys just turned up and started … Well it's a massacre in there. Did you say that Hank is dead too?'

'It's happening all over,' said Denny. 'We've got a houseful of refugees at the moment. But we didn't know about *this*.'

'Can you help me?' said Dawber. 'I have three thousand employees in there, and they're dying.'

'Just get us in there,' said Tamar. 'How did *you* get out?'

'I have a special access in my office.'

'I was hoping you were going to say something like that,' Tamar told him. 'Back door then. Come on.'

'They're extremely vicious,' warned Dawber.

'But not too bright,' said Denny. 'We can handle them, don't worry.'

* * *

Inside it was a nightmare. The power had been cut, and black masked figures flitted about like oversized bats in the gloom. But lurking in the shadows can work both ways. Not to mention that fighting in the dark is always a tactical advantage when your enemy has greater numbers than yourself.

'You start getting them out,' Tamar told Stiles – meaning the Agency employees. Stiles crept silently away, while Tamar, Denny, Hecaté and Jack (who had begged that he was old enough to help now) made as much noise as possible. And, like a demon through the smoke, came Death with a long, shiny sword in the form of Tamar spitting vengeance and fury, to the terror of the warriors.

* * *

Jack Stiles was trapped. He had managed to get the employees that he had rounded up as far as the exit point, known within the Agency as the "teleportation room", although what it really was and how it really worked was anyone's guess. The whole of the Agency headquarters was housed within the TARDIS like expansion of a disused Djinn bottle, and someone had corked it. All the employees had "Master" cards, adapted to the bottle's frequency in order to allow free passage in and out. But it was not working.

Hence, Stiles was trapped. In fact, they were all trapped. On the other side of the door, the creatures in black were forcing a way through. It would not take them long to break in as Stiles was frantically aware. There were so many of them, they were a battering ram all by themselves.

He had no doubt that either Denny or Tamar would find a way to break the lockdown which no doubt extended to the exit point in the Director's office. But they were not here. And he had no way of getting to them. He was cut off by hordes of – whatever they were (must *give* them a name) and people were starting to panic.

It was all about energy, he thought. The specific frequency of the energy that made the bottle into a trap, only opened to the specific trigger that it was tuned to. A sufficient burst of kinetic energy, sustained for long enough, should force a gap in the energy field and let everyone out.

Well, he could not save these people by himself. But perhaps Leir could.

It was the only chance. Stiles drew on the gauntlet of Leir [*] and accessed the power of the ancient god who had created it.

His own mind directed the power of the gauntlet, but it was not his power, it resided in the gauntlet itself.

The energy was invisible but powerful. A gap began to open up in the wall. A bright white light leading to a tunnel, through which the outside world could be dimly perceived.

'Go, go,' he yelled. And everybody ran.

Stiles did not know how long he could keep this up; it was draining him to the point of exhaustion, and the gauntlet was red hot. But he was determined to hang on until everyone was out.

He was on the point of collapse. Just as the last one ran through, he let go, too exhausted to follow, and all the energy that had been forced aside sprang back like a steel-trap closing. A massive surge of power travelled back through the energy stream up Stiles's arm, and lifted him off his feet. He hung there for a moment, suspended in a lighting storm, then the field shattered. Like a bottle being blown outwards (which, in this case, is more than just an analogy) and Stiles was lying in a

---

[*]Which he now carried with him whenever he thought there might be a chance he would need it – like a fight. Most of the time, really then, but he rarely used it.

field, burned black all over, and surrounded by anxious faces that he did not see.

From the point of view of those still inside, it happened like this: a bright white but soundless explosion and they suddenly found themselves outside standing in a field. The remaining black masked warriors fled, so that was handy, but there were still plenty of people around; standing in a large huddle around something that they could not see.

The words. 'Is he dead?' were enough to make all of them run towards the crowd and force a way through. Despite the fact that Stiles was unrecognisable, Hecaté let out a wail of horror and despair. She grabbed at Denny for support, and he held her up as Tamar bent down to Stiles.

'He's breathing,' she announced. And she concentrated hard, trying to heal him. But she sat back with a gasp. 'I can't,' she said. 'It's not working.'

'Hospital,' said Denny decisively. Tamar nodded. They had nothing to lose at this point. A moment later, they were gone.

* * *

Stiles was placed in a tank full of water with breathing tubes and monitors all over him. But the doctors shook their heads gravely and looked pessimistic.

'They asked questions like: 'Does he have a living will?' and, 'who is his next of kin?' and, 'is he an organ donor?'

They said he was brain-dead. The machines were keeping him alive. But there was no hope.

They tried to talk Hecaté into switching off the machines.

She agreed. 'I always knew I would have to let him go one day. But not so soon. Not so soon.'

Tamar disagreed; she had a hunch. The gauntlet, despite their best efforts had yet to be removed. Only Stiles himself could take it off, until he died, at which point it would naturally remove itself. He was still alive.

'It was an artificial life,' the doctors said. But Tamar was insistent. Give it a bit longer,' she said. 'Or don't you believe in miracles?'

The doctors did not. They believed in cold hard facts. But without permission, they were unable to do anything.

Hecaté believed in miracles. She had been the author of more than a few. She withdrew her permission.

They offered Hecaté a bed in the hospital, so that she could stay with him. She accepted. It would have seemed ungracious not to. She did not expect to use the bed. It was a wet night, thunderstorms. It seemed appropriate. The others went home.

'Where's Uncle Jack?' asked Iffie. 'Where's Auntie Hecaté?'

Tamar told her, and Iffie cried, but Tamar told her there was hope.

'There's always hope,' she said. And later, she cried herself to sleep in Denny's arms.

* * *

'One down!' Ashtoreth was feeling extremely pleased with himself. Not only had his early forays all gone exactly as planned (like his mother, he believed in testing the water before diving in) but one member of that hated household had already fallen. True, it was not the one he most wanted to die, but it was a start. Not that he had planned it that way. It was simply an unexpected bonus. And his enemies would be grieved by his loss. Or ... would they? Did the evil feel grief? On reflection, he thought not. But they would be dismayed by his fall at least. Afraid for their own skin.

As well they should be. 'So shall all tyrants fall,' he muttered. (It never occurred to Ashtoreth to consider the actions of Jack Stiles as heroic.)

He was conscious, though, of an element of regret. *She* would be grieved, and the thought of her grief hurt him. A weakness. Oh but she *had* pierced his armour; pierced it to the core. Thanks to her, it would never be quite whole again. His mother had tried to keep it so. He understood so much more now, about why she had kept him here, away from the world and its dangers. She had been trying to protect him. And now she was dead.

The man responsible was going to pay for that, no matter *who* got hurt in the process.

So much for regret then. It would not be allowed to interfere with his ultimate goal. And she would come to understand in the end. Good must always triumph over evil.

Here, in this palace by the sea, he would stay, safe until the time came. Spending his armies in the fight against evil. The place had changed since his mother's time. Now it resembled nothing less than a barracks. Filled from end to end and top to bottom with quarters to house his soldiers.

As he sent each division out on their missions he would call them before him to bless them before they went out to face the forces of evil what he was doing at these "blessings" was disseminating his power among them. As each one died, the power returned to him, but in the meantime, he was temporarily weakened. He was able to "bless" upwards of one thousand soldiers at a time. Any more, and their borrowed power would be too weak, too thinly spread, to be effective.

But, at the moment, only seven stood before him to be blessed. For these soldiers, he had a special mission. To accomplish this mission they would need the maximum power he was able to spare. But, should they succeed, he would have more power than any being on the face of the Earth and beyond.

'It may take you many months to complete this task, perhaps a year or more,' he told them. 'There will be hardships. There will be moments of despair. You must not give up. The key to our victory is out there. It is up to you to find it, should you have to search the four corners of the earth. I know I can rely on you. Now come forth and receive your blessing and your tools.'

The "tools" he referred to were laid out on a table before him. One each, wrapped in a cloth woven from a shimmering material of indeterminate origin.

He did not expect them all to succeed. Perhaps one or two. He was even prepared for the fact that one or more of them might find what he sought and never return, keeping the power for himself. It would not matter.

It might be a long time, as he had told them, before the outcome of this search was known to him. He would just have to possess himself in patience. In the meantime, there was much work to do.

Had anyone else been doing what he was doing, planning what he was planning, he would have been the first to condemn them. He now had the same hubris as any god that you care to mention. He would not have accepted the same argument from another, but, as far as he was concerned, it was right because it was he who was doing it.

* * *

The war in ------- came to an abrupt close last night after the deployment of an airborne toxin at the sites of military bases belonging to both sides. Approximately fourteen thousand soldiers in total were killed. Rebel troops known to belong to the ------- that have been seen in the area have refused to claim responsibility for the attack, and it is presumed that protesters against the war have orchestrated this heinous attack. The protesters, going under the name "The -------" have refused to comment.

Neither government has agreed to make a statement. There have been no civilian casualties reported.

Severe burning over several square miles of the ground just outside the city has been identified by helicopter as words burnt by an unknown medium into the ground. The words read. WARMONGERS BE WARNED.

There is no explanation forthcoming for this extraordinary circumstance. No fires were reported the preceding night, and the fires needed to cause such a large area of burnt ground would have been seen for miles.

This was Ashtoreth's favourite so far. As far as he was concerned, the overall reaction to this proved that the world was so corrupted that several groups of humans were actually suspected of perpetrating this action against their fellow creatures. It was amazing. No one questioned it. No one was even surprised.

* * *

It was a nightmare; well there was a lot of it about lately. Everywhere was a nightmare at the moment. This particular nightmare had all the usual features. Black masked devils looming, by the several hundreds, through the effectively created smoke, brandishing weapons of all shapes and sizes and attacking in virtual silence. It did not seem to matter who they were going after, witches, centaurs, small gods – whatever, their MO seemed to be the same every time. Slaughter, slash and kill by whatever means necessary.

They had attacked the house a total of six times until they apparently got the message – that they were wasting their time and forces on pointless diversions that were not working anyway.

As Tamar sliced and diced with vicious precision, her mind was actually elsewhere. What was it this time anyway? The Covenant of Eeeee.* Magicians and Sorcerers.

As she fought, she kept half an eye on Denny – a procedure that she had never felt necessary before, but he was not himself at the moment, although he seemed to be doing all right for now.

There had been times recently, when Tamar had seriously wondered if she would not be better off fighting on her own.

Jack was a competent fighter and a reasonable substitute for Stiles, but still, she always felt as if she needed to watch his back. Experience was what was lacking there. And now Denny seemed to need more backup than he had previously done, (i.e. none at all).

One thing, though, that she had determined on – and she knew that Denny agreed with her – was that no matter how desperate things became, they would not be bringing Iffie into

---

* Also known as the crew of magicians who couldn't think of a better name.

---

the fighting. If she was distracted now, she thought, how much worse would *that* be?'

And then she saw him go down, six warriors behind him bore down immediately, and he had not seen them, she was sure of it. She turned and brought down her sword, and six heads rolled as Denny leapt to his feet. He nodded shortly at her and continued to fight apparently unaware of his narrow escape. Not that he was so easy to kill. Even if he had been hit, he would probably have survived. But it should not have happened at all; that was the truth of it, and it worried Tamar.

* * *

It was one of those rooms. You know the kind, without windows and with large, incomprehensible maps and diagrams on the walls.

Several suits sat around a large table, and a military uniform stood at the head of the table. He looked grim.

These men met in times of crisis. The rest of the time they did not know each other at all.

A young man in uniform who nevertheless had "secretary" written all over him, from his neatly parted hair to his shiny shoes, passed out folders and then sat down in a corner to take the minutes.

'It comes down to this,' said the man with the General's stripes. 'Mayhem!' He thumped the table. 'Mayhem and bloody chaos.' He glared at the assembled company as if daring them to disagree with him. No one did.

'It's a fortunate thing for us, that the government departments of this benighted country mostly have right hands that don't know what the left hand is doing.' He reviewed this sentence in his head and decided to let it go. 'Only *we* know the full extent of the damage being perpetrated. Only *we* have made the connections. And it's a damn good thing too. This sort of thing is very bad gentlemen, very bad for business. So what do we know?'

'We know,' he continued, answering his own question. 'That several random groups, and I use the word "several" only to avoid using the word "hundreds" in any kind of official capacity, have been targeted and destroyed around the globe apparently by the same group of insurgents, and again, I use the word instead of saying "maniacs", which is not an official term.'

The men nodded solemnly. It was a bad business, and a bad business was bad for business.

'So what do we have? Not much to go on, unfortunately. We have no idea who is behind this. No kind of warning beforehand or explanation afterwards apart from the random scribbling left behind at each scene. This group has made no attempt to identify itself in any way. No demands have been made. And yet, thousands of people have died apparently for simply doing what people do.

It would seem we have a religious maniac on our hands, yet religious maniacs are rarely this organised. Most set themselves up in a disused barn somewhere in Iowa or some such place, have themselves a good time procreating with several wives and end up in a shoot out with the F.B.I. I think we can assume that is not going to be the case here.'

He cleared his throat and continued. 'So far then, this group has made its point by laying waste to "several" large business corporations. More than a few brothels, escort agencies and gentlemen's nightclubs. Every modeling agency on the official charter (for the sin of "vanity" I believe) newspapers and TV and radio news corporations ("deception") a large number of army bases regardless of the affiliations of the soldiers within. Indeed this group single handedly ended the war in ----- by decimating the forces on *both* sides with extreme prejudice and yet a refreshing lack of *bigotry* I must say.

'As well as every "alternative" religious group, they could lay their hands on. On top of all this, it seems that several hundred individual citizens seem to have been targeted at random all for various "sins" and there may be many more than we know about in this last case. How many of these attacks have been put down as ordinary murders? We may never know. The cities all around the world are losing their homeless populations. Vagrancy is a nuisance gentlemen, but *not*, as far as I am aware, a sin. And, as we all know, it is a *necessary* nuisance. Although don't ever quote me on that of course.

'In summation gentlemen, we have a very large problem, and what are we going to do about it?' He put his knuckles on the table and glared again at the men sat around it.

The silence lengthened. There were no answers forthcoming at all.

* * *

'So far they've attacked the witches, the forest creatures – centaurs, fauns, satyrs, unicorns *et al*, the small gods, the warlocks, necromancers and mages. Brownies, gnomes and probably the Djinn.' Tamar summed up the situation succinctly while pacing up and down the floor restlessly. 'Then they went after the Agency,' she continued. 'And we don't know if that was a part of their plans or not. After all, they were tracking their movements they may have just been getting too close or something.' She stopped and faced the room. 'So who's next? And why? And who's doing all this? And … and *why*?' She threw the floor open helplessly. 'Anyone?' she said.

A room full of magical beings all simultaneously looked at their feet, hooves or paws.

'Well, that was a waste of time,' said Tamar. 'They all come here expecting us to just *sort it all out* somehow – they could at least *try* to help. What do they think we are? Why do they just assume that we can fix everything?'

'Because we always do,' said Denny. 'And we'll fix this too, sooner or later. You'll see.'

'How?' said Tamar.

~ Chapter Twelve ~

TAMAR LOOKED AT the newspapers on the front doorstep in deep suspicion. The last time someone had left her an anonymous newspaper it had caused an argument with Denny that had left the house in ruins and led to her walking out for six months – and the trouble that *that* had caused was nobody's business. People who left anonymous newspapers were *not* her friends.

However, what were the chances of that happening again? She picked up the papers as carefully as if they were wired to explosives and took them into the house.

She read the headlines and the attached stories with increasing alarm. How had they missed this? Had they become so insulated, so wrapped up in the magical world that they had forgotten that the rest of the world was still out there? The first story in particular was unnerving, to say the least. Black masked men fleeing the scene? They had apparently not been seen since, but that only meant that they had become more careful.

And the words scrawled at the scenes of these different crimes. That was an obvious link if ever she saw one. A link not only between these crimes but to recent events in the magic community. This was not a magical problem only, as they had assumed. It was far bigger than that.

'*Den-eee!*' This time the house shook.

She thrust the pile of newspapers at him in silence. One look at her white face was enough to tell him that this was no joke.

He read the papers while she sat in silence. An occasional expletive escaped him as he read the first story, but by the time he had finished, he had lapsed into a kind of horrified stupor.

He dropped the papers on the floor and stared out of the window blankly. He looked, for all the world, as if he would never move again.

Once or twice he looked as if he were about to speak, but no words came out.

Eventually Tamar lost patience. 'Lust,' she said. 'Avarice, *Idolatry*?'

'I know,' said Denny. 'I know.'

'Warmongers. False *Idols*,' she continued inexorably.

'I *know*,' said Denny.

'And what's all this stuff about the homeless going missing – how is "vagrancy" a sin. But that's what it says.'

'We let them die,' he said in a hollow voice. 'We didn't even *try* to stop it.'

'We didn't *know*,' said Tamar.

'We *should* have known,' he said.

'Well, we know now,' she said. 'It stops here.'

'What?' said Denny. '*What* do we know? That it's not just magical? That it's happening all over? We still don't know *why*! Or *who*!'

'Oh, I know who,' said Tamar. 'I don't know *how*, but I know who.'

And a light dawned over Denny. 'Ashtoreth!' he said.

'He has to kill all the evil people, remember? Sinners! We thought he was going to start with *us*. But he must have changed his mind. He has a questionable definition of evil if you ask me. But I can see how it might make sense to a twisted religious nutcase. It's him all right.'

'I don't think this was his plan all along,' said Denny. 'It certainly wasn't Cindy's, I'm sure of that. Something must have changed.'

'Whatever,' said Tamar. 'It doesn't matter anymore.

'But, who are all those guys that are actually *doing* this stuff?' said Denny. 'Where did he get them from?'

'I *said* they were brainwashed,' said Tamar, as if this answered his question. 'It's like a cult or something.'

'But who *are* they? What if he's got an endless supply? He'll never leave that sanctuary again. He'll just stay there and keep sending out more and more of them and, no matter how many we stop, there'll always be more.'

'Don't exaggerate,' said Tamar. 'He can't have an *endless* supply. Although he might have enough to keep us busy for a long time,' she ended gloomily. 'Depends on where he got them from.'

'It's *him* we have to stop,' said Denny. 'If we stop *him*, it *all* stops.'

'So, we keep trying to find him,' she said. 'And until we either find him ourselves, or he comes out of hiding, which he *will* eventually, we run damage control.' she clenched her fists. 'No one else dies.' she avowed.

'What makes you think he'll *ever* come out?' said Denny.

'Denny, you are not being your usual intelligent self today. All this has upset you, made you slow. We *know* he'll come out. He's sworn revenge, hasn't he? I know his type. He'll keep his word, if it kills him. And let's face it his little minions, whatever the hell they are, can't do it for him. Even if they could, he won't get any satisfaction out of that. He's the up close and personal type. He wants to *see* us suffer.'

'He won't come back until he thinks he's ready,' said Denny. 'Until he thinks he's got the power to kill us – or me at least.'

'I think you're right,' she said. 'And that could be any time.'

'Sometime, no time, anytime, never,' said Denny gloomily. 'How do we keep tabs on the whole world?' he asked, changing the subject. 'I'm good at the Aethernet. But I'm only one man.'

'If only we had access to a worldwide Agency with spies and Aethernet connections all over the mainframe,' said Tamar.

'It exploded,' said Denny.

'The people didn't,' said Tamar. We'll set up a command base here. I'll contact Dawber.'

'Who do you think left us those newspapers?' said Denny. 'That was weird.'

Clive probably. Who else?'

'Clive's still furious with us for breaking the mainframe. We fractured quite a bit of reality you know.'

'It wasn't that bad. They got *most* of it sorted out. Besides, that was fifteen years ago, he's probably over it now.'

'Tamar, there are *still* bits of history flapping loose because of what I did. Clive isn't speaking to us anymore.'

'Maybe that's why the newspapers, instead of coming and talking to us like he used to. Does it matter?'

'I'd just like to know who it was.'

'Know who what was?' said Iffie, coming into the room.

'Whoever delivered these papers,' said Denny without thinking.

'Well, the old guy at the paper shop has the pretty unlikely name of Arthur Charpentier,' said Iffie. And she laughed.

'I *know* that name,' said Denny.

'He's a nice old guy, he used to give me free sweets, and he never asked to see my knickers or anything,' said Iffie.

Tamar was shocked, but Denny just laughed.

'And I think he knows I'm a witch too.' continued Iffie. 'He makes jokes about me turning him into a frog and stuff. He's a very witty guy,' she added sarcastically.

'Sounds like Clive to me,' said Tamar. 'And that's just the sort of name he'd come up with too.'

'What's so important about a bunch of newspapers anyway?' asked Iffie. 'Who's Clive?'

Tamar and Denny looked at each other. 'Clive is ... irrelevant.' said Tamar.

'Secrets, mother?' said Iffie, rolling her eyes.

'Don't call me "mother",' said Tamar. 'It makes me feel like I ought to be knitting. And Clive *is* irrelevant – at the moment. We'll tell you all about it some other time. As for the papers … go and get Jack, there are some things you both need to know.' And suddenly she grabbed Iffie in a tight embrace. 'It's a terrible world,' she said. 'But we can't shield you from it forever. I wish we could.'

'It's okay mum,' said Iffie considerably startled. She hugged her back and put her face in her hair. 'It's okay.'

Iffie had never seen her parents like this before. They seemed worried, uncertain, vulnerable. Her mother looked strange and sad, and Dad ... For the first time she noticed how weary he looked, in fact, he really looked kind of ill. 'Are you okay?' she asked him. 'You look a bit off colour.'

'What?' Denny jumped guiltily. 'No, no, I'm fine,' he said hurriedly.

Iffie frowned at him in puzzlement for a moment then her face cleared. He must be up to something, she guessed. It was not as if he ever did get really ill; it was flatly impossible. So there must be some other reason why he looked like that. He never did anything without a reason.

But afterwards, when she had been left alone, she wondered. What possible reason could he have for looking as if he were dying?

* * *

'No wonder you didn't want to tell me what you were doing,' Iffie said incautiously. 'I think it's terrible.'

'How did you find out?' he asked her.

'That doesn't matter. I know… Ash, how can you do these things? Don't you know how wrong it is?'

'Are you going to tell your family?'

'Ash, did you hear what I said?'

'I need to know. Are you going to betray me'?'

'Well, when you put it that way …' she thought. 'No of course not,' she said. She knew instinctively that her mother in particular, would not want Ash to know that his secret was out.

She rather regretted bringing it up at all now, but she had just been so distressed.

'*I can still help him*,' she thought. '*It's not too late.*'

'I know that you don't understand,' he was saying now, 'and that's all right. I don't blame you. You have a good heart, but your loyalties are misguided. But you *will* understand one day. You will see that it was necessary. I have been chosen to purge the world of evil.'

'I don't think I will ever understand Ash,' she said sadly. 'But I might be able to forgive you one day.'

* * *

Ashtoreth was perplexed by Iffie's final remark to him. '*Forgive me?*' he thought. He did not understand that there was anything to forgive. Oh, he knew that she did not understand but still ... the outrageous presumption of her. 'Forgive *me*? *Her*!' How dare she*?*' The arrogance, the impudence!

The truth was, he was angry because he was hurt by her reaction. He had allowed himself to dream of her by his side, meek and acquiescent. Even though he knew she was not of that nature at all. But she *would* be adoring and grateful. Grateful that he had saved her from the iniquities of her evil family.

But he must be patient, that day would surely come. For the moment, she was still ensnared in the bosom of that nest of vipers.* A mere victim of circumstance. It was not her fault. Once she was by his side, she would understand. She would see.

* * *

There was no change in Stiles's condition and Hecaté was close to despair. Only Tamar's continued insistence kept her from signing the papers that cunning nurses continually slipped under her nose. It was not that she wanted him to die, far from it; it was that, according to the doctors, he was already dead. If she could be allowed to let him go, perhaps she too could die

---

*This was a mixed metaphor too far even for Ashtoreth. Sometimes he really did sound like a bad Victorian novel. It was a wonder he could follow his own train of thought. No wonder no one else could.

and end this agony. She had once sworn that she would not hold on to him beyond his time, to see him become first senile and then atavistic as mortal men did if they extended their life span beyond what was allotted. How much worse was this?

Her children were crying out to her. There were witches in pain out there still, but she did not hear them. The sound of her own misery overwhelmed her senses. How had this happened? A goddess and a mortal man – well that *had* happened before, but how had he come to mean so much to her?

Perhaps gods and men were not that different after all.

~ Chapter Thirteen ~

THE HOUSE HAD now undergone another change. Banks of computer consoles lined the rooms; all being industriously used 24/7.

The Agency had moved in. It was like being taken over by the F.B.I during a kidnap situation, said Iffie, who had taken to contacting Ash down at a local abandoned warehouse, since the house was now so full of people there was no privacy anywhere. There were dour looking agents standing around in dark suits waiting to give reports.

The mainframe was being monitored around the clock. This was not easy considering that it contained the whole of space and time but Tamar insisted they try and, so far, they had been forewarned of several attacks on various fronts. The Warlocks, the Necromancers and several more covens of witches had been saved as well as three soldiers' barracks and four more temples.

Ashtoreth seemed to be stepping up his activities to an alarming level.

Denny's original prediction that Ashtoreth would simply keep turning out more and more of his soldiers, while remaining in safety himself, was turning out to be depressingly accurate.

It really did seem as if he had an endless supply. The more they knocked down, the more sprung up somewhere else. It was getting difficult to keep up.

And Denny was exhausted. Sometimes he wondered how he stayed on his feet, let alone managed to fight, yet somehow, he managed to keep going. So far, he had managed to hide his failing health from Tamar, but he was not sure how much longer he could keep it up. The power of the Athame was fighting back, keeping him on his feet somehow, but it was not enough.

'Got something,' shouted a voice from one of the consoles. Denny rubbed his eyes. 'What?' he said wearily.

'Looks like the ... do you want to hear this? You look knackered.'

'I'm fine, what's going on?'

'Okay, looks like they're going after the money makers again. Two corporations and about a dozen large businesses have been hit.'

'When did it happen?'

'Tomorrow,'* said the operator.

'What all at once? This is getting ridiculous.'

'He certainly is getting busier sir,' agreed the operator.

'Yes he is, the bastard. And don't call me sir,' added Denny. 'Do I *look* like a sir to you? You can call me Denny. You don't work for *me*.'

'Another hit on the small gods, sir,' another voice called across the room. Saturday. I've got the locations.'

'You know, he's got to be wondering by now, how we keep getting there before him ... before his lackeys,' said Denny, ignoring the "sir" this time.

'We don't, always,' said Director Dawber coming into the room. 'That's the problem.'

'Often enough, though. He's got to wonder why.'

Dawber shrugged. 'Any new Intel on these "warrior" freaks?' he asked.

---

* *All* of space and time – remember?

'Nada,' said Denny gloomily. 'We can't get hold of one to find out anything about them. And whatever the hell they are, there's no data on them. As far as we know anyway.'

'Got to be a record of them in the mainframe somewhere,' said Dawber.

'You'd think,' said Denny.

'We'll keep on it,' promised Dawber. 'Personally, I think they came from Hell.'

'Well, I never saw them when I was there,' said Denny, causing Director Dawber's eyebrows to shoot up into his hairline. They never stopped surprising you, these people, he thought. If anyone can crack this, it's them.

'Oh, *no!*' there was a cry from across the room. Dawber looked over in surprise. These people were highly trained and, moreover, were used to this sort of work. What could have elicited such a response?

He looked at Denny, and they raised their eyebrows at each other and shrugged. One way to find out.

* * *

Father Donaldson was a pretty conscientious priest. He never stole the collection money, or recorded the confessions, and he certainly did not diddle the altar boys. So all in all, he really did not deserve what was about to happen to him.

He was sitting in the vestry, conscientiously bringing the parish records up to date on the new fangled computer thingy. If Father Donaldson had a vice it was a relatively harmless fascination for all modern technology. Was that any reason for six black masked men to burst in on his solitude, tie him up and set his church on fire?

* * *

'He's attacking the Church? The *Christian* church?' said Tamar blankly. 'But that's *his* mob, isn't it?

'He's accusing them of the sin of "Pride".' said Denny.

'I can see that,' said Tamar. 'But still … we can't let him.'

'Of course not. According to his manifesto….'

'What manifesto?'

'Oh, yeah, that's being published afterwards, if our information is correct. He's coming out of the closet. Not that he's leaving his stronghold personally, but … anyway, the manifesto says, among other things – it's really just a list of the sins of mankind – anyway, it says that the churches of Rome and England have become complacent, indolent, wasteful. Spare the rod and spoil the congregation, sort of thing. I think he's pretty appalled that we don't all go to church every Sunday and send the kids to Sunday school and all that, like the olden days. He's blaming the Church itself.'

'So he's wiping them out?'

'A clean sweep.'

'But it's nonsense. You can't *force* people to go to church. How are the Church to blame?'

'Supposedly for letting us get away with it. We're all supposed to be too terrified of Hell to even *think* of not going. Look, it doesn't *have* to make sense – he's off his chump, remember?'

Well, there is that, of course … sounds like he reckons he's got them on Sloth as well as Pride.'

'He doesn't say as much, I don't think.'

'What about Greed? The church of Rome has been accused of that for centuries.'

'He could be accusing them of washing their feet in the font. It doesn't matter. He only wants an excuse.'

'What would that be then, sacrilege?'

'He's going for the big leagues now,' said Denny, ignoring this. 'Maybe attendance is down, but the Christian church is still a mainstay of society over a large part of the world. He's got plans. There are several governments on the manifesto too.'

'Church and government,' said Tamar. 'The *other* mainstay of society, for better or worse. All he needs is an excuse to go after the governments, and let's face it, how hard could that be?'

'He's gone way past purging the world of evil,' said Denny. 'He's moved into taking over the world mode. They always do in the end,' he sighed.

'*Evil maniacs*!' she said. 'Funny how so many of them have it in for us personally.'

'It just means we're doing something right.'

'We *have* to find him.'

'We haven't got *time* to find him. He's keeping us too busy.'

* * *

Despite what Denny had said about them having no time to look for Ashtoreth, they realised that finding him was the best way of stopping the slaughter. Tamar had been talking again about the historical files where belief in the gods still existed. But not with any real hope.

Of course, if we're speaking of the historical files,' said Denny. There is *one* place we haven't looked.'

'We've looked from one end of time to the other,' said Tamar dispiritedly.

'No, we haven't,' said Denny. 'We haven't been to the *end* of time.'

The end of time,' echoed Tamar in a horrified tone. 'But that's … sorry, what *is* that then?'

'An empty place, it's not filed. Well, there's nothing there. Except the *beginning* of time, of course.'

'And that's not filed either I suppose?' said Tamar.

'It's a gap,' said Denny. 'The space of time between then and now, shorter than a click of your fingers. But there is no time there. It's eternity too. How do you file eternity? But you could hide there forever.'

'And you know how to get us there?' she asked.

'Oh yes,' he said smugly. 'Dunno about getting us out again … I'm *kidding*,' he added when he saw her face.

'The end of time,' said Tamar. 'What are we waiting for then, the world to end?'

To reach the end of time, Denny simply entered the file closest to it; the end of the year five hundred gazillion or something like it, and waited.

It wasn't exactly nothing, not like the void. It was a howling wilderness. Tamar pointed this out.

'There's a lot of temporal energy being funneled through here,' said Denny.

'I can't believe Cindy ever came here.' said Tamar. 'It's horrible. Like being stuck inside a blender.'

'Wait!' said Denny holding up a finger.

'Wait for wha…' silence fell; silence and absolute stillness and then a light fell.

'Welcome to eternity,' said Denny.

'My God, it's beautiful,' said Tamar in awe.

'A perfect moment,' said Denny. 'Everyone has this inside them. The ability to make a perfect moment last forever.' he smiled at her.

'You've been here before.' It was not actually a question, it just sounded like one.

'How would you have liked me to describe it?' he said.

'You couldn't have,' she conceded.*

'Exactly,' he said.

'I feel like … like … like falling in love, like the first time I kissed you.'

'I know,' he said. 'A perfect moment.'

'You soppy git,' she said.

'Mind you, I know what you mean,' she added, leaning her head on his shoulder.

'It's the most romantic date anyone ever went on,' she said. 'I wish we could stay.'

Denny would have liked very much to stay here. It was peaceful; no nasty dreams could haunt him here. He would get no weaker. But they could not stay. It was obvious to him that Ashtoreth was not here. It would hardly have been a perfect moment if he had been. Denny, having been here before, had known that he would know immediately if he was here.

'He isn't here,' he said reluctantly.

---

* And I'm not even going to try – use your imagination.

'At least it hasn't been a waste of time,' said Tamar. 'And even if it had been, I wouldn't be sorry we came.'

* * *

'The Army of Righteousness?' Tamar was reading Ashtoreth's "Manifesto". 'Is that what he's calling it? He's not just barmy. He's not very imaginative either.'

'Doesn't matter what he calls it,' said Denny. 'But it's a pity he doesn't give away what the army's made up of. 'You know, 'my army of – insert name of species –.'

'That would be helpful I suppose, but, on the other hand, it's not as if we're having any trouble beating them up.'

'But every time we get rid of one lot …' He left the sentence hanging. It had been said too many times before.

'What does it matter?' she said. 'The only way to stop them for good is to stop *him*. And we can't. Not until we *find* him.'

'Or, we could assume that we're going about this the wrong way,' said Denny. 'It wouldn't be the first time. Find a way to take his army away from him, and he's got nothing.'

'But we've tried to find out what they are. It's getting us nowhere.'

'Maybe we've been asking the wrong questions. We need Jack … He's better at this investigative thing than us,' he added lamely. 'Sorry, I shouldn't have brought him up.'

'That's okay. Hecaté says his burns have mostly healed up. The docs are at a loss to explain it. Anyway, we're not just going to pretend he doesn't exist, are we? He deserves better than that.'

'He always assumed that everyone was lying to him until they could prove they weren't.' said Denny. 'He suspected *everyone. All* the time.'

'Guilty until proven innocent,' said Tamar with a reminiscent smile.

'He was usually right.'

'Yeah, sad isn't it? You can't trust anyone …' Tamar broke off, frowning.

'What is it?'

'I think Jack may have just solved our problem for us,' she said. 'I think we have been proceeding under a false assumption because *I* believed a lie.'

'A lie?'

'How does Jack do it?' she said. 'Proceed on the assumption that you already know they did it, and let them tell you all about it as they try to keep up with you?'

'Who are we interrogating then? Are you sure we have time for this? The next attack is scheduled for ...'

'Ah, but that's the beauty of it,' she said. 'Where we're going, there *is* no time ... No time, now *there's* an idea.'

* * *

'If you expect me to apologise, you've got another think coming,' said Satan. 'My days of cowering before you are over ... Okay, okay I'm sorry.'

Tamar had hardly moved a muscle; it was just the look on her face.

She and Denny looked at each other. She had been right. They had barrelled in here acting as if they knew for a fact that he had lied, and he had confirmed it before he had had time to think.

'So, Ashtoreth's army are *Nephelim*?' said Denny. 'You *did* send out fallen angels to corrupt the human race. Dawber was right. They *did* come from Hell – indirectly anyway.'

'Who is Ashtoreth?' said Satan.

'A Nephilim.'

'Not one of mine,' said Satan firmly. 'Never heard of him. And as for an *army* of Nephelim running around in these times, well, that's ridiculous. They are *long* gone. Their descendants would have no power left now.'

'We've seen them, fought them,' Tamar told him. As if to say: "Get out of that one".

Satan shrugged. He simply did not believe it possible.

'They *are* pretty weak, though,' said Denny. 'Just not completely powerless. Maybe the race hung on to their powers better than you would have thought.'

'Impossible,' said Satan. But now he looked uncertain. 'The Nephelim were all male. In order to breed they would have had to dilute their genetics with humans. If there *are* descendants, they would be almost completely human by now – no powers whatsoever.'

'Almost isn't the same as absolutely,' said Denny. 'They are still part Nephilim. And it all fits. The fact that they are all willing to serve Ashtoreth, the sheer numbers of them – there must be millions of them by now – and the fact that we never knew about them before this. They must have been living as ordinary humans for centuries. No wonder we couldn't find them in the mainframe. They didn't exist as Nephilim until Ashtoreth called them up. You say they wouldn't have any powers left by now, but you aren't certain – are you?'

'Well ... it seems unlikely,' faltered Satan. A slow smile spread over his face as if he could no longer contain his pleasure. Tamar caught the look. 'This is what you planned,' she accused him.

'Nonsense,' said Satan. 'All I wanted was to corrupt the human race. The Nephelim are not intrinsically evil, but they *are* far more susceptible to corruption than humans. Much of the weakness in the human race comes directly from what I did. They were not originally designed that way – the first men were sickeningly strong and noble. Find an evil man, a weak and easily corrupted man and the chances are he is a descendant of the Nephilim. But, no I did not plan *this*.'

'But you're pleased it happened?'

Satan shrugged as if to say: "What do you expect? – I *am* Satan".

'And so they sin, come to hell and get turned into demons and sent out into the world to tempt others into sin and so it goes on,' theorised Denny.

'The cycle of sin,' said Satan. 'It's been working beautifully for thousands of years. And there's no way you can stop it.'

'Just give me time,' muttered Tamar.

This would have been the ideal note to leave on, but Denny was not about to let it go at that. A perfect dramatic exit – ruined.

But *C'est la vie*, as they say.

'You're telling us that you *didn't* plan all this?' he said. 'Just how stupid do you think we are?'

Satan rolled his eyes at Denny but said nothing. He did not have to.

'Well, after all, perhaps I'm giving you too much credit, after all,' said Denny turning away. 'Seems like all the evil plans you ever took credit for, turned out to mere accidents. Why should this be any different? Just because you're denying it, doesn't mean you don't want us to believe it. I know that trick.'

'ACCIDENTS?' roared Satan indignantly. '*My* evil plans have the beauty of subtlety. Such subtlety that such an ignorant creature as yourself could not hope to understand. What you take for accidents … ha! *My* plan was to corrupt the human race and begin the cycle of sin. And I did it so well that no one has ever been able to see how I did it, let alone stop it.' He paused. Denny continued to stare blankly at him. 'But if you insist,' Satan resumed resignedly. 'I will tell you this much. What has happened was foreseen … Long ago. There was a prophecy made back in the time before the cycle of sin began. It predicts the Rise of the Nephilim to cleanse the Earth.

'I have seen this prophecy. It said that one more would appear to lead the others into the light … whatever that means, lot of blah, blah, blah, I can't remember it all. It didn't say *when*, but we don't need to wonder about that anymore do we?

'Perhaps what I have done was instrumental in the fulfilment of the prophecy, but it was known long before that, that this time would come. But not by me, not until later.'

'So, it *was* accidental – at least as far as *your* part in it goes?' said Denny.

'Not accidental,' said Satan. 'A part of the grand design. I have my place too, you know. As do you.'

'The Rise of the Nephilim?' said Tamar. 'To cleanse the Earth? What does that mean? Cleanse it of what, and why?'

Satan smiled. 'I think you already know. And if you want the truth, I'm not too happy about it either. If I'd known then what my creation would lead to ...' He shrugged. 'Maybe I wouldn't have done it.'

'I'm guessing that's not a humanitarian sentiment,' said Tamar caustically.

'Not exactly,' Satan agreed.

'You don't still have a copy of this "prophecy" do you?' asked Denny.

'No, no, sorry. I put stuff down in this place and never see it again. You know how it is. This place is full of thieves.'

'And liars,' said Tamar.

* * *

Being in the underworld had triggered a random thought that had begun earlier when Denny had mentioned the hall of images. The Fates.

Now Tamar knew that the Fates were no longer in existence; she knew it better than anyone. She had been the one to destroy them. But there was another. Now that they knew that Ashtoreth had gained access to an apparently inexhaustible supply of Nephelim, and it was becoming increasingly obvious that he intended to take over the world with them, it had become even more imperative that they find him and soon. It might also be important to discover not only where he was but where he was going and even, in light of the Nephilim army, where he had been.

The goddess of Destiny might be able to help them with that one.

Few people, Tamar knew, realised that Arachne, the spider goddess who guarded the Fates in the underworld, was no mean weaver of the destinies of men herself. She had been demoted for unspecified reasons to a mere guardian of the Fates until Tamar had destroyed them. Now she was back behind the spinning wheel so to speak. Actually Arachne did not need a spinning wheel what with being part spider and a natural weaver. And best of all, Arachne was an old friend.

'You never call, you never write,' said Arachne only half jokingly as Tamar entered the cave with Denny in tow.

She looked archly at Denny, as if she knew something he did not. Which was probably the case when you came to think about it. She knew something about everybody that they did not know themselves – such as everything that was going to happen to them. But Denny knew that she would keep it to herself.

'I know why you are here of course,' she said. 'Saw it coming. She shrugged multiple shoulders. 'Can't help you I'm afraid.'

'Can't or won't,' said Tamar.

'Both actually,' said Arachne. 'God, it's so dull having a conversation that one has foreseen. Say something to surprise me – no wait! I remember saying that, and I know what you are going to say so don't bother. And you can shut up as well,' she said, just a microsecond before Denny started to laugh. He stopped, startled.

'Okay, since I know you're going to ask anyway, I can tell you that your boy Ashtoreth has fallen off the map as far as I am concerned. He has no destiny – that is, he appears to be making his own. And God only knows how *that* will turn out. I certainly don't.' she sighed. 'I'm only telling you this much because it can't hurt anything. But … there is something funny about it all. It's as if there are *two* futures, and that is all bound up with him somehow. And you too for that matter. But it's not clear.' She shook her head.

'Can't you tell us *anything*?' said Tamar. 'What about his warriors, where did *they* come from? I mean that's the past. You must be able to see *that*!'

'You don't need me for that,' said Arachne firmly. 'You *know* what they are. But if there's any confusion I will tell you this, the only thing any of them are likely to have watched in the past is Television. And if that helps you one iota then I'm a greenfly.'

Denny decided to try something, just by way of an experiment. The fact that the last time they had met Arachne had likened him to an upended broomstick might not mean anything, he thought. Cindy had once been pretty contemptuous of his looks too. He smiled at Arachne – that's all, just a smile.

It worked immediately. 'Oh, all right then,' she said. She leaned forward and said conspiratorially. 'I cannot see *his* destiny, nor where he has hidden himself, but I *can* see yours. You will face him within the year. Until then, nothing can be done against him.'

'Thank you,' said Denny gravely aware that she had not been much help really, but it did not hurt to keep on friendly terms. You never knew.

Tamar was despondent though. 'It seems as if we're never going to find the bugger,' she said. 'Everything we try just… just *fails*!'

'If Arachne's right,' said Denny. '*He's* going to find *us*! In the meantime, damage control?'

'In the meantime,' said Tamar fiercely. 'We *don't* just give up. If *he* can control his own fate, then I'm damned sure *I* can.'

* * *

'… And in the time of men, after the age of myths is over, and the age of magic is done, the age of metal and wheels powered by the harnessed lighting will come. And that will be the age of the greatest sin.

'And one will rise up from the legends of the past and take his place among his ancient brethren who have been here from the beginning hiding in the light while all around the darkness falls.

'And he will gather his brethren and lead them in the way of the light.

'And he shall blaze forth his light into the dark corners of the world and destroy the darkness …

'And so shall the sins of the world be cleansed and the age of sin be over.

'But …'

'But *what*?' said Tamar, as Denny stopped abruptly.

That's all it says,' he said. 'There's some missing. At least there *is* a "but".'

'Yeah, "but" it could mean anything.'

'I never heard of a prophecy that said "but" though.' said Denny. 'Could be a good sign.'

'What, like, "but … then he gets killed, and everyone lived happily ever after"?' she said her voice dripping with scorn. Denny did not appear to notice.

'Well, yeah that sort of thing,' he said, 'but probably a bit more obscure than that. I mean this doesn't mention him by name or anything. It doesn't even call him the Nephilim.'

'No, but it sure sounds like it's about him.'

'Well, I still say that "but" sounds like an opening,' said Denny. And wondered why Tamar suddenly fell about laughing.

* * *

'Speaking of time,' said Tamar, who had developed a bad habit of returning to earlier conversations that she been having (sometimes several days previously) without warning. 'I don't know why I didn't think of this sooner.' And she stopped time.

'That should give us some time to catch up with these bastards,' she said. 'I mean we *know* it works on them,' she shook her head. I should have done it earlier. I don't know why I didn't,'

'Dirty tactics,' said Denny. 'We don't usually, and let's face it, we never thought it could get so bad so quickly. It sort of crept up on us.'

'Well, dirty tactics or not, we need the advantage. They're all over the damn place now, attacking in unison. We need time to catch up.'

But it did not quite work out that way. Ashtoreth, who as it turned out, was clearly not affected by time, as it was passing in the real world, soon caught on to this trick.

They had not been there five minutes, dispatching frozen warriors with a nasty feeling that they were somehow cheating, when *another* batch of warriors appeared as if from nowhere

Obviously, they had been sent directly from the stronghold where there was no time to stop. Well, they were in the real world now. Tamar considered restarting time and stopping it again, thus trapping this lot too and any more that had been sent out elsewhere. But she knew it was no good. Not if he could just keep sending more.

Stopping time would only help them short term, during a battle (and they did not really need that kind of help) but as a long term plan, it had tanked. They would still be dealing with the problem piecemeal.

In fact, the only thing stopping time had probably achieved was to prevent Ashtoreth's hapless victims from fleeing when fresh warriors were sent out.

In view of this, it was only fortunate, that, having been given the idea, Ashtoreth was not able to stop time himself, or he most certainly would have done.

* * *

Another sleepless night for Denny, and Tamar decided to stay up and keep him company, without having the slightest notion that this was the last thing he wanted.

She was lying on the bed, and Denny was reading – more research, this time about the Nephilim though. He would not do his "secret" research in front of Tamar.

'How many angels can dance on the head of a pin?' said Tamar suddenly.

'Is that supposed to be funny?' said Denny. I'd rather know how many half-angels can dance on the end of my sword.'

'Very bloodthirsty,' said Tamar approvingly. 'You're coming on. But I only asked because I've been thinking.'

'About angels dancing on pins?' said Denny, frankly disbelieving.

'They say an infinite number of angels can dance on the head of a pin,' she said.

'Christ,' thought Denny, 'she really *has* been thinking about it. And I thought I was the one cracking up here.'

'There's a lot of blather about divinity and all that, but it got me wondering … is there any truth to it?'

'In an infinite universe, anything is possible,' said Denny sententiously.

'Bollocks,' said Tamar. 'The universe isn't infinite. You should know that. On the other hand … This isn't the only universe – is it?

Denny remembered the void after the lights went off and his certainty that there was more out there – in the void, or beyond it.'

'So?' he said.

'So if a lot of angels, I don't say an infinite number – just a lot, could dance on the head of a pin,' she said. 'And for the purposes of this discussion we are assuming they can, how would they do that?'

'A giant pin?' said Denny.

'Or very small angels,' she said.

Denny sat up and looked at her. 'Okay, he said. 'You're clearly going somewhere with this. Let's have it.'

'Mini universes,' she said.

'What?'

'It's like a microcosm inside a microcosm. Like rock pools. You said that our universe is inside another larger one. Well what if it's like – Dutch dolls? One inside another?'

'I think you mean *Russian* Dolls,' said Denny.

Tamar waved a dismissive hand. 'Whatever!' she said. 'You know what I mean.'

'Yes, and it's an interesting idea. As well as parallel universes there could also be diminishing universes on a purely physical level. And it wouldn't be any problem to a god or an angel.' He stabbed a finger at the discarded book on his lap. 'Or half-angels for that matter. If *we* can shrink down to any size we want, then there's no reason why they couldn't. It would be a self-contained universe with its own mainframe so any data pertaining to it wouldn't be in our mainframe. Very cool.'

'I can see you've really taken to the idea,' said Tamar dryly.

'But why not, it could be the answer. And even if it's not … fascinating!' he looked more animated than she had seen him in a long time.

'Dweeb!' she said affectionately.

'That's *geek*, thank you, and this was your daft idea in the first place.'

'But … how do we find such a thing?' he wondered.

'Ah,' said Tamar, 'that's where quantum comes in handy.'

'You mean magic?' said Denny. 'The art of finding a thing without looking for it.'

'Beat you to it!' challenged Tamar.

Denny raised an eyebrow. 'Given your history of stacking the odds in your own favour,' he said, 'that remark can only mean that you've already done it.'

Tamar gave a grimace of deep chagrin. 'You know me too well,' she said.

Denny waggled both eyebrows at her in such a comical fashion that she burst out laughing.

'Lead on MacCheat,' he said.

'I don't have to,' she said. 'I brought it here.' And she held out a hand.

On it – just barely visible was …

'The head of a pin?' said Denny incredulously.

'Not exactly,' she said. 'However …'

'That's what gave you the idea,' finished Denny. 'And … there's really a *whole* universe in there?'

'Yes, a whole universe. But it's okay, we won't have to search it all.'

'Thank god for that. Why not?'

'Quantum,' they both said together.

'Will it be like our universe?' asked Denny.

We'll soon find out.' said Tamar. 'But I'm betting on no.'

'How are we supposed to get in?' asked Denny.

For answer, Tamar held up a little bottle marked "Drink Me".

'Very funny,' said Denny. 'You're saying we just have to be the right size?'

'Yes, we should be drawn in by the natural gravity of this universe once we're small enough. As long as we're close enough to it.'

Tamar would have won her bet hands down had Denny been foolish enough to take her up on it. For one thing, the planets were cuboid and had a silvery mirror like sheen that was just translucent enough to see through and all the land and trees and so on appeared to be *inside*. And once inside the only habitable one, the *people* ....

'It's like the land of the Cyber-men,' said Tamar unkindly. It was in a way, but much worse. They were bipeds, so that was a relief in a way, but so squat and square that they looked almost like they were trundling along on wheels. Their skin was metallic, not like human skin covered in metallic paint but truly metallic, shiny and smooth, but not reflective. Yet it seemed flexible enough to allow facial expression. Whatever else they were, they were clearly organic creatures and not artificially made. The eyes, although black and shiny, were the eyes of living creatures. Close up it was possible to see rainbows of swirling colours in them, like oil on water.

Besides, robots did not wear clothes and these did, indicating a sense of modesty peculiar to sentient creatures everywhere.

To call them ugly was being charitable. The features were squashed up within a tiny squared off area of face making them look like a lot of flattened tin cans with faces painted on them.

'I daresay they look nice enough to one another,' said Denny. 'We probably look like hideous monsters to them.'

Tamar did not like this idea, and was even considering changing her appearance to match the inhabitants, when she realised that Denny would laugh like a drain if she did so. And would probably never want to look at her again either, not with that image in his head. So she refrained.

She made herself invisible instead. Denny though this was a good idea and followed suit. They were getting frightened stares.

And then they went for a look around.

It was evidently a city of some sort. All the buildings, tall and small were built around the same principle. They were all round or cylindrical – just as we make most of our building square and flat. This civilization went in for curved lines and domes. It was like a city of pipes and igloos.

Fascinating as all this was, it was not why they were here. 'Let's get into their mainframe,' said Tamar.

Denny was not listening; he was looking around, eyes wide with wonder. 'Wow!' he kept saying. 'Wow! It's like being on an alien planet. Look at that!'

'I think it's a garbage truck,' said Tamar dryly. 'And not a mega space buggy whatever you might think.'

'Killjoy,' said Denny.

Then Tamar stopped and stared herself, but not in fascination or wonder but rather in horror. '*Not* a garbage truck,' she said pointed forgetting that she was invisible. 'Well, not unless you consider dead citizens as garbage,' she added.

'Bring out your dead,' said Denny in a hollow voice. 'It's a plague. Look at the marks on the doors. And they're incinerating them in that thing.'

This appeared to be true. As the doors at the back of the truck closed, a bright flash of light shone out for a second then the doors were opened again to reveal an empty space.

'A horrible plague,' repeated Denny. 'Do you think Ashtoreth…?'

Tamar shrugged. 'Not sure it's really his style. But … maybe. It'd be a good way of clearing the place out for his soldiers to take over I suppose.'

'Well there's only one way to find out,' said Denny.

'I don't like this,' said Tamar reaching for Denny's invisible hand.

'There's nothing we can do here,' he admitted. 'Close file?'

'We can but try,' she said.

The mainframe of another universe was disturbingly like their own mainframe. Only the colour scheme was different. Denny was disappointed, but it just went to show, he said, that bureaucrats were the same everywhere.

'I wonder if there's a little metallic Clive running around in here somewhere,' said Tamar.

'Who cares?' said Denny. 'Can we use this mainframe? 'It's all in a different language.'

'Shouldn't matter,' said Tamar. 'After all, we managed to get in using just our intention.' She concentrated and miraculously the language became English. 'Virtual reality,' she said. 'It's enough to make you wonder if *anything* is real.'

'Course it is,' said Denny dismissively. 'It's as real as you want it to be.'

Tamar liked this idea, and it earned Denny a kiss. 'What would I do without you?' she said.

'I dread to think,' he said. 'Now can you find out anything or not?'

'Can *you*?' she said. 'You're the expert and what do you mean you dread to think?'

Denny ignored this as too difficult. 'We need the central files,' he said. 'This way.' And he set off.

It did not take long to ascertain that neither Cindy nor Ashtoreth had ever been in this universe. With the ease of long practice, Denny found his way into the central mainframe hard drive and did a quick search. It turned up nothing.

'Well, said Tamar philosophically, 'it was worth a try.'

Tamar, unable to stop herself from well intentioned interference, had sneaked in to a file while Denny was busy doing this, to find a cure for the plague and sent it, as a bolt of inspiration (a pretty easy program to run – the "muse" program) to a doctor type. So, she was feeling relatively satisfied with herself, despite the fact that their personal objectives had not been fulfilled by coming here.

'Cookie?' she asked. 'It had "Eat Me" iced on the top.

'You can take a joke too far you know,' said Denny. However, he took the cookie.

* * *

Denny was wrong if he thought that Tamar had not noticed his declining health and strength. Night after night she had lain awake watching him twitch and moan in his sleep. That had been at the beginning. Now she had noticed that he hardly slept at all, she had seen him in the night, stumbling about clutching the Athame, trying desperately to keep awake. She had watched him grow paler and thinner and seen the lines of weariness stretch across his face, seen the hollowness of his eyes increase. It was as if he was being tortured from within or prey to some hideous internal malady. And it was getting worse. Every day he seemed weaker, it tore at her heart to see it, until she felt like she could not stand it anymore. Whatever it was, it was eating away at him like a vicious parasite and turning him into a shadow. Now she lay awake at night, without him, staring into a future that had somehow become terrifying. Never had she imagined something like this. He was so weak now she was afraid he might die.

It was a quarter past midnight when Denny woke sweating and shivering and rose silently and went downstairs. The situation was taking serious toll now. He could not stay awake forever, but every time he gave in to exhaustion the hag returned to strip him of yet more of his strength.

'Tell me about the dreams,' said Tamar from the study door. So, she had known all along. He realised he had been a fool to think she would not have noticed.

She had been watching him for longer than he realised. The familiar contours and hollows of his face glowing gently in the light of the computer screen filled her with a sudden surge of tender love. She would *not* lose him now, not ever.

'Tell me about the dreams,' she insisted.

Although Denny was accustomed to calling himself an old married man, he still looked on Tamar with the incredulous eyes of a lover. It was still hard to believe that this fabulous creature was really his and, what was even more amazing, she seemed to feel as if *she* were the lucky one. Denny knew different. He was, therefore, determined never to do anything to hurt her, and the dreams, although his actions were anything but voluntary, seemed like a betrayal of the worst kind. How *could* he tell her? But, then again, if there was one person he just could not lie to …

Denny told her.

'I see,' said Tamar. Her tone told him nothing. 'So they aren't just dreams then. Will it happen tonight?'

'No.' he said positively. That was the funny thing; it had never happened more than once in a night.

'Do you feel better, now? Could you sleep?'

Yes, I think so.'

'Good. We'll look into this tomorrow. We'll get to the bottom of this,' she reassured him. 'We always do don't we?'

Denny fell asleep almost immediately, taken over by exhaustion. But Tamar lay awake in the dark for hours staring into nothing and wondering.

* * *

His name, he was sure, had been Thomas before the blessing time. He had been a pretty ordinary family man and petty thief on the side. A small corner of his mind still wondered how on earth he had ended up here. Standing here, shaking with terror, outside the mouth of surely the largest, darkest, most sinister cavern in the world.

The sounds from the inside were not encouraging either. He had climbed for days in one of the coldest regions of the world. His faith had driven him on. And something else. It was as if he ~~was not the master of his own~~ destiny any more, which he knew

* Apparently, for all his preoccupation with the sins of mankind, Ashtoreth had not bothered to screen his army of Nephelim for possible previous convictions. As long as they did what they were told now, he did not care who they were.

to be true, but... surely he should still be the master of his own limbs? No, that was blasphemy. He had been blessed. If he got this right, he would be redeemed for all his sins forever. Moreover, he had no control over his actions any more. Whoever Thomas had been, he looked out from behind the eyes of the Nephilim now. And the Nephilim was the Lord Ashtoreth.

He entered the cave. From the shadows was the glow of a pair of red slitted eyes. He was not afraid; there was no room for fear in a heart filled to the brim with exhilaration and exultation.

~ Chapter Fourteen ~

TAMAR HAD NO ideas about what the dreams meant, other than the fact that they were apparently real enough to be wearing Denny out. She had noticed for some time that he had been growing weaker and had spent a considerable amount of wakeful hours herself, wondering whether or not to confront him about it. When, only the day before, she had seen him stagger and almost pass out from sheer exhaustion, she made her mind up. She simply could not watch this anymore.

She decided that, rather than waste any more time on pointless research, she would take the problem to Hecaté. Her instincts told her that there was something decidedly witch-like about this, and witches were not Tamar's area of expertise.

'There is no need for research,' said Hecaté, drawing the curtains around the hospital bed, as if this would give them more privacy. 'I have knowledge of this phenomenon that Denny is suffering from. The creature is known as the Succubus. Considering the history of Denny's almost fatal attraction for supernaturally gifted women, perhaps he was bound to attract the attention of a Succubus sooner or later.'

'As if we don't have enough to worry about,' said Tamar.

'No,' Denny argued. 'I read up on those, it doesn't fit. The Succubus, is supposed to be very pretty and seductive, this isn't like that.' He looked sidelong at Tamar. 'Honestly, I'm not lying about that,' he added, slightly defensively.

'I believe you,' said Tamar. 'You *are* a fool sometimes,' she added. 'Did it never occur to you that the beauty of the Succubus might be a glamour? And *you* can see through a glamour.'

'I never thought of that,' he admitted.

'What *is* a Succubus anyway?' asked Tamar.

It is a kind of demon,' said Hecaté.

'Oh, well, that *proves* it then,' said Tamar confidently. 'Demon glamours never work on other demons, and the Athame is a demonic weapon – technically.'

'Actually it's a bit of a relief,' said Denny. 'I thought it might be … well it doesn't matter what I thought. What do we do about it?'

'Catch her at it. She will have no power over a woman. How long have these visits been going on?'

'A few months, on and off. Just lately it's been getting more often though – every night.'

'Amazing,' said Hecaté. 'Most men would have been totally and permanently exhausted by now. The Succubus takes the strength of a man. But she has a weakness of her own. She needs the man, his strength, his power and most of all, his love. You must not give her what she wants again.'

'How do I stop her? I feel so weak when it happens. I can't fight. I can hardly move.'

'You can keep your mouth shut, can you not? No matter how desperate you feel you must not tell her what she so longs to hear.'

'I thought it was just a dream,' Denny said. 'Although lately it *has* seemed more real. I thought I was having prophetic nightmares again.' He shook his head wearily. 'I've been waiting for this thing to turn up for real, and it was real all along.'

Tamar put her arms around him. 'You're just irresistible aren't you?' she said.

Denny rolled his eyes. 'Only to demented power crazed lunatics,' he said. 'Present company excepted.'

'Besides,' he continued. 'It's not me, is it?' He withdrew the Athame. '*This* is what attracts them. The power, not me. I mean this sort of thing never happened to me before I got this thing.'

'Yeah?' said Tamar. 'But to look at it another way, before you got that thing, as you call it, you never really had much to do with magical women did you? You don't *know* that it's not just you.'

'Well, I don't think so,' said Denny stubbornly. 'I reckon it's the Athame. I mean ordinary women still don't think too much of me, which is par for the course and always was. But magical women – they sense the power. At least that's what I think. After all, *I'm* nothing special. I mean the Faerie queen didn't look into my soul or something and decide I was just what she needed, did she? And Hecaté said it. *This* one is definitely about the power. That's what she wants. That's what she's taking.'

'And I think it *is* you,' argued Tamar. – 'But then again, maybe I'm biased. But remember *I* liked you before you ever got that thing.

'That's different.'

'And remember the Succubus also wants your love.' added Tamar not to be outdone in an argument.

'Maybe it is a little of both,' said Hecaté. 'You have changed since you received this power you know. You no longer hang your head as you once did.'

'That wasn't the Athame that did that,' said Denny. 'That was Tamar. If I've changed, it's because of her.'

'Well, I suppose we'll never know,' said Tamar. 'But whatever the reason, it certainly does cause a lot of problems, and this is the worst one yet. What are we going to do?'

'Denny must resist,' said Hecaté. She turned to Denny. 'You must not give in to her. You must not say the words.'

'The problem is, it *feels* like a dream,' he said. 'I don't actually seem to have *any* control at all, even over what I say.

Do you think I *want* to say it? I try not to, I really do. But I can't seem to help it.'

'I have an idea about that,' said Hecaté.

* * *

By the light of an early dawn, the sun sparkled on the Mediterranean. Down there somewhere there was a cave, the Nephilim (once known as Julius – but he no longer had a name) knew, and in that cave, he also knew, death or glory awaited. The boat he had charted was now far from the shore – the cave was actually a crater in the seabed straight down towards the earth's core.

Without hesitation, he dived off the boat. His Lord would protect him.

The pressures at this depth should have killed him long before he ran out of breath. Neither happened, and eventually he saw what he was hoping for; he had not mistaken his location. In the pitch dark at the bottom of the sea, a light glowed, as if the very fire at the centre of the earth was shining through the great cave mouth beneath him. It spanned at least a mile in length, so there was no chance of him missing his entry. From above it looked like a volcanic vent; great swaths of steam rose from its depths, superheated water that would scorch the flesh from an ordinary man, bubbled all around the area. If this place was ever seen by mortal eyes, it would be taken as a perfectly ordinary geological phenomenon. But once inside, the truth was revealed. But no ordinary man would ever get so far. And if he did ... he would certainly never return, not from this place. It was enormous, not just the cavern, which was as large as a city and as deep as the ocean again, but its occupant.

Below him, as he trod water, the water parted as if streaming off the sides of a vertically rising missile, and coming up fast, from the depths of the cavern rose two bright golden glowing eyes like small suns.

The Nephilim smiled.

* * *

'Love me, love me,'

Denny opened his eyes and sat up abruptly, throwing the hag-like creature sideways off the bed. 'I don't think so,' he said.

'*What*? What is this?' shrieked the hag, leaping to her feet.

'I'm just not feeling it,' said Denny. 'I guess you aren't my type.'

The hag leered gruesomely at him. 'No man can resist my power,' she said and grasped him by the throat.

Denny took hold of the skinny claw and forced it backwards slowly and inexorably. A weird look of triumph and cruelty sat oddly on his face.

'Ah, but I'm not an ordinary man,' said Denny. 'In fact ...' And he transformed before the hag's eyes into Tamar. 'I'm not a man at all.' And she reached out, quick as a striking cobra, and grabbed the hag by the hair, twisting the head around painfully.

'He's *my* man,' she said, indicating the comatose figure on the bed – which, disturbingly, still looked like her. She struck out with the flat of her hand at the creature's chest sending her flying to the corner of the room.

'Why does *everybody* want my man?' she asked plaintively. She stalked over to the crone and kicked her down to the floor as she tried to get up.

'Can't find one of your own?' she sneered. She delivered a staggering roundhouse to the head.

'Why can't you all just leave him *alone*?' she shrieked. 'I saw him *first*.' She kicked again. 'He's *mine*!'

'A Faerie queen, a crazy witch and now *you*!' she said. 'I just want him to my-*self*!' On the last syllable she took the Succubus by the head and twisted, throwing her over her own heels in a kind of awkward somersault.

'Is that too much to ask?' she said calmly. 'Is it?'

'What makes *you* deserve him so much?' asked the hag standing up slowly. Apparently unhurt, despite the pounding.

Tamar thought this an odd question under the circumstances. 'Well. I'll kill anyone who tries to take him from me,' she said, as if this was an answer.

'Threats,' sneered the hag. 'That's all you've got?' And she raked her claws across Tamar's face, drawing blood.

Tamar staggered back in shock. According to Hecaté, the Succubus was pretty defenceless against a physical assault. Suddenly this was not going according to the script at all. The hag struck Tamar full in the face and sent her flying across the room.

'Okay, so not so defenceless. I can handle that.' Tamar stood up shakily. The unexpected assault had left her slightly stunned.

'You don't deserve him,' shrieked the hag looming over her as she hovered a little way in the air. 'You never did, you just got lucky. What's so great about *you* anyway? He could have been mine. He *should* have been mine.'

'I know that whining voice,' thought Tamar. She recognised the sentiments too. She grabbed the Succubus by the wrists and held the hands firmly (while the Succubus struggled wildly) looking at the fingers. On the third finger of the left hand, was a golden ring. Tamar made a light and looked at the face. A raddled, distorted travesty of a face but Tamar recognised the eyes. *Cindy!*

'He never could have been yours,' said Tamar gently like someone trying to talk a suicide off a rooftop. 'But you know that really, don't you?'

The Cindy-Succubus cackled hideously. She broke free and leapt to the window sill and hung there for a moment. 'So, you've won again,' she said. 'For now at least. But don't think for a moment that it will last. They're all the same. He betrayed you once. He'll do it again. He's a *man*. None of them can be trusted.' And with this parting thrust, she dropped off the window falling in a steep dive and vanished.

As soon as the potent influence of the Succubus left the room, Denny awoke. He ran over to Tamar who was trembling and bleeding.

'She's wrong you know,' he said. 'I'll never do that to you again.'

Tamar looked surprised. 'You heard all that?'

'Everything,' he said. 'But I couldn't move you know. Like a bad dream.'

'Could you put your *own* face back on?' said Tamar. 'You're kind of freaking me out – you look so much better than I do at the moment.'

Denny shook his head briefly and his own features returned. 'Oh, I don't know,' he said. 'I think a black eye suits you. You look like Iffie. Except she wears *two* black eyes.'

'It's the red eyeliner that gets me,' said Tamar. 'It makes her look like she's having a brain haemorrhage.'

'I think that's the idea,' said Denny.

'I won't you know,' he reiterated insistently taking her hands and looking her plaintively in the eye. 'You *can* trust me. After all where else could I find a woman willing to fight a Succubus for me?'

'Almost anywhere,' thought Tamar. 'On current showing anyway.'

'It was Cindy.' she said. 'And Iffie was right. She still has her godlike powers.'

'I noticed that,' he said, touching the bloody streaks on her face gently. 'But we'll be ready for her the next time.'

'She won't come back now that we're on to her.' Tamar laughed. 'Just how irresistible do you think you are?'

'Revenge is what's pretty irresistible,' Denny pointed out. 'Not me.'

'It was *you* that drew her here in the first place,' she said. This was unarguable. At least, Denny did not feel like having this argument again.

'We have to catch her,' said Denny. 'If Hecaté's right, then she'll go looking for a substitute.The Succubus *needs* a man. That's the nature of the beast. She could start attacking at random if she gets desperate.'

'How did she get to be a Succubus anyway?'

'Maybe Hecaté can tell us, she seems to be the expert.'

Hecaté could. 'The Succubus is a type of Demon usually,' she told them. 'But there have been cases of a broken hearted witch becoming a Succubus. Trying to steal what she could not get in any other way – love. It is a rare and extreme reaction. I am sorry, I did not even think of it.'

'So, before, those *were* just premonitions – dreams?' said Denny.

'Yes and no. Cindy became the Succubus from the moment her heart became broken. And yet she did not, because of the Rheingold. I can only theorise, but it seems to me that that part of her was only in her subconscious. The Succubus was out there – looking for you. But it had yet to take physical form. What the ring destroyed in Cindy, when she forgot to forsake her love, was her self control. Her heart was finally allowed to break, and the Succubus was released. Before that, I doubt that even Cindy herself had any idea that she was reaching her mind out to yours in this fashion.

'She came to you because you were the focus of her heartbreak. But you are right. She will attack others if she cannot have you. Those in the most danger will be those who remind her of you.'

'If the Succubus has been a part of her psyche the whole time, why did the dreams only start a few months ago?' said Denny.

Tamar looked alert. This had been puzzling her too.

'We may never know that,' said Hecaté disappointingly. 'There are dark places in the mind that cannot be explored or understood, but it is clear enough that, even before she faced you, she was already beginning to lose control. Perhaps, because of her plans, you were on her mind recently more than you had been before.'

'And now she's out there, doing God knows what to skinny blond men because of me. And *he's* out there too, Ashtoreth I mean, also doing God knows what, also because of me. I seem to be right at the eye of the storm these days, don't I? I knew I should never have crashed the mainframe. It's really buggered up my Karma.'

All through this conversation, Denny's face had been turning increasingly red. He hated this sort of thing; he was finding it acutely embarrassing to talk about Cindy's obsession with himself. He had never wanted it; all he had ever really wanted was to be left alone, invisible – except to Tamar of course. And it was not as if it was comprehensible in any way, not once you took the Athame out of the equation, and Denny knew instinctively that, with Cindy at least, he could not blame the Athame for her feelings, much as he would have liked to. The Athame had nothing to do with it; Cindy had wanted *him*, not his power. He was not handsome; he had never had the slightest illusion about that. Even at the height of the "Geek Chic" era he had been just a little bit *too* geeky for general attractiveness. And Cindy had always seemed to prefer big handsome men in any case. Well, right up to the moment when she had suddenly turned her attention on him with the concentrated focus of a well-trained sniper.

'You said she would go after men who reminded her of Denny?' said Tamar suddenly.

'Yes, that seems most likely,' agreed Hecaté.

'Then I know *exactly* who she'll go after first,' said Tamar.

* * *

Slick had been reasonably easy to find. He was now living in a run-down flat at the top of a derelict building in a dodgy area. The kind of place where the people live like cockroaches and the cockroaches live like kings; where it was not a great surprise to find a used needle floating in the toilet bowl and vermin in the sugar, and where it was not advisable to use the lift without a gasmask.

'If we'd known, we would have been able to track him by the smell alone,' said Tamar. 'This place is even worse than where I found Denny.'

Denny, naturally, was not with them. Them being Tamar and Hecaté. It had been deemed "inadvisable" to bring Denny back into Cindy's immediate orbit. And Tamar had flatly refused to risk it. Hecaté had not wanted to leave Stiles's bedside, but she would do it for Tamar and Denny, and Tamar actually though it might do her some good anyway. Besides, she needed her.

'People live any way they can,' said Hecaté. 'I have seen worse places in my time believe me. What makes you so certain she will come here?' she asked Tamar

'Oh, I should have seen it before. Slick always reminded *me* of Denny, at least when Denny wasn't around. And he knew it too – Slick I mean. It's not that he looks like him exactly, but he can *make* himself look like him. I reckon that's why he went to Cindy in the first place. *You* were the one who said he liked her. Tonight won't be the first time he's played the substitute; I'd stake my life on it. But it was never so dangerous before.'

'Shhh!' said Hecaté. 'He might hear you.'

Slick was sleeping peacefully on a foam-filled pull-out sofa bed that was covered with stains instead of blankets.

Shortly after midnight, the windows rattled, and a shadowy figure slipped across the room.

'Pay dirt,' said Tamar. 'I told you.'

The figure straddled the sleeping Slick who stirred and moaned softly in his sleep. The tender maternal side of Tamar was stirred by his helplessness. She clenched her fists in anger and made as if she was going to step out of the shadows.

But Hecaté pulled her back. 'Not yet,' she said.

Tamar sat back down, but it was hard to watch; in some ways, even worse than Denny. Poor Slick had no magical defence against this attack; he could easily die. Nor was *he* the reason for Cindy's hunger. He had done some questionable things maybe, but he did not deserve this.

Cindy leaned forward over her victim. Where before she had been wary, looking around the room for possible threats, now suddenly she was intent, focussed – preoccupied.

'Now!' said Hecaté, and Tamar leapt out. 'Want another ass kicking,' she said, 'or will you come quietly?'

Cindy hissed at her in furious amazement. She leapt for the window and was thrown back by an invisible barrier.

'No getting away this time,' said Tamar. 'We were ready for you. You know you can't win against me.'

Cindy merely stood there grinding her teeth, uncertain what she should do. Any minute now, Tamar realised. She would attack.

'*Suscitatio suscitatio exorior ex vestri somnus patefacio vestri oculus quod animadverto orbis terrarum.*' Hecaté muttered over the prostrate body of Slick.

He sat up suddenly, like a reanimated corpse. 'What the hell is going on...?' Then he saw ... '*Tamar?*' He blinked in disbelief. Then he saw Cindy.

'Cindy?' he said. 'I thought you were dead.'

'No, she said bitterly, 'just badly disfigured.

But Slick did not appear to have noticed any change in her. 'I thought it was a dream,' he said. 'But you're really here – aren't you?'

Hecaté stepped forward to intervene between them. Cindy was dangerous, but Tamar held out her arm to stop her. Something interesting was happening here, and she wanted to let it play out.

Slick put a hand out to touch Cindy's face, but she shied away. 'Don't touch me,' she yelled. 'Don't look at me.'

'It's all right,' he said tenderly. 'Don't you know by now that it's all right? You don't have to cast spells on me to make me love you. You cast a spell on me a long time ago. Why do you tell me to love you Cindy? I already do.'

He took her hands. 'You took this ring as a symbol of your commitment to power,' he said. 'But power can't love you back. *I* can. Isn't that what you want? To be loved? Isn't that what this is all about? You never really gave up on love, did you? Take off the ring Cindy, take it off and come back to the world, with all its pain and heartbreak and loneliness. It's still better than this. Take it off Cindy.'

'You love me?' she asked.

'Yes, I love you.'

'And it doesn't matter to you, what I've done?'

'Oh, it matters, it matters a lot. But it doesn't matter if you never love me back. It won't change how I feel. I just want you to be free.'

'There's a lesson in there somewhere,' thought Tamar. 'An "after school special" kind of lesson, but a lesson just the same.'

'Tell me your real name,' said Cindy.

He told her, and Tamar had to stuff her fists in her mouth to stop herself from ruining this beautiful moment with a huge guffaw of laughter, as Cindy slowly took off the ring and let it drop to the floor.

'Denny was the dream,' she said. 'Seeing him again only reminded me. For fifteen years, *you* were the reality. Say you forgive me.'

'I forgive you.' This was no time for any sophistry about there being "nothing to forgive". There was a lot to forgive, and she needed to hear it. 'I forgive you.'

The Succubus let go its hold on Cindy, it was like watching someone shed their skin to reveal a different person underneath.

Tamar darted forward to retrieve the ring. 'I'd better take this,' she said. 'Not that I don't trust you,' she added, grinning at Cindy, who understood that she was forgiven in this quarter too.

'Now,' said Tamar, 'how about taking us to this secret lair of yours so that we can round up your son too? Before he does anything else that might get him grounded for a million years.'

* * *

Have you ever hidden something so well that you cannot even find it yourself?

Cindy was genuinely anxious to help, but she simply could not find it. She no longer had the power.

This was a considerable blow. But Tamar was not ready to give up easily. Slick was canvassed. 'How had *he* found her?' But it turned out that because he had found her so easily, she had moved her base of operations to a much more secure location immediately. And he did not know where.

It seemed ludicrous, that Cindy could have lived somewhere for fifteen years and have no idea where that place was, but she just said. 'It wasn't that kind of a thing. Not a *place* as such.' Which was a clue, but not a very helpful one.

'Where will you go now?' asked Tamar, realising that Cindy was not ready to come back to the house yet and face Denny – or Hecaté for that matter, who had vanished back to the bedside of her husband the moment Cindy had become herself again.

'We'll find somewhere,' she said, taking Slick's hand possessively.

'Well, keep in touch,' said Tamar, realising suddenly that she had been foolish to expect things to just go back to normal after everything that had happened.

'Oh, we will,' Cindy promised.

'We have quite a lot to talk about, though,' said Slick.

'Good luck,' said Tamar as they vanished. As soon as they had gone, she burst into a fit of uncontrollable laughter. *'Veritas! Oh my God!'*

* * *

'So, we *still* have no idea where he is or how to find him,' was Tamar's final summary of the situation, when she returned to the hospital to pick up Denny and fill both he and Hecaté in on what had happened.

'Or what he's planning to do,' added Denny. 'I mean to us.'

'Take his revenge,' said Hecaté.

'Sounds familiar,' said Denny.

'Yes, it does,' said Tamar. 'And Cindy went into hiding for fifteen years when *she* vowed revenge. We might not be hearing from Ashtoreth for a long, long time.'

'Perhaps Cindy can do something,' she wondered aloud. 'He's *her* son. She made him what he is.'

'Don't think she isn't telling herself that every minute of every day,' said Denny. 'But it doesn't mean she can *do* anything.'

'He's forgiven her too,' Tamar thought. 'Perhaps he always had. He always felt as if he was more to blame than her anyway.'

'If she could just see him. Talk him down ...'

'Got to be able to find him first, though,' said Denny.

Iffie rolled her eyes to the ceiling, when she heard all this later on. 'Oh, my God,' she said. 'Lies, betrayal, murder, unrequited love and a secret plot for revenge – then *another* secret plot for revenge. It's a supernatural Soap-Opera?'

* * *

'Ash, there's something I have to tell you,'
He waited courteously.
'About your mother,' she added,
'I don't want to discuss that,' he snarled, his expression changing in an instant.
'But Ash, you see, she …'
'I have to go now,' he said quickly and vanished.
'He *knows*,' Iffie realised with a shock, 'even if he's not aware of it. Somewhere deep down in his secret heart or his subconscious, he *knows*, he's probably *always* known. And he doesn't want to hear it. Because where's his reason for revenge, if he hears the truth? And he *wants* to have his revenge. He's looking forward to it. Better play it carefully then. I won't bring it up again for a while. Get his confidence back and then throw it at him, the truth, when he least expects it. I'll need to get some proof to show him anyway. Otherwise, he'll just call me a liar, say I've been corrupted or something equally ridiculous.'

* * *

What he really needed, he thought, was a suit of armour. That would have been appropriate. He did not understand this mission, not that he was allowed to question. But if he had been, he might have asked himself, why his master, who took his power from the Lord, needed this Earthly power source. But of course he never asked himself that. The part of his mind that was the Nephilim might have answered, had he asked such a question, that the lord helps those who help themselves. But what Gerald Wassermann, really wanted to know right now, was: "Why him?"

He was not afraid. Not afraid, bloody terrified was more like it. But that was Gerald, the Nephilim was not afraid at all.

The power, oh yes, the power was all very well. But it was the great big obstacle to getting the power that was worrying Gerald. A suit of armour, indeed, would have been most welcome round about now.

He needed to have faith. Faith yes, that was it, faith was the thing. He surrendered his will and let the Nephilim become his armour. After that it was easy.

* * *

It was a little after midnight in the real world. There was no time here, not in the normal sense. Oh time passed, but it was in the mind. He could stop it altogether with the right force of will. But there was little point for the most part. *She* had stopped time in the real world – now *that* was power. Power such as he coveted.

Even Ashtoreth himself was aware that he had changed. He could not hide from himself that he had become power hungry and lustful. But he excused himself. It was what the Lord had had in mind for him all along; that was evident. He was the instrument of the Lord's divine retribution and his own sins would be forgiven since they had been committed in the execution of that duty. Sometimes, though, he doubted. It happened whenever he pictured Iffie's face. She would be repulsed by his actions he knew, and a part of him did not want to do anything that would cause her to turn from him, to think less of him. But he reckoned it a weakness, perhaps the Lord had thrown her into his path and not her evil family – as a test of his faith.

She knew what he had done, a part of it anyway. But she did not know the whole, nor did she know what he was planning to do next. She would be horrified if she knew. In his heart he knew this. In his heart, he himself shied away from the next step – because of her.

If he gave into these feelings, he would go back to the world and take her away somewhere, to live in peace. He would even forsake his desire for revenge on her father – for her sake.

Every battle he did not fight, every time he found himself reigning back his atrocities, it was because of her. She was his conscience, although he did not see it this way. To him, she was a flaw, a hole in his armour, and it was all the more insidious because he could not tell himself that she was evil.

There were two paths before him now. He could take her as his standard of behavior. Act solely as if she were watching his every move and passing silent judgment on him. And take her into his heart where she could watch over him forever. If he did this he would be happier but would he be righteous? His war on sin would, of a necessity, have to stop. She would never condone it. Hers was the gentle way. She would have him lead people back to the path like a shepherd. (It never occurred to him that, actually, Iffie's "way" was to pretty much leave people alone to get on with their lives as they saw fit).

Or he could continue to follow the path he was on, the path of the butcher, not the shepherd, follow it to the end. Whatever the consequences.

And if he lost her, so be it. The sacrifice was necessary. He knew what he had to do. There had never really been any doubt; his task was clear.

He had a premonition that, if he allowed her to, she would destroy him one day.

* * *

The cycle of sin notwithstanding – and Tamar had not forgotten about this – there were more important issues to be dealt with at the moment. Ashtoreth, safely hidden away where they could not get him was now organising several strikes a day, more than they could possibly hope to keep up with. "Damage control" was rapidly turning into a desperate scramble to keep one step ahead in an increasingly losing battle.

They had lost two comrades in arms when Stiles had fallen, and the news on him was not encouraging. Hecaté was a broken reed.

However, they had Cindy back, and Slick came with her. Not to mention the hundreds of volunteers from both the

Agency and the magical community, but it was not enough. They needed tens of thousands, and they just did not have them.

As the Church was crushed and governments fell (accused of the sin of corruption, which was a particular irony considering what they now knew from Satan) and still no way of defeating the armies of the Nephelim was found, despair began to pervade, not only Tamar and Co, but the whole world.

'If Ashtoreth *doesn't* leave his stronghold,' said Denny. 'We'll be fighting this battle forever.'

'Then we'll fight it forever,' said Tamar, 'if we have to.'

I Am The Angel Of Your Redemption And This Is My Manifesto.

For the cleansing of the sins of the world.

The following sinners will be cleansed, for the sins of -

Corruption and Deception. All the major governments of the world. To be replaced with one World Government of my construction.

Pride and indolence, hypocrisy and greed. The Holy Catholic Church and the Protestant Church of England. All will follow the teachings of the Lord in my Name.

Idolatry. The Holy Catholic Church of Rome for the worship of the idols of the saints who were but men and not angels. All other churches, temples and faiths of all kinds who follow the teachings and perform the worship of false gods and idols.

The Performing of Black Magics and Idolatry. Witches, Pagans, Wicca's, Voodoo Practitioners, Hermetics. Warlocks, Mages, Necromancers.

Warmongering. For the sin of making war on their neighbours for their own pride, profit, or the exploitation of others, all the armies of the world (apart from the holy army of the Righteous, shall be wiped from the earth and peace restored.)

Pride (vanity
Envy
Gluttony
Lust
Wrath
Avarice (Greed)
Sloth

Idolatry (the worship of false gods)
Cruelty
Corruption
Black magic
Deception
Exploitation
Pusillanimity (cowardice)
Addiction
Hypocrisy
Non-conformity People who dress, behave or live in a style likely to cause discomfort or embarrassment to their fellow citizens.
Vagrancy.

Any and all individuals found to be practising the above named sins against the teachings of our Lord shall be purged from humanity

Ashtoreth.

~ Chapter Fifteen ~

IT WAS ONE YEAR after the death of Finvarra, and events had combined to make it a year of horror. What had begun as a rash of sadistic raids had turned into a reign of terror that they had no hope of stopping.

If they had thought it was bad at the start, from the time Ashtoreth published his manifesto, he had shown the world what he was really capable of. There had just quite literally been no stopping him.

Every day Ashtoreth's armies of death squads marched the streets of the world rounding up the "evil" citizens and taking them away for "trial" never to be seen again.

The terrifying "manifesto" had been posted up on streets, and over flyovers and large buildings all over the world but at first, of course, no one had taken it too seriously, it was dismissed as just the ramblings of some religious nutter – until the marching boots were heard coming down the street.

Then Ashtoreth broadcast his manifesto on worldwide television and radio. And pretty soon, his was the most well known face in the world. Even those who had never seen a television in their lives could not fail to see at least one of the immense images of his face that began to spring up on the fronts of official buildings everywhere.

People who had lived in a democracy all their lives, learned to cower behind false walls or under false floors in their homes when the sound of the booted feet of the Army of Righteousness was heard marching down their street. And there was nothing anyone could do to stop it. Tamar and Denny could not be everywhere at once. But the Army of Righteousness could.

In the early days, troops had been marshalled worldwide and sent out, on foot and in tanks, to meet the death squads, and, for a time, there had been massive fire fights in every place from city centres to ordinary back streets, and from small rural villages to urban centres and even the campsites of the voluntarily dispossessed.*

With the fall of the governments, most countries were brought under a state of martial law "for the duration of the current emergency". For a short time, there had been hope. But only for a short time.

As Tamar and Denny had discovered, for every Nephilim warrior that was knocked down, ten more would appear in his place. It was a hopeless fight. And, as evil warmongers, the army troops that tried to stand against Ashtoreth were shown no mercy.

When the armies fell, the citizens got armed. Those who had not already been anyway, and there had been a considerable number of these, and armed gangs of refugees now roamed the streets, but Ashtoreth's army was mopping these up too. There was always some excuse. When you are determined to wipe all the sinners in the world, no one is safe.

And Stiles was still in a coma. Some brain activity had been noted; a miracle according to some doctors, a mere anomaly according to others. And, a few months earlier, Hecaté had seen some colour return to his face. Unfortunately, the colour in question was green. Not a good sign according to the medical staff. But it was a weird luminous green and, strangely enough, it gave Hecaté hope.

---

* Also known as New-Age Travellers.

But today was a day for remembrance. Today the fighting would stop for a while, even if the world went to hell, as they gathered to pay their respects to the first to fall.

A grave in a green place, away from the resting places of mortal men, surrounded by trees and covered in yellow flowers.

It had been tended with reverence over the past year. Jack had not been here in all that time – so who...? Denny looked over at Cindy as she laid a flower on the grave, and he knew.

It was cold – November. But the flowers grew, and the trees were green and gold as the sun sparkled through them. The power of the Faeries lived on.

Jack bent his head in respect, and not to hide the tears that he was not ashamed of. Iffie took his hand in silent sympathy as she had done a year before. 'I'm sure he's watching over you from somewhere,' she said. It sounded trite, and she wished she had not said it. But suddenly Jack's face glowed.

He knew that his father was not watching over him from anywhere. The thing was flatly impossible. Faeries did not go to heaven; his father was now a part of the ether, he lived on in the trees – the flowers – the gilded sunlight. The sudden light in his face was due to a sudden, blinding revelation that had come to him from Iffie's casual remark.

His father was not in heaven, but he knew whose *was*.

* * *

The area was full of sinners, but that was not his task. He turned his back reluctantly on the village and headed for the river.

By the river was a cave. The local people shunned it for reasons of what the rest of the world would describe as superstition, but he did not. Sinners all, they had strong reason to fear the river and the cave. But he was not afraid. Fanaticism burned in his eyes. Of all the travellers that Ashtoreth had sent out, he was the most dangerous, the most determined. Even before the blessing, Henry Blenkinsopp had had an unshakable belief in himself. He had always known he was meant for greatness. He said his faith was in the Lord, that the Lord was always right, but what he meant was, he had faith in himself, that he was always right. Such men are dangerous even without the explicit encouragement given to him in the form of a holy mission.

He entered the cave boldly and struck quickly.

Once he had taken the power (and he fully intended to return to his master and deliver it as instructed). But surely, since he was here, the sinners within his grasp should not be allowed to escape retribution. The fact that the villagers had taken him in and shown him hospitality meant nothing to him. He was doing them a favour. Sinners needed to be cleansed. It was for their own good, before they sank deeper into sin, that he would take them away from temptation.

He clutched the new source of his power to his breast and stalked purposely toward the village.

* * *

Tamar kept in regular touch with Cindy, who seemed happy with Slick but filled with a horrendous self-reproach that was threatening to overwhelm her. For her sake, as much as anything, Tamar was determined to sort this out. If only it were that easy.

It seemed not unlikely that Cindy knew more than she realised. Perhaps with enough subtle prodding, something useful might come back to her, or slip out accidentally.

In any case, it was good to have her back on the team; indeed, it might prove, in the end, to be invaluable.

Cindy herself was certain that she had nothing to remember. The person who had done those things was not herself. She was not capable, could not believe herself capable or perhaps she did not *want* to believe herself capable, of such blind hatred, such incalculable cruelty. She considered that she had been possessed. Looking back, that was what it felt like. As for how she had created a secret base – she could not remember. She remembered the palace, but it was as if it had been a dream. No, not a dream – more like a living nightmare. She had lost herself for a while; even the mind living helplessly behind the eyes of the goddess had not quite been her own but that of the pathetic Succubus. No wonder her memory seemed scrambled.

It had occurred to her, as it had to Iffie – witches tended to think alike even ones as different as these two – to ask Slick how he had found her in the first place. What had been going through his mind at the time?

'I used the Agency,' he said. Which was not really helpful, since the Agency had been unable to find her or her son since she had moved her base of operations.

'I erased all my findings as soon as I knew where you were anyway,' he said. But I had a good idea where to start, in any case. I knew you would be close to the source of the power – the origin of the ring. It's what *I* would have done, stayed close until I was sure it was going to take. And I knew we thought alike in some ways. Reading people was my business if you remember. I understood you far better than you would have ever believed back then. So I used the Aethernet to scout likely locations. No one knew I was any good at computers, I kept that to myself, I'd always been secretive anyway, and there were only two possible locations that fitted the bill – the Rhine itself which was obviously out of the question and the ancient forge where the ring was cast the first time. And hey presto, there you were. But as to where you took us after that. I don't know any more than you seem to.' He frowned. 'How is that you don't remember?' he said.

'It's like there's no room in my head to understand what I did then. My mind was so different then. So much more power. It's like I wrote a paper on quadratic equations in my sleep then woke up and tried to read it and found I couldn't understand a word of it. I can see the words, but they make no sense to me.'

'Ah,' said Slick, finally understanding.

'What do *you* remember about that place?' she asked. 'And about how I was then. There might be a clue in that. You said you were good at reading people, when I was a mad goddess, what sort of a home would I have chosen do you think?'

'Somewhere safe, yet somewhere ostentatious. That place was like a fairy tale palace I remember, but it was like a fortress underneath, and like a fantastic dream on the surface.'

'Try to be more specific,' said Cindy slightly acerbically.

Slick raised an eyebrow. 'Did you just tell me off?' he asked. 'Thank God for that. I was beginning to think you never would again. It's okay, you know. It's all very well to be penitent, but you can't let it crush you down forever.'

'I did some terrible things,' she said. 'Things I can never pay for, and it's like I'm not even being punished for it. I feel terrible.'

'*That's* a punishment,' Slick pointed out.

'The only one I'm getting,' she said. 'I deserve more.'

'There's your son. That's a punishment too.'

'Well deserved,' she said, and bowed her head.

'Everyone has *forgiven* me!' she howled suddenly throwing her head back. 'Well, everyone except Hecaté. I haven't ... I can't face her yet.' (Cindy had not yet faced Denny either, but she knew from Tamar that he had forgiven her too.)

'But the others ... How can they? I don't understand it. I'm not sure I *want* to be forgiven. It would be easier if they all hated me, but they don't – *you* don't.'

'And you don't think you're being punished?' said Slick shaking his head. 'Perhaps forgiveness is the most potent revenge of all. Although I'm sure that's not why they've done it,' he added insightfully.

'We should go back to help them to find my son,' she said suddenly. 'It's *my* fault this has happened. His crimes are on *my* head. I don't think I can handle any more guilt. We have to stop him before he does anything else.'

Anything else?' thought Slick. He remembered once thinking that Ash needed to let off some steam. He was certainly doing that now, he reflected. Fifteen years of inactivity had built up a considerable head of steam too. And now that he had started Slick, for one, didn't think he was going to stop any time soon.

'And do you think you will forgive him if he does?' he asked.

'I wouldn't be so cruel,' she said.

* * *

He had done it. Oh blessed be the beloved master. Whose power he could feel burning within him, who had nursed his weary limbs and fed his soul with the strength to carry on when his suffering had been almost too much to bear. He had done it at last. Young Frank had no need of faith in the ordinary sense; he believed because he had seen and felt and knew his master's power. Frank was an idealist and Ashtoreth was his hero.

And now, here he stood at the door of his destiny, in the depths of the Amazon jungle. Beyond the waterfall, he could see the reddish glow that signalled the end of his quest. He was almost unbearably excited. He pushed the creepers aside with shaking hands and plunged through the rushing water. The glowing green eyes that shone through the misty air behind the falls faltered and shrank back as Frank raised his weapon and shouted. 'I am the power of the Lord.' Then he struck.

* * *

For Cindy, coming face to face with Denny this time was even worse than the last time. There was an awkward silence that extended into a black hole of dead time into which all hope of ever being able to speak again was sucked into an interminable void of embarrassment. They had met accidentally, after avoiding each other for three days, at the foot of the stairs. Cindy wished she had followed her first instinct and turned on her heel and walked away.

'Fancy a coffee?' said Denny eventually.

'Got anything stronger?' she said in a strangled voice.

'In *this* house? Naturally,' he said with a grin.

'Vodka?'

'How many would you like?'

'About ten I think,' she said.

'I think I'll join you,' he said.

They did not talk about the past; they did not talk about the impending doom of the future (which would have been like a rebuke to Cindy). It was a rambling conversation that covered a multitude of extraneous subjects from football to music. But it breached the barrier and let Cindy know that she was forgiven, and Denny know that he was forgotten.

Denny had made Cindy grow up and shed her superficiality – never again would she judge a person on their looks alone. She had truly loved him, in spite of all her previous convictions. But a person can fall out of love. She would always have a soft spot for him. Actually, the truth was, if he had offered to run away with her, she probably would have gone like a shot. But he would never do that. And that was okay now. All that mattered was that he had forgiven her, and they could be friends. Cindy had an intuition that, in the coming days, she was going to need all the friends she could get.

Jack was not going to be one of them; he did not want anything to do with her. And who could blame him? Cindy certainly did not.

'I'm only surprised that he doesn't hate me more,' she said to Iffie who had relayed this sentiment.

'Oh, he hates you a good deal,' said Iffie candidly. 'But Jack's a pretty gentle person. He won't give you any shit. Just stay out of his way for a bit. I reckon he'll come round eventually.'

'He has no reason to,' said Cindy. 'What I did was shameful, and he was hurt the most by it. You care for him very much, I can see. I don't know how you can bear to even talk to me yourself.'

'We all make mistakes,' said Iffie. 'I can deal. I'm not perfect either. What happened to you could happen to me one day. Being a witch is a dodgy business if you ask me. I mean, I wouldn't mind some extra power. It's like … being a witch is good, but it means that you get to know that there's more out there. More power, you know. Kinda tempting, if you can get hold of it.'

'Take a lesson from me,' said Cindy. 'It's not worth it.'

'Oh, I know, I know, you're right. God, *you* ought to know if anyone does. And mum too, she was a *slave* for 5000 years before she got powerful. And dad nearly turned into a *demon*. It's never that easy, I get that, I do, really. All I'm saying is I can see how it happened, you know. I don't judge.'

'You have that luxury,' said Cindy. 'I didn't do anything to *you*.'

'I met Ash, you know?' said Iffie suddenly.

'Yes I heard.' Cindy clearly did not want to talk about that. But Iffie was relentless and somewhat inconsiderate when she wanted something. 'I thought he was okay,' she said. 'He's a good guy I think, just a bit messed up.'

Cindy winced, but Iffie did not notice. She thought she was being comforting.

'Even if he *did* try to kill my dad,' she went on. 'He didn't mean it. I mean if he *knew* him … My dad's the best man in the world,' she finished, having gone completely off the original topic.

'I can't argue with that,' said Cindy.

And Iffie blushed a deep crimson as she realised her *faux pas*.

'One day,' said Cindy, to change the subject. 'You'll realise that someone else can fill that title, for you at least.'

'I can't think who,' said Iffie.

'I can,' said Cindy as Jack walked into the room and then abruptly walked out again.

'He'll come around,' Iffie reiterated, as they both watched his retreating back.

'Don't feel sorry for me,' said Cindy. 'For one thing, I brought it on myself. And for another, I may not look like it, but I'm a survivor.'

And she thought to herself, 'I wonder if she realises how her eyes shine when she talks about him?'

* * *

'So, you have come to kill me?'

The Nephilim formerly known as Janeck shook his head.

'Many have tried.'

Janeck was a bit bewildered by this turn of events. He had charged in here ready to take the power for his master, and the next thing you know, he was being asked to please slow down and wipe his feet. That sort of thing can put the most gung- ho warrior off his game.

'I usually offer them a cup of tea,' said the voice in the darkness. 'Would you like one?'

'Tea?' Janeck's thoughts skidded to catch up.

'I used to tear them limb from limb of course, but I've mellowed. Sugar?'

'Have I got the right place?' wondered Janeck. He had never been the sharpest tool in the box, and he was painfully aware that he was easily confused. It was happening now. He had never in his life felt so confused.

The Nephilim was not confused. This was a ploy, and he was not falling for it.

'This foolish boy might be easily confounded,' he said, apparently referring to himself. 'But look into my eyes and see who I am.' Two orange glowing eyes moved cautiously closer to his face.

Then he struck.

* * *

The army was coming. This was such a common occurrence nowadays that the people had an almost Pavlovian response. They heard the distant sound of marching feet and emptied the streets instantly like cockroaches when the light comes on. As the Army appeared suddenly in the street, row upon row of black clad warriors marching in long lines like a parade, only a few people, maybe forty or so, remained, and they were all armed to the teeth. Except for a small group who had once been rather dismissively and discourteously described as a "rag tag band of adventurers", and this was what they looked like too. Anyone who had been told that these few represented the strongest concentration of power in the world would have laughed out loud. Until they saw them fight.

To see the women, who looked as if they might be more at home on a catwalk in Paris or, at least, in the case of one of them, between the pages of a lingerie catalogue, swing swords almost as tall as themselves with the viciousness of Berserkers, cutting a swath through the enemy as if they were straw dummies, was an unlikely sight at best. And where had those swords been concealed? They had not been carrying them before the fighting started.

Then there was the badly dressed slacker type with the untidy blond hair and the slight build. Who looked as if a strong gust of wind might knock him down. Who would have thought that such a specimen would have the strength of ten men, but this was apparently the case – at least, ten of the Army of Righteousness were not enough to bring him down. It was quite something to see him disappear under a scrum of hammering fists (perhaps with your heart in your mouth) and then watch the pack fly apart in all directions as this man stood up and threw them aside as easily as if they had been rag dolls.

The obvious teenager among the group looked the most likely fighter – tall and well-built with a greasy rebel look about his longish hair and battered leather jacket, but far too young to be in this situation surely. Yet his self-possession in the face of the oncoming hordes was phenomenal in one who clearly had not been shaving more than a year or two.

He fought methodically with a knife and short sword – standard slash and parry not as flamboyant as the others in his style but quite effective all the same.

And occasionally the dark haired woman or the fair haired man would throw what looked like explosions of light – some sort of grenade? – into a crowd of warriors and disperse and decimate twenty or sometimes fifty at a time.

They were only four against hundreds, but they were taking the enemy apart.

The others who were armed and fighting alongside them were mostly the members of the magical community who had been roped in to help and several members of rebel groups made up of ordinary citizens who had discovered that they were not so ordinary after all. Not when the chips were down. But it was becoming increasingly obvious that none of them would have survived had it not been for the efforts of the mysterious small group who had apparently appeared from nowhere just when they were needed.

The small contingent of magical people who had been waiting for the Army had not been expecting Tamar and the rest to turn up here, but they were extremely grateful to see them.

And as suddenly as it had started it was over. The Army – what was left of them was in retreat. At least for now.

Tamar stuck her sword into the road as if she were sticking a knife into a pie and leaned on it wiping her brow.

But it was not over. Denny had seen something happening away in the distance.

A truck full of civilians was being driven away at top speed. Denny knew that they were being taken away for "trial". Experience had taught him as much. The battle had obviously been a diversion – he had *thought* it was too easy. There was no time to explain. He leapt on a handy motorbike, and gunned the engine, using a spark from his finger to start her up, and took off at warp speed after the truck.

'Where the hell is he going on that thing?' asked Cindy.

'He's following the truck,' said Tamar who had just realised what was going on. 'You can't teleport after someone if you don't know where they're going.'

'Get off it,' said Jack dismissively. 'He's a speed demon, and we all know it.'

'That may be true,' said Tamar. 'But in this situation, do you really think he'd be indulging himself? He's going after them the only way he can, and you know it.'

'I hope he catches up with them,' said Cindy.

'Oh, he will,' said Tamar confidently. 'After all, most motorbikes don't get up to five hundred miles an hour which is the fastest I've clocked him at – of course that was a Harley Davidson, but I still reckon he was cheating.'

Denny was cheating now. After all, *they* were. No truck in the history of the world could go *that* fast.

Five hundred – six – seven hundred miles per hour. No human could have stood it for long, fortunately Denny was not exactly human. But still, he was afraid he was going to lose them.

They obviously knew he was after them, but fortunately seven hundred seemed to be their limit. Enjoying himself immensely, although he would never admit it, Denny gunned the engine – which had long since run out of fuel – and passed them, swerving the bike to an expert stop right in front of the truck which skidded alarmingly and began to spin.

Denny leapt off the bike and caught the side of the spinning truck; he hauled himself up onto the footboard and put his heel down onto the asphalt using it as a brake until the vehicle came to a screeching stop.

Without pausing for breath, he jumped down and wrenched the driver's door open. 'Bugger off,' he suggested to the driver, who did so with alacrity, as did the guard in the passenger seat.

There were two more guards in the back of the vehicle who also appreciated Denny's suggestion and the opportunity to act upon it. They would, no doubt, have been less generous if the circumstances had been reversed, but Denny was no murderer.

Denny surveyed the shaking passengers and decided that they would be all right. They were shaken up, and there were a few cuts and bruises but nothing serious. They were all gawping at him in astonishment, but he barely registered this anymore, it was an all too common reaction these days.

A teenage boy hopped off the truck and beamed in elation. 'Wow!' he said. 'That was so-oo, *cool*! That was like just so-oo *cool*!'

'Denny gave him a wry grin. 'Yeah,' he said. 'Don't try this at home folks.'

He handed the keys to a solid looking citizen. 'Truck's yours now,' he said. 'Here,' he handed the man a card. 'This is the address of an undercover group that'll hide you. It's up to you of course, but you aren't safe in your homes anymore.'

The man took the card in a bemused fashion.

'But aren't *you* going to take us?' said a woman coming forward and giving Denny a look of embarrassing devotion.

Denny turned away. 'No,' he said. 'You'll be okay now. I have to get going. Er … sorry.' And he ran for it. Some things were scarier than others. Hordes of Nephelim – no problem. Adoring admirers– terrifying. He was not going through all that again.

He looked back, though, just for a second. 'Drive carefully,' he said and gunned the bike and shot off at the speed of light.

* * *

'Time I returned this,' said Tamar, holding up the Rheingold. 'I kept meaning to do it, but I never seemed to get around to it.'

'I suppose I should go with you,' said Cindy resignedly. 'To apologise or something.' She shrugged. It was hard to know what she could possibly say – especially to Woglinde.

Tamar held up the ring. 'You know,' she said. 'It's almost a pity that we can't use this. Any port in a storm you know, and right now, I'd say we need all the help we can get.'

'It's okay,' she added. 'Denny and I will take it back. You don't need to go.'

'Not Denny,' said Cindy sagely. 'You don't want him near those Rhine maidens. I mean they were distracted the last time they saw him but …' She shrugged expressively.

'You mean no magical woman can resist him?' said Tamar with a laugh. 'I'm not too worried about the girls. They're too self-involved to cause *that* kind of trouble.'

'So was I,' Cindy pointed out.

'No-o,' said Tamar thoughtfully. 'You never were really, not like *they* are – they take vanity to a whole new level believe me … But okay, I'll go alone if it'll make you feel better.'

'I have to come too,' said Cindy. 'I have a lot of apologies to make. Gotta start somewhere.'

'Well,' said Tamar, thinking it over. 'I wouldn't have made you do it. But on the whole I think it's the right decision.'

'I was about due,' said Cindy.

The waters of the Rhine were churning discontentedly.

'It's been like this for... ever since ... Let's just say they aren't pleased,' finished Tamar awkwardly. She looked at the ring in her hand thoughtfully. 'You know I'm not so sure we should hand it back in this condition,' she said, and she closed her hand tightly over the ring and clenched hard. When she opened her palm, a small lump of gold sat there instead of the shiny ring.

'That's better,' she said. 'Seeing it as a ring ... well, its oil on the flame really, isn't it?'

Cindy was shaking with nerves by this point and really could not give a decent answer to this.

Then Tamar called the Rhine maidens.

It need not be said that they were not best pleased to see Cindy, at least at first. But when Tamar handed back the gold, they did thaw out a bit.

'I'm sorry,' said Cindy. 'I don't know what else to say.'

'Maybe a vault in the future,' put in Tamar. 'I mean it's not as if this was the first time this had happened.'

'That's true,' said Flosshilde. 'And if memory serves, it was Woglinde's fault the last time too.'

'It *wasn't* her fault,' said Cindy. 'I never intended to steal it – not at first. It was just when I saw it, and I was feeling so... at the time. But she couldn't have known what I would do. I didn't know it myself.'

'Huh,' said Wellgunde. 'That's what you say *now*... Anyway at least you brought it back.' She shrugged. 'So I suppose we have to forgive you, since you *are* sorry.' Her voice dripped with acidic sarcasm as she said this last part.

There was an awkward silence that was eventually broken by Woglinde. 'So,' she piped up suddenly. 'Where's that nice young man I saw you with the last time we met, you know, the blond one? You didn't bring him with you, did you?' she added hopefully, looking around her.

'I *told* you,' said Cindy. 'What did I tell you?'

'I'm getting him a T-shirt printed,' said Tamar crossly when they got back, 'that reads "PROPERTY OF TAMAR BLACK".'

'Why?' said Cindy. 'He never sees anyone but you. *I* should know. And if you do that, you'll have to wear one too. I mean it happens to you all the time too – *more* really. I mean, it's all types with you, magical or not, but you never see him getting all bent out of shape about it.'

'He isn't the jealous type,' said Tamar. '*I* am.'

'Oh, I don't know,' said Cindy. 'I reckon if you didn't give them all the old ice maiden treatment he might be a *bit* bothered.'

'Just a *bit*?' said Tamar, with a slightly plaintive edge to her voice.

'We-ell, just enough to break their arms and legs maybe,' said Cindy.

'He'll never have to,' said Tamar complacently, having got the answer she wanted.

'Never say never,' warned Cindy.

* * *

Having made a beginning on her apologies Cindy had one more to make, and this was a big one.

It was almost like a ceremony. Cindy knelt before Hecaté and begged her forgiveness for straying from the path. Hecate's eyes were cold and Tamar and Denny looked at each other and shuddered at the look on her face. They had never seen her like this before. A goddess, and an *angry* goddess at that. Only Stiles had ever seen her like this, just once. Stiles, who was now lying in a hospital bed only a few feet away, in part, because of what Cindy had done.

Suddenly Denny felt a firm pressure on his hand. Tamar was gripping it so hard that she was cutting the blood off; she was white to the lips.

Suddenly Cindy raised her head. 'No I suppose not,' she muttered. 'If I deserved forgiveness then I wouldn't have to beg for it. But I don't, do I?'

Hecaté smiled suddenly. '*Now* you do,' she said. 'But you will have to continue to earn it every day of your life from now on. You understand that, do you not?'

Cindy fell on her face.

'I do not mean by your abasement,' said Hecaté. 'I mean by righting the wrongs you have done. We will all help you. We are your friends Cindy. Get up now.'

Tamar breathed out. Even Denny looked relieved. Just for a moment there, there had been doubt. They had, just for a moment, seen another side of Hecaté to the one they knew, the vengeful goddess within had emerged and there had been a definite possibility of smiting.

Tamar had realised this might happen before they came here. She had known of this aspect of Hecaté, Denny understood with a shock, it was the reason for the white face and clenched knuckles. The question was – had Cindy? On reflection he believed she had. She was braver than he had thought then, if that were true.

'Well,' he said afterwards as they walked out of the hospital just like normal people, 'I suppose if you're going to be struck down by a god, the hospital's the place for it. I mean the morgue's only downstairs.'

Tamar showed her disapproval of this tasteless remark by her stony silence.

'That doctor's checking you out,' he said suddenly with a wicked twinkle in his eye. 'Want me to beat him up?'

'He's allowed to look,' said Tamar calmly.

'No secrets in *our* house,' she thought irritably.

'I can't say I like it, though,' said Denny seriously. 'But there's nothing I can do about it, is there?'

Tamar smiled. There would be no need for the T-shirt after all.

* * *

It had all gone quiet. At least that was how it seemed – until they heard about New York. Ashtoreth had got quite excited about New York it seemed; decided that he had found Babylon. He cited the statue of liberty as the largest false idol in the world and had it torn down and smashed to bits before raining fire and brimstone down on the city.

Liberty, he said was not a proper goal for mankind, not a right ideal to worship. Obedience was the first virtue, and those who worshipped at the altar of Lady Liberty were the most corrupt people in the world. Just look at the way they behaved.

The problem was that it was quite hard to argue with the logic of this argument. You knew it was wrong; it was just hard to say exactly *why* it was wrong.

'I thought he thought *we* were the centre of all evil,' said Denny after hearing all this.

'I thought that all large cities were the centre of corruption in their own little corners of the world,' said Tamar. 'Just goes to show you doesn't it?

'Aaaaaagh!' Denny pulled at his hair in frustration. 'We can't let this go on. We just *can't*. What do we *do*? If he carries on like this, he's just going to blow up the whole world and be done with it.'

Tamar closed her eyes. 'We stop fighting,' she said. 'And we concentrate all our efforts into finding him and stopping him. It's not as if we're making much of a dent by fighting anyway.'

'We've *tried* to find him. We can't.'

'Not hard enough obviously,' said Tamar. 'We've allowed ourselves to be distracted trying to take out his army piecemeal. This is bigger than that. We can't save the world one person at a time, not this time.'

'I suppose he's got to be *somewhere*,' conceded Denny wearily. 'So where haven't we looked?'

~ Chapter Sixteen ~

JACK HAD NEVER walked the halls of mainframe before. It was quite an experience. The layers of reality that overlapped made it difficult to keep your footing. He wondered how Tamar and Denny could be so *blasé* about it. He was finding it horribly disorienting. It had taken him a week to get up the nerve to do this, and now he was almost wishing he had not.

Any file would do. The point was to escape the mainframe into a different place – one that existed apart from reality. Denny had gone to Hell. Jack wanted to get into Heaven.

Faeries do not go to Heaven; it is not their proper sphere. He wondered how he would like it. Not at all, he suspected, and there was a fair chance that, if he was discovered, he would be ejected without ceremony.

'My Father,' he blasphemed. 'It's just like all the pictures. White fluffy clouds and everything.'

Even the fabled Pearly Gates. There was an intercom. Jack shook his head in disbelief. Well, there was certainly no question him of announcing his arrival. He spread his wings and fluttered gently over the gates. There was no one around.

'Must be further in,' he muttered, looking around, and he chose a direction and began to walk. It was like walking on a thin sheet of glass that was just under water, his feet sank a little way under the surface before they hit resistance. Only these were fluffy clouds not water, and he found that he could kick up small cotton wool-like tufts, as he walked, like autumn leaves.

After a while, he became aware that he was surrounded by wraith like presences. He did not know what they were, but they were all heading in the same direction with definite purpose. Very definite – they were in trememdous hurry. He decided to follow the crowd. They led him eventually to – 'What the...?' He stared in shattered disbelief. Rising high before him were the Pearly Gates.

The wraith like figures passed through and continued on, further in.

Jack gathered his wits and followed them. He continued following until once again they came to the gates.

What the hell was going on, he wondered. Was heaven built like a puzzle box? Worlds inside worlds on and on *ad infinitum.*

Was this how the virtuous spent their eternity? Some reward!

He realised at this point that the wraith like figures around him were the departed souls making their way through the many levels of Heaven. Perhaps it was a different experience for them – a spiritual journey of some kind that had a meaning on a level that he just could not see. Perhaps they could see things here that he never could. Maybe each of them was having a very different experience. It was an intriguing thought. But what it also was, was a not particularly helpful conclusion.

He decided he had no choice. The intercom was apparently for visitors. At least, the dearly departed had made no use of it. Although how many visitors could Heaven get? And who? However, he *was* a visitor, and he clearly was not getting to the management this way. He would have to use it after all.

He pushed the buzzer. A burly and unfriendly looking angel manifested and looked down his nose at him. 'Yes?' he said in a supercilious tone. 'Can I *help* you?'

Jack immediately wished he was invisible. He had never suffered from excessive vanity, despite his handsome looks. But it was hard to be made to feel as if you were as ugly as a deformed toad and as worthless as Monopoly money.

He gathered his courage, what there was left of it, this was *important*. 'I want to speak to an angel called Erasmus,' he choked out.

'*Do* you?' said the angel curling his lip.

'It's all right. Telemenculus,' said a voice. 'I'll speak to him. I know why he is here.'

The angel disappeared with a dismissive "poof"

'Take no notice of him,' said the friendly angel. 'He's just in a bad mood about being put on gate duty.

'Are you Erasmus?' asked Jack, his courage rising with this friendlier approach. This one did not seem to think he was worthless. In fact, there was admiration in the gentle eyes. Admiration and understanding.

Erasmus nodded. 'And you are Jack,' he told him, just as if he did not know his own name.

'Many people here do not know their own name,' explained Erasmus, although Jack had not spoken. 'The nature of death. It's a force of habit to remind them. I apologise.'

'You said you knew why I was here?' said Jack. 'I'm beginning to see why.'

'I have been expecting someone for some time. You wish to find my son?'

I don't *wish* to find him. I have to.'

'I understand.'

'You *have* been watching him, haven't you? I mean I figured you *are* an angel, and on top of that, he *is* family.'

'Two excellent reasons why I should have been watching him, indeed,' agreed Erasmus. 'I have been watching over him.'

'Not very well,' said Jack tartly.

'A rebuke,' said Erasmus. 'You are no doubt wondering why I have not … intervened. I am forbidden. I intervened in human affairs once before and was banished for it.'

'So, you don't want to risk it again?' said Jack contemptuously.

'You misunderstand. They watch me closely after my transgression. Were I to attempt to interfere, they would step in and prevent me before I could even begin.'

'Are they really so heartless?' said Jack. 'He's your *family*.'

'I was not supposed to *have* a family. I am supposed to be divine. Being forced to look on as my son destroys the world and his own soul, while being able to do nothing to stop it, is my punishment. One of my own making.'

'So, I guess you shouldn't really be talking to me, should you?'

'You came here of your own free will, to ask me a question. Ask.'

'Where is your son?'

'In an in-between place.'

'I don't understand.'

'I hardly expected that you would.'

'Look,' Jack was losing his temper. 'Are you going to tell me where he is or not?'

'No.'

'To hell with you then …'

'I am going to *show* you. It is the only way to understand.'

'Oh! Er… I'm sorry.'

'Come with me.'

'She really was very clever, you see?'

'Yes.'

'The mind of a god. A powerful thing.'

'It's incredible. No wonder we couldn't find him.'

'What will you do now?'

'I'm going in there.'

'He will kill you.'

'Maybe.'

'So alike and yet so unalike,' said Erasmus, looking sidelong at Jack.

'Everybody says that,' said Jack, feeling a little nettled.

'Ah, but not everybody can see what I can. The differing souls. The one so pure and clean, the other so tarnished – yet it is not his fault. What others see, is perhaps an echo of the same thing. They *feel*, rather than *see* the difference between you.'

'I'm supposed to be the tarnished one really,' said Jack. 'Evil Faerie changeling and all that.'

'It seems that a fallen angel has more evil in him than a Faerie,' Erasmus said. 'The sins of the father. But your father didn't really sin all that much, did he?'

'*Is* he evil, though, or is he just …?'

'Mad?' As a Hatter, I assure you. Be careful in his realm. I will give you one piece of advice. Not everyone will be able to see what I can see.'

Jack thought about this. Then he spread his wings. The wings shimmered in the light and became the large feathered angel wings that Ashtoreth sported.

'I'm going to end up doing a comedy, glassless mirror routine aren't I?' he said suddenly. 'I can just feel it coming on.'

'Not unless you also shorten your hair,' said Erasmus.

Before he left, Erasmus gave him one more piece of advice. 'Forgive her,' he said. 'Nothing was ever healed by holding on to resentment and bitterness.'

'It's too late for that,' said Jack.

'It's never too late,' said Erasmus.

* * *

Not a slow boat, but a fast plane to China, the wonders of modern technology. However, now that he was here, he would have to rely, not on modern technology, but ancient magic to find what he was looking for.

He had definitely drawn the short straw here, he realised. Not only had he taken the longest journey of all the Nephelim, but the one least likely to succeed. He knew that the power he had been sent to find was up in the sky – in the clouds somewhere and how was a man supposed to find that without wings?– Which had not been a part of the power package the master had "blessed" him with.

Nor was there likely to be any more glory in his journey than the others. Quite the opposite, in fact. Of all the quests, this one was the least likely to please the master by its success. Eastern magic did not appeal to him as much as the more familiar western kind. Not that it was any less potent, but the master considered it heathen. And he was against that – in principle anyway. He was not sure how he knew all these things, but he was sure that he knew them.

Arron had found that the further away from the master he travelled, the more he was having these traitorous thoughts. The more, in fact, he was thinking for himself, and what he was thinking mostly, was that he was wasting his time.

* * *

Jack crept through the corridors of Ashtoreth's palace. Dark corridors with burning torches for that delightfully gothic effect. He felt like a fugitive here. Like *he* was the one in the wrong. The convict haircut may have contributed to this feeling.

'Pull yourself together,' he told himself. 'You're acting like you have a bag marked swag over your shoulder. Ashtoreth wouldn't be creeping like a burglar through his own palace.'

He straightened up. Forced himself to walk tall. Straight into the throne room. He stopped with a gasp. Ashtoreth had grown up *here*? No wonder he was crazy. Everything was wrong. Beautiful, but all wrong. It reminded Jack of Heaven. A puzzle box of worlds within worlds. A place outside of reality.

Outwardly lovely but twisted up. All inside out. You could wander through it forever and never get anywhere, always ending up back where you started. Its infinite size was both real and a mere illusion. An illusion that Jack's Faerie eyes could see through, to the *other* reality hidden beneath. The reality that everyone knows, that everyone lives in (under normal circumstances). It was as disorienting as walking through the mainframe. Five minutes in here was giving Jack a headache and Ashtoreth had been here for sixteen *years*. Ashtoreth probably was not able to see it the way he did, but it would still have had a subconscious effect.

And to think, this place had been right under their noses the whole time. Hidden in plain sight.

He had no idea what he was looking for. He did not really want to run into Ashtoreth, whose power was far greater than his own and whose homicidal instincts were unparalleled in human history.

Half a dozen Nephelim warriors entered the room and bowed. For a moment Jack was nonplussed. Then he remembered what he looked like – *who* he looked like.

'Report!' he hazarded, hoping fervently that Ashtoreth would not suddenly appear. He was evidently expected.

'Our quest is complete my lord,' said a gruff looking fellow with a nasty scar running down his face.

'Good,' said Jack.

'*What quest?*' He looked nervously beyond them for the arrival of Ashtoreth. This action was evidently misinterpreted, however.

'Yes, Arron did not return with us my lord. He chose to betray you. But you will no doubt punish him when the power that we who are loyal have gathered is surrendered to you.'

'No doubt,' said Jack absently.

'We are ready to make our sacrifice my lord,' said the spokesman.

Jack hurriedly held up a hand. 'Not yet,' he said as he desperately tried to think. He had no idea what was going on here but sacrifice did not sound like a good idea. Neither did surrendering their power.

'My lord?' asked the spokesman in a perplexed tone.

'It is not yet time,' said Jack thinking on his feet.

'Oh I think it is exactly the time.'

Six heads whipped round, and Jack fled through an archway behind him only to end up face to face with Ashtoreth standing before the throne.

'A bloody puzzle box,' he thought. 'I *knew* it.'

Ashtoreth grabbed his arm, and Jack did the only thing he could think of. This world was built from the imagination, and Faeries have power in the realm of the mind. If he could just catch Ashtoreth off guard ... He concentrated and shut down the illusion it only lasted for a second before Ashtoreth caught it, but it was long enough.

Still hanging on to Jack with an iron grip, Ashtoreth spun round in confusion dragging Jack with him. 'What is this place?' he demanded.

'Abandoned warehouse,' said Jack. 'I hate to tell you this, but this is where your palace *really* is.'

Ashtoreth let go of his arm and stared around the place.

'How did you do that?' he said.

'Faerie magic,' said Jack. 'The magic of the mind. Your *palace* is nothing more than an illusion made real.'

'It's more than that,' insisted Ashtoreth.

'Well, yes. But only in a manner of speaking.'

But Ashtoreth did not want to know. 'I *will* kill you,' he said.

'I don't doubt it,' said Jack calmly.

'Faerie magic ...' mused Ashtoreth. 'That's how you penetrated my fortress? And you are the last of your kind.'

Jack bowed his head. 'Yes, I am,' he said sadly.

'So, even if you were not evil, I would still have to remove you, you can see that?'

Jack raised his head indignantly; his face was flushed with anger. This was *too* much! To stand here while this maniac made out his justification for the fact that he was going to murder him. 'You're calling *me* evil?' he spluttered. '*You*?

'*I* haven't slaughtered thousands, no *millions*, of innocent people,' he raged on. '*I* didn't kill the only man who was willing to be my father without knowing *where* the hell I came from. He was a good man. He took you in and looked after you, and you ... you... And *I* didn't take the best man in the world and lock him up in his own nightmares because I was afraid to face him head on.'

'AFRAID?' roared Ashtoreth. The other accusations seemed to have gone right over his head, but he picked up on this one all right. 'I was *not* afraid. I was following orders. Obedience is the first virtue.'

'And now *you* give the orders,' said Jack. 'So that works out well for you then?'

Ashtoreth just smiled complacently. 'Yes, yes I do,' he said. He spread his wings menacingly. 'Time to die – Faerie scum.'

Jack tensed; his own wings outspread. He was breathing heavily.

'No one here to save you this time,' mocked Ashtoreth.

'*Jack?*'

Jack never drew his eyes away from Ashtoreth's menacing gaze. He did not have to, he knew that voice.

Ashtoreth knew it too. It haunted his dreams. He turned; his attention diverted temporarily from his step-brother. Then he headed towards her, but Jack was quicker, flying up he sped across the warehouse and landed with a heavy thump interposing himself between Iffie and the approaching Ashtoreth. His wings hunched as he raised his shoulders into a defensive pose, then spread out fully as if to shield her. 'You leave her alone,' he snarled. 'You fight *me.*'

But Iffie, to his great horror pushed him gently aside. 'It's all right Jack,' she said, holding out a hand to Ashtoreth. 'He won't hurt me.'

Jack was appalled to see her take his hand and go to stand with him. Ashtoreth laid one hand possessively on her shoulder the other curled around her waist, still holding on to her hand.

'Please understand Jack,' she willed him. 'If I don't choose him, he'll kill us both. I can't let you die. I *can't!*'

But Jack – usually so sensitive to the thoughts of others – was too shocked and bewildered to hear her.

Iffie squeezed Ashtoreth's hand. 'Let's go, Ash,' she said. 'Never mind him. He'll keep.' And she threw Jack a disdainful look that pierced him to the core.

Ashtoreth smiled; the triumphant smile of the victor. 'I will deal with you in due time,' he said. 'Come and visit again, why don't you? Bring the family. Soon I will have more power than the world has ever seen. I would be happy to see them all in my humble home. You can watch them all die before I deal with you.' And he vanished in a flash of light, taking Iffie with him.

'If only it meant he was dead, like those minions of his,' thought Jack bitterly. He was incapable, at the moment, of more constructive thought (such as, what *kind* of power?) heartbroken and devastated by Iffie's betrayal. And if *he* felt this bad, how were Denny and Tamar going to take it? There was little that was selfish in Jack, even in his grief.

He remembered vaguely that she had been carrying something as she came in. She had dropped it near the door.

Slowly and wearily, like an old man, he forced his legs to move. To walk as far as the door and pick up whatever it had been.

A bundle containing some oddments. A candle, a crayon, a kitchen knife, a small gas stove with a small non-electric kettle and a box of matches. This collection might not have meant much to the average person, but it told Jack that she had been intending to do a spell of some kind.

He looked around. There were marks on the floor to indicate that she had been here before, crayon marks that might have been in the shape of a circle once, before they had worn away. What had she been doing here?

The question distracted his tortured mind away from the recent events that had torn his heart asunder so brutally. It was also a delaying tactic, he realised. He was dreading going home to face her parents with the news that he had lost her to Ashtoreth. It was all *his* fault. If he had not brought him here … His eye was caught by a torn scrap of paper, carelessly dropped, by the grime on it, some time ago. He picked it up indifferently, expecting nothing really, but he looked sharply again as he recognised Iffie's handwriting. It was a summoning spell, a spell for summoning *angels*.

Jack did not bother fooling himself by even considering the possibility that it was Erasmus she had been after contacting. It was Ashtoreth, no doubt. And she had been here several times

– perhaps many times, the betrayal went back much further than today. He noted that she had been shocked to see Jack himself here, but had shown no surprise at seeing *him*. He had not really noticed at the time.

He was shaking all over, blind with tears. He never knew how he made it home.

Denny found him lying on his bed staring blankly at the ceiling several hours later.

In the end, Jack lied. He only told Denny that Ashtoreth had taken Iffie away, that he had been unable to stop him. That he was sorry. He made it sound as if she had been kidnapped against her will. Why should they have to know the truth? It would only hurt them more and what difference could it make now? He was willing to take all the blame if it made it easier on them. If it let them remember her in a good way. He felt totally responsible anyway.

He told them later, what Ashtoreth had said about gaining great powers and improvised about what else he knew – about the six Nephelim and their "sacrifice".

"Bring the family," Ashtoreth had said. And Jack pondered on this. He *could*, but was it a good idea? Ashtoreth would be expecting them now, thanks to his foolishness. And he had not been bluffing about the new power. Jack's own encounter with his soldiers had taught him that.

On the other hand, once that power was his, he would be coming after them anyway. Would it be better to face him on *his* home ground or theirs? That was what it came down to.

The advantage of routing Ashtoreth within his palace was timing, it would be their choice. The disadvantage was the armies of Nephelim all over the place. But he might bring them along anyway.

In the end, he resolved to let Denny and Tamar decide what to do.

* * *

There was some consternation among the Nephelim. Had they or had they not seen *two* masters? Was it a test? Even more worrying – had they passed? It was not that they were afraid of being executed. Weren't they all going to die anyway? But if they failed him in any way, Ashtoreth had made it pretty clear that they would not receive their heavenly reward. And they were all looking forward to it so much.

Then Ashtoreth arrived with a strange young woman. Women were strictly forbidden here. What were they supposed to do? Was this the impostor? Was it another test? They were all very quietly panicking.

Ashtoreth dismissed then peremptorily. He wanted to be alone with Iffie.

After a moment's hesitation – what if it was the impostor, the master would be furious – they left.

When they had gone, Ashtoreth turned to Iffie and surveyed her with satisfaction.

'I knew you would make the right choice in the end,' he said. 'I never had any fears for you, and soon you will witness my crowning moment, when I receive my power. Praise the Lord. And after that you shall become my queen. Hmm, I shall have to have another throne made for you. Only the very best for my queen. How do you like my palace?'

Iffie understood from this unbroken soliloquy that Ash wanted to talk, not listen. He wanted to boast. It was a relief actually. She could listen with half an ear and think her own thoughts at the same time, which were considerably bewildered. It had all happened so fast, she felt she needed time to assimilate it all and think of a safe way to get out of here – his queen indeed!

'It's beautiful,' she said dutifully, and he continued to rattle on, about his plans, his power, his great and powerful self. Yawn!

At least she had saved Jack. When she had seen them squaring off against each other, a revelation had come to her. She wanted Jack to win, but there was no way he could. She had thought fast and done the only thing she could think of to save him. She had, she admitted it now, been attracted by Ash, very much so, in fact. Dangerously so. But when it had come down to a choice between him and Jack, Jack had won hands down. In fact, a terrible hatred of Ash had flowered when she had realised that he might kill Jack. For the one who took Jack away from her, there could be no forgiveness. And Ash had been ready to do just that. He might yet.

How could she prevent such a catastrophe? She had believed for a long time that she could save Ash from himself. She no longer entertained such hubris. He was long gone, so far past sanity that there could be no drawing him back. Not by any power that she possessed. And she was not so sure, anymore, that she even wanted to.

She had known of all the terrible things he had done, but it seemed that seeing really is believing. Not until she had seen him ready to murder Jack with his own hands, had she seen the truth. The truth that she had not wanted to see. Had it been anyone but Jack, it might have taken her even longer to see.

She had been so wrapped up in Ash that Jack had seemed to fade into the background. But he had always been there, she understood now, in Ashtoreth's face. Every time she saw him, it was Jack she was really seeing. Like looking in a mirror and seeing your own face. She had recognised him in his reflection, but it was not him. Odd how meeting Ash had finally helped her to truly see Jack. She had never been able to see him when she had been looking directly at him. Like her own face, she had only been able to see him in his mirror image.

And Jack. He had not understood. She had seen the pain of betrayal on his face. If she could only get back to him, he would understand. She would *make* him understand. But how was she ever to get back? Ash would certainly never let her go and the only other person who knew the secret of this place was apparently Jack himself. And if he was foolish enough to return here for her, Ash would kill him instantly.

How had he figured it out anyway? Oh, Jack was clever, very clever to have found his way in here. But ... clever enough to figure out a way to come back now, without being caught? Well, if he wasn't, Mum and Dad would think of something. They wouldn't just leave her here. Even if Jack told them that she had chosen to come. Dad would never believe it anyway.

'... And what do you suppose is the greatest power in the world?' Ash broke through her thoughts.

She forced herself to attend to the question. What on earth had he been talking about anyway?

'Er, it's the Djinn isn't it?' she said, giving him a hopeful smile.

'Hah! You might think so,' he said. 'Many do. But even a Djinn whose power is not dependent on a master is not as powerful as I will soon be. I have found the oldest and greatest power ever to reside on this Earth.' He smiled. 'Can you really not guess what it is?'

Iffie though he was talking metaphorically now, and, given his obsession ... 'God?' she said.

'I can hardly take the power of God himself for my own now can I?' he laughed. 'No, I was talking about an Earthly power. The oldest power. It has survived to this day although few know it. They are the eldest. They walked the Earth before human life was even thought of, and their later brethren cannot come close to matching their power and majesty. There were seven, so I sent out seven warriors – six have returned. One would have done.'

Now Iffie knew what he was talking about. 'The conclave of Cetus?' she gasped. 'Dragons!'

'Six dragons,' he affirmed. 'The first, the eldest, the most powerful dragons in history.'

'Such noble creatures,' he continued. 'They were from a time before sin existed.'

He adopted his lecturing tone and began to declaim. 'Before the time of men, was the time of the dragons. There were seven at the beginning living all over the world. The father of those dragons was Cetus, one of the dragons of Joppa, the other was unnamed, and no one knows what became of him. It is ridiculous rumour to suggest that he was killed by a man. No mortal man has ever had that power. Cetus was of the sea, the greatest power this world had ever seen.

'The dragon called the Tararque was different from his brothers. They say he has six legs the head of a lion the paws of a bear and a scaly body with a barbed tail.

'And in the West there were four dragons known only as the Drakon in Greek and Draco in roman the British refer to it as the Drake. If they ever had names they have been long forgotten. These dragons have the characteristics that many of the typical fantasy dragons do. They have four taloned feet, a pair of wings that are like that of a bat. Their heads have a crest and a beard underneath their chin. Some have horns or antlers. They have tough scales; their stomachs are like that of crocodiles. It is said that the blood of these western dragons have powerful healing properties and the blood also allows the understanding of other languages. It is also said that these brother dragons have a gem in their head known as the Draconce or Dragon-stone it is a brilliant red it is said to have curative powers.

'And then there were the eastern dragons. Chinese dragons play with a ball of light known as the sacred pearl; this is thought to be the source of the dragon's power. Chinese dragons have the power to polymorph (change their shape). The father of these is a dragon named Chiao, who is the supreme Dragon of the earth.' He stopped abruptly he seemed to have finished his lecture for now, so Iffie ventured a question.

'And ... and they still exist?'

'Oh, yes, and I shall be immortal, as they were, until their power was stripped from them.'

'How...?'

'These,' Ashtoreth took from his robes what was unmistakable to Iffie as an Athame. 'I'm not above stealing a good idea,' he said. 'Demons make these, and a demon is merely a corrupted angel. I forged these in the place where my mother once forged her ring ... She never realised that I knew about that. But ...' He shrugged. 'Servants talk.' he looked at her, his eyes shining.

'That's amazing,' she said, as she was evidently meant to.

'And he's going to use this power to kill my family. I've got to find a way to stop him'.

* * *

When Tamar heard about Iffie she hit the roof, and in her case, this was not a metaphor. Denny had to bring her down quite carefully. She was so angry that she completely missed the point at first. At last – Ashtoreth had been *found*. Of course, this opened up a whole new set of problems – such as what to do with him.

'I'll kill him,' she snarled through gritted teeth. She grabbed a sword (part of Denny's old collection) off the wall. 'Slowly,' she added viciously.

'You can't,' said Cindy coming into the room.

Tamar turned. 'Look, I'm sorry you had to hear that,' she said. 'I understand how you must feel but…'

'No,' said Cindy. 'I mean you literally *can't*. At least not with that.' she indicated the sword. 'He's part angel. His flesh is incorruptible. No blade will pierce him. Not even yours,' she said to Denny.

'But the Athame will cut through *anything*,' said Denny.

'Not him,' Cindy assured him.

'Damn,' said Denny. 'I was kind of counting on being able to draw his power without killing him.'

'Really?' said Tamar sounding surprised.

'Oh I wasn't being merciful,' he said. 'Death would be merciful in comparison to that. At least for him.'

'Isn't there any way round it?' asked Tamar.

'You can't ask her that,' said Denny. 'It's not fair.'

But Cindy answered. 'It's okay. I never really had much hope that you would be able to show mercy in the end. The only way is if he is no longer pure. Why do you think I kept him locked away from the world for so long?'

'Pure?' said Denny. 'You mean like … as long as he hasn't … um …'

'Right as long as he hasn't "um",' said Cindy.

'So he's immortal?' asked Tamar.

'No, no, he will not live forever. He's the exact opposite of you in that respect. He will grow old and die eventually, but he cannot die an unnatural death.'

'How do we know he hasn't – "ummed"?' said Jack who was pretty certain that he had. Or would have soon.'

'He knows as well as anyone what would happen,' said Cindy. 'Why would he risk it? He won't, not yet anyway.'

'Do impure thoughts count as corruption?' said Jack. 'Because if they do I reckon we've got him.'

Cindy did not think so. Neither did anyone else. At least, they were not about to risk their lives on the possibility.

Because that was the other problem. What was this mysterious power that he had mentioned to Jack before he made his standard villain's exit?

'Are you sure he wasn't bluffing?' said Tamar.

'I *know* he wasn't,' said Jack. 'He looked so ... so ... *satisfied* with himself. I could just tell. Besides, I *saw* the guys who were going to make the "sacrifice". They thought I was him.'

'You know, the sooner we go in after him the better,' said Tamar. 'Before he takes on this power would be best. But even if it's too late for that, learning to use a new power takes time. *I* should know. We can tackle him while he's still finding his feet. Better than later on, when he's had some practice.'

'And do *what*, exactly?' said Denny. 'If we can't kill him ... wait a minute, if we can't kill him, why did he run? What was he afraid of?'

'It wasn't fear,' said Cindy. 'At least, not for his skin – so to speak. He knew that if he couldn't die at your hands, neither could you die at his. Not then. He didn't have the power. But now, who knows.'

'So, he had a plan. He ran because there was no point in hanging around?' said Tamar.

'He always was horribly logical,' said Cindy. 'Like a machine.'

'Well, it's a pity he wasn't programmed better,' said Jack nastily.

Cindy flinched.

'Jack,' said Denny sternly. 'You can take us to Ashtoreth's palace?' he ended surprisingly. Jack had been expecting a reprimand.

'Yes, but you have to sort of … let me.'

'*Let* you?'

'I'll have to sort of … kind of … But not exactly… er, take over your minds.

Just for a minute,' he continued hurriedly, 'and there's really nothing sinister about it. It's not like mind control … well it is, but … you see, you have to see the world the way I do. I have to show you.'

'Where exactly *is* this place?' said Tamar.

'It's a realm of the imagination.' said Jack. 'Down at the old warehouse on Culiver Street.' he pointed at Cindy. '*She* imagined that the old warehouse was a huge palace and because she was a god at the time she made it real. Gods understand the power of belief better than any other beings – the power of sustainable creation. Zeus created a palace on the top of mount Olympus. Odin … well you get the idea. When you go up there, there's no palace that you can find. It's not really there. But the gods lived there anyway. I'm sorry I can see it better than I can explain it.'

'That's all right,' said Denny. 'I think I get the general idea. How do you know all this anyway?'

'I … someone told me – well *showed* me,' said Jack awkwardly. 'He doesn't want to be involved, I promised I wouldn't say. He could get into trouble or something.'

From this, everyone jumped to the same conclusion; that it was Clive he was talking about.

'I've seen Olympus,' said Tamar inconsequentially. 'And we've *all* seen Valhalla.'

'And now Iffie's seen … what did you call it anyway?' said Jack to Cindy.

'It has no name,' said Cindy. 'Naming it would have been dangerous – made it too real. A thing with a name has an existence. And anything that has an existence requires a file.

You would have been able to find it in the mainframe. The home of the Olympians has no name. Only those taken there by the gods can enter. Valhalla is accessible to anyone because it has a name.'

'You couldn't have told us all this before?' said Denny impatiently.

'What difference could it make?' asked Cindy in a perplexed tone.

Denny took Cindy by the shoulders and gave her a gentle shake. 'Give it a name *now*,' he told her.

Cindy's eyes widened. 'Oh!' she said in shock.

~ Chapter Seventeen ~

IT REALLY WAS a magnificent dress, Iffie had to admit. But it just was not *her*. And she felt horribly exposed without her heavy makeup and several tons of jewellery. But Ash had insisted.

Iffie could feel the resentment burning away inside her. This was his idea of a relationship, was it? 'He tells me what to do, and I do it?'

The truth was, although she knew she was a pretty girl, she did not feel that she had inherited her mother's singular beauty, and her way of dealing with this was to cover her face up as much as possible, so that it was quite hard to tell what she really looked like. For all anyone knew, she might look like anything underneath – even her mother. It was a "look" rather than a natural appearance. She glanced in the large mirror at her naked face and saw quite a lot of her father's features looking back at her. His eyes for sure, and his razor like cheekbones, but her mother's dark hair and brows. The effect was striking but not beautiful, she thought. She looked like a million other girls, unlike Tamar, who looked like no other girls anywhere.

But what the mirror did not show her was that, in her own way, she looked like no other girl anywhere either. The fire behind the eyes, the shifting colours within that changed like a stormy sky with each different thought. Hypnotic eyes. Denny's eyes. (And he had never seen his own face as others saw it either. Never understood that when people looked at him, they did not see the thin, pale unshaven face, all they saw was his eyes.) And the faint blush under the skin that made her look as if she were lit by an inner glow. That same glow that she saw in her mother's face, but never in her own.

The best of both of them; that was what people saw in her, and what she would never be able to see in herself.

She stared at her reflection with dissatisfaction; it was worse than just a lack of her usual armour against the world. Her hair was scraped back into a demure pilgrim style, and the dress, although lovely, was white. A terrible colour on her she felt. She looked like that princess in that movie who lived a long time ago in a galaxy far far away. "Liar" or something like that.

Well, that was appropriate anyway.

* * *

It was not going to be a big ceremony or anything, far from it. Ash wanted to keep this pretty quiet for some reason. Perhaps the purloining of power from ancient dragons did not quite fit in with the image he wanted to project to his followers. But she was to be there. Ash needed an audience it seemed, even if it was just an audience of one. Why else would he be making such a big deal about this?

It was pretty horrible. Six fools all just lined up to die. No need for Athames here. Apparently the power would just pass to Ash naturally, as the power he had bestowed on them earlier passed back to him.

Iffie was unsure how this would work. That the power he had given them himself would return to him when they died made sense. But the power of the dragons resided in the Athames surely?'

Could another Athame take her father's power, for example? Did that power reside within him or the Athame or both?

She had always understood that if he lost the Athame he would lose his power also. But ... he *owned* the Athame, and, therefore, its power.

'All that is yours, surrender to me,' Ashtoreth was saying.

'All that is ours we surrender to you,' parroted the men.

And then each man stabbed himself with his Athame. And in a blinding flash of revelation, Iffie understood. It was damnably clever, in a horribly twisted sort of way. She was sure she never would have thought of it.

The power had nowhere else to go but back into Ashtoreth. It could not go into the Athame – it was already there, and it could not go into the man using it – he was using it on himself. It could only follow the direction of the only other power transfer taking place within these men as they died – and that was back to Ashtoreth. The path of least resistance.

The only change in Ashtoreth was a beatific expression that Iffie found particularly nauseating under the circumstances. There was no thunderclap, no flash of light, nothing.

'I hope you're happy with yourself, you murdering bastard,' she thought, bending down to look at the dead men on the floor as Ashtoreth stretched his limbs luxuriously. The poor things, they may have done terrible things, but *he* was ultimately responsible. For *their* deaths too. She hoped they would be forgiven and go to Heaven, after all. She would pray for them. No one else would. This man for example, she lifted his head, he looked as if he might have been quite nice (under different circumstances).

'What are you doing there?' asked Ashtoreth suspiciously.

'Praying for them,' she said truthfully. What did he fear she was doing, she wondered.

'Of course,' he said indifferently. They were nothing to him now.

'*Monster*,' she thought.

Then the change in him became apparent as he spread his wings. They were no longer the white, fluffy wings of an angel but the bat like wings of a dragon. Iffie took an involuntary step backwards, just in time, as Ashtoreth blew out a stream of fire from his open mouth.

He put a hand over his mouth and gave an embarrassed giggle as if he had just burped. 'Oops! Sorry,' he said. 'I didn't singe you did I?'

'No,' she said coldly. 'I'm fine. The tapestry is on fire, though,' she added, stalking swiftly from the room.

She ripped off the hated dress, pulled down her hair and changed into her customary black rags. She was just thrusting her fingers angrily into her rings as Ashtoreth entered without knocking.

She turned as he came in and gave him such a look as would have stopped most men in their tracks.

'You're angry,' he observed.

'No,' she said in wilful contradiction of the evidence.

'You are,' he insisted. 'Why?'

'I'm not angry,' she said. 'I just wanted to get changed.'

'You didn't like the dress?' He seemed puzzled.

'No.'

'Why didn't you say so?' he asked, so reasonably that she wondered if she had not, at least in some respects, misjudged him.

'Because I'm afraid of you.' Did not seem like the tactful thing to say at this point. 'I don't know,' she muttered.

'I thought it so much more suitable,' he said. 'These rags do not do you the justice you deserve. But if it's what you prefer …'

Iffie looked at him in wonder. There were two of him; it really seemed as if there were two of him. Three if you counted Jack … but that was being silly. Jack was Jack, but Ashtoreth was clearly schizoid. If only *this* Ash, the one looking at her now with the mute appeal in his eyes, was the *only* one. But there was the other one. The one who would kill followers, who had given him their trust and deserved his consideration, for his own gain. The one who could plot to murder innocent people including her own family. She must not forget that.

She had never told him that Cindy was alive and well and living with Slick. It had never seemed the right time and now, after all this time, was it a good idea? He was so unpredictable. He might choose to accuse her of lying. Or decide that if it were true then his mother had also betrayed him. And knowing Ash, it would not take a great leap from there to conclude that Iffie would betray him too one day and he might as well kill her now and save time. And all this was true, from a certain point of view. That was the trouble really. He had been brought up, not on lies exactly, but on such a twisted version of the truth that he had learned to twist everything he heard into a warped reality. It would be easy to pity him, but Iffie only had to remember his face when he had been about to kill Jack in order to harden her heart.

'I'll think about it,' she said. She wanted to get rid of him, but he did not seem to want to go.

She sat down quite deliberately in the window seat, gazing out on the fake stars twinkling prettily over the fake sea. But he did not take the hint. Instead he came and sat beside her.

'So, are you a dragon now?' she asked conversationally. Removing her hand from underneath his.

'No,' he said eagerly. Glad that she wanted to talk. 'No, I'm still me, I just have the power.'

'And the breath,' she said with a forced laugh.

'Oh, the dragons' power is far more than just breathing fire,' he said. 'That's just a little bonus.'

'Immortality,' said Iffie. 'But I never heard that dragons did magic at all. I mean I know you said all that stuff about morphing and healing and understanding foreign gibberish but …'

'Doesn't mean they couldn't,' said Ash. 'Fire magic, the most powerful magic in the universe. Fire is life.'

'Oh, god, it's cryptic nonsense time again,' she thought. 'He's never going to tell me. I might as well not bother.'

He moved closer to her and she tried to wriggle away, but there was no room on the window seat, he had her trapped. He was stroking her hair.

'I have learned a lot since we last met,' he told her. 'I can make you happy Iffie.' He leaned in and brought his face closer to hers. It took all her self-control not to rear back. He took her chin in his hand and lifted her face to his. She returned his gaze steadily and coolly, and he sighed and stood up. 'Not yet then,' he said and walked away without looking back. Iffie closed her eyes and gave a sigh of relief. *'Please, please, someone get me out of here!'*

* * *

'And it can't be a name that's already been used,' said Tamar. 'No Shangri La or Avalon or anything like that.'

'I know, I know,' said Cindy a little nettled. 'What did you think that I was going to call it Xanadu? Just let me think for a minute.'

If Cindy was stalling no one could blame her, but Denny, at least, did not think she was. It was hard to think of something like this, a name that had never been used for any place in the world anywhere. Particularly under pressure. Denny was trying too and could not come up with a single idea.

Cindy's brow was furrowed in thought. 'Slick's good at this sort of thing,' she said eventually.

'No, it has to be you,' said Tamar. 'No one can help you, it's your world. If you don't name it, it won't work.'

Denny stopped trying to think of something.

'But my mind's a complete blank,' wailed Cindy.

'So, what else is new?' muttered Tamar unkindly.

'You're not helping,' said Denny. 'Let's leave her alone to think, come on.'

'He's going to kill us all, you know,' said Denny gloomily.

'Depends on exactly what this new power of his actually is,' Tamar said. 'It might not be as great as he thinks it is, at least not against all of us together. But supposing it is, at least we *do* have a secret weapon against that eventuality,' she said.

'Cindy,' said Denny. 'Alive and well. *If* it works.'

'We nearly lost her,' said Tamar thoughtfully. 'The ultimate irony. *He* was the one who *actually* tried to kill her, without even realising it, when he went after all witches. If he'd succeeded … What do you mean, *if* it works?'

'He might not believe it's really her.'

'Let's not dwell on that eventuality shall we?'

'You were right you know, the faster we get to him the better.'

'Maybe we should try letting Jack take us in,' said Tamar.

They were not completely comfortable with this idea. They had all had Faeries in their heads before. It had not gone well. Mind you, if they could not trust Jack … After all, he could have been in and out of people's heads for years if he had wanted to, and he never had.

'Give her a bit longer,' said Denny.

'But Iffie … we don't know what he's doing to her in there.'

'I don't think he's doing anything to her,' said Denny wondering how much he should tell her about his suspicions.

'You mean because they were friends?' she said.

'Maybe *he* still thinks they are,' said Denny. 'He's got no reason to think otherwise, has he?'

'He called her a betrayer,' said Tamar with distressingly accurate recall.

'Jack didn't tell us everything,' said Denny.

'Well, anyway, even if you're right. He could still turn on her at any minute.'

Denny knew it – he was trying not to think about it. It was hard always having to be the voice of reason, the calming influence. Especially now, when all he wanted to do was rip the world apart to find his daughter.

'We'll find her,' he said

'And make him pay,' said Tamar clenching her jaw.

'Oh, he'll pay all right,' said Denny with a chilling calm that made Tamar shiver. There was something infinitely terrifying about this coldly furious Denny. He was like a distant stranger.

'He'd kill him without a second thought,' she thought. She herself was not so certain that she could do that.

'Anyway, no splitting up this time,' she said. 'We all go in the same way and if it works it works and if it doesn't we try the other way.'

'It'll work,' said Cindy from the doorway. 'Denny, open the mainframe we're all going to Kaya-Noelani'

* * *

Iffie was right about Ash. There *were* two of him, and both of them were in two minds at the moment. Making a total of four minds.

On the one hand, he was positively salivating for his revenge. He could hardly wait to use his new powers on his enemies and destroy them forever. On the other, he was sensing that Iffie was still not at a place where she could easily accept that. Then again, she had chosen *him*, which must mean that she believed in him. And there was, of course, the sense of an anticlimax. It was going to be far too easy in the end. And, despite the salivating, there was also a temptation to put it off, savour the moment. Do some private gloating over their inevitable destruction.

There can be no mind in the world more tortuous than that of an indecisive schizophrenic. Round and round he went – chasing the various arguments in his head. He was about to have the decision taken out of his hands entirely.

Iffie was wandering through the palace. She drew some curious looks from the various Nephelim around the place, but they all shied away from her as she approached. She could not tell if his was because she was from the unknown species known as "female" or because Ash had warned them off. Either way, it made it easier to move around the place. She was, however, under no illusions that her every move was not being reported back to Ash. If only she could give them the slip. She knew where she wanted to go. And she did not want him knowing about it. It was impossible to teleport in here, wherever the astral plane was it was far away from here, which also put invisibility out of the question.

'Come on Iffie, are you a witch or aren't you?' she chastised herself. 'There must be *something* you can do.'

The six men who had sacrificed themselves in such a dramatic manner had not exploded in the flash of white light that had become so familiar to them all. They had been drained and left as desiccated husks. Iffie did not know why it had happened this way with them and frankly she was not that interested. But she *did* want to see the bodies. Ashtoreth's reaction to her interest in them had been suspicious in the extreme.

'What are you doing there?' he had snapped.

And she had wondered at the time, 'what does he *think* I'm doing?' She had decided to find out. The problem was, if she went directly to the room where he had ordered them taken, (and she had no idea where that was, but one problem at a time) he would find out immediately, what with his goons spying on her the whole time.

She might not be able to make herself invisible here, but there was a trick that was less dramatic but almost as effective. She could fade … make herself, if not actually invisible, then at least, unnoticeable. It was called "ghosting". No one saw ghosts because they did not want to. It helped that not one of them would look her in the eye anyway. She made them nervous, they would much rather *not* notice her, despite their orders. She concentrated and sank into herself until she felt no more than a mere shadow on the wall, then she stepped out deliberately in front of one of them. He nearly walked right into her. He simply had not seen her. It took a lot of concentration to keep it up, and the Nephelim were so numerous that she had no respite as long as she was in the corridors.

'At least he hasn't got CCTV,' she thought. 'There's no way I could hide from that.'

A handy side effect of the ghosting was that sometimes echoes of you appeared in other places. There could easily be reports going to Ash that she was in the throne room or the south corridor or heading for her room. Anywhere, in fact, that she had passed through recently. It came from splitting your focus for a bunch of technical reasons that she had never bothered to master.

Her concentration was beginning to falter. That one had almost seen her, she was sure. He had done a double take and scratched his head anyway.

She dodged into a room hoping fervently that it was empty. It was not.

There were no Nephelim in here, nor was it the room where the bodies were stored. But, nonetheless, there *was* something in here. The answer to her question. 'What did he *think* I was doing?'

* * *

'What's that sound?' said Denny suddenly looking up from his keyboard. They were in the private study, away from all the clatter of the Agency, while Denny checked that the name Cindy had given her kingdom had been filed.

'I can't hear a thing,' said Tamar.

'Yes, strange isn't it?'

The whole world had suddenly gone silent. No screams, or cries for mercy. No marching feet. Through various feeds connected up through the mainframe, they had been keeping tabs on most of the Army of Righteousness' activity in the world and suddenly it had all stopped dead.

Denny typed frantically, checking file after file. 'It's everywhere,' he announced. 'He's recalled his armies – he must have.'

'What, *all* of them? Why?'

'Because he doesn't need them anymore?' said Denny shrugging.

'Oh *shit!*'

'We're going to need more help,' said Denny.

The phone rang.

* * *

Stiles stirred and opened his eyes. Well, they were in the place where his eyes should be anyway, inside the sockets were glowing orbs of light. He sat up stiffly like Frankenstein's monster. He turned his head to look at Hecaté who was staring at him with her hands clasped and her eyes shining almost as much as his.

The light faded from his eyeballs, and he gave his well-known grin. 'Don't suppose you've got a cigar on you have you?' he asked.

Hecaté manifested one for him. 'To hell with the rules,' she said uncharacteristically. 'This is a celebration.'

Stiles now took in his surroundings. 'I'm in hospital?' he said in surprise.

'You were very dead my love, but you have been reborn.'

Oh, yeah?' he said, 'as what?'

This was meant to be a little levity to distract him from the idea of having been dead, which was not a pleasant thought.

But Hecaté answered him seriously. 'That remains to be seen,' she said.

'What? What do you mean?'

'You are no longer human,' she said. 'You were dead for a long time. Only the gauntlet of Leir has saved you. But to do that it must also have changed you. No human can do what you have done.'

Stiles looked curiously at his arm. 'I'm still wearing it,' he said in surprise. 'I didn't realise, I can't feel Leir. He's not here.'

'It is a part of *you* now,' she said. 'Leir has gone.'

'Are you sure?' he said. 'I feel exactly the same as I always did. Maybe it's just drained of power, and as for the other thing, I mean you'd be surprised, maybe, how long a human can survive brain death … it can be as long as …'

'A year?' said Hecaté dryly.

That shut him up. He opened and closed his mouth like a fish, but no sounds came out.

'You are a god,' she said briskly. 'Accept it. It is not as if such things have not happened before. As long as you do not disappear swearing vengeance and build some castle in the air somewhere, from where you can harass the world it will be all right.'

'What are you talking about?'

'A lot has happened,' she said. 'Shall we talk about it?'

'We don't need to,' he said, his eyes widening in shock. 'I *know*.'

'I *told* you,' she said smugly.

When Stiles appeared with Hecaté, a large cigar sticking out from between his grinning teeth, it was as if time had suddenly spiralled backwards. Even the unaccustomed silence from the mainframe added to the effect. It was almost as if none of it had happened. With Cindy in the house and Iffie away, it was almost as if the last sixteen years had never happened at all, but had all been a very vivid dream. Stiles even looked as he had when they had first met him. Many lines of care and age had been smoothed from his face in the transformation. It was a profoundly disorienting feeling.

And Denny suddenly understood what Tamar had been trying to explain to him about his agelessness. Time stood still for you when you had eternity. For a moment, he was the same old Denny he had been when he had first met her all those years ago. All those years ago were just yesterday. He was not older; he had just been around longer.

Tamar ran to Stiles like an excited child greeting a favourite uncle and flung herself into his arms. But she drew back quickly afraid of hurting him. Her power was dangerous to humans; death was often the result of prolonged contact and she did not want to risk losing him again.

However, Stiles gathered her back up and swung her around joyfully until she was dizzy. When he put her down she gazed at him in wonder. 'What happened?' she asked. 'You aren't human anymore.'

'What, did you think I'd had a quick face-lift while I was in the hospital?' said Stiles.

'It was Leir,' said Hecaté. 'He sacrificed himself for Jack, and now the power is his.'

'There's a lot of it about,' said Denny.

'Speaking of which,' said Stiles. 'Don't we have a fairy tale palace to raid?'

Tamar laughed. Only Stiles could put the Herculean task before them that way.

'Uncle Jack?' said Jack coming into the room and, with those two innocuous words, time started up again properly.

He had come to tell them what they had already surmised. That the armies of the Nephelim had retreated, and that the Agency guys had no idea what was going on.

'We have to go now,' he said dancing up and down excitedly. He tugged on Denny's arm like a child after sweeties. 'Now, Denny, *now*,' he insisted.

'He's right,' said Tamar. 'Shortcut,' she added. 'No time to check the file exists. Straight into mainframe. 'Everybody – close file.'

* * *

'So this is your palace, is it?' said Tamar conversationally. It's ... nice.'

'It didn't look like this when *I* lived here,' Cindy said a shade defensively.

'No, I didn't think this gothic look was very you,' agreed Tamar.

'Is this the time for comparative décor?' asked Denny a little testily.

'Are we sure we've got the right place then?' asked Stiles.

'This is it all right,' put in Jack. 'I've been here before remember?'

'It certainly is,' said Denny, just seconds before they were attacked.

'I was just going to ask where everybody was?' said Stiles from the heart of the mêlée.

'Do be careful Jack,' said Hecaté anxiously. 'You don't want to hurt your back.' (It was going to take her some time to get used to Stiles's new situation).

* * *

Knowledge is power, and Iffie now had certain knowledge that gave her a lot of potential power. The question was – should she use it?

She had been sent for. 'Like a bloody skivvy,' she thought resentfully. Still, it probably meant that Ashtoreth was planning some other horrible thing that he wanted her to see. She ought to go and see what it was this time!

'Ah, he greeted her in the throne room. 'I'm glad you are here.' He frowned at her appearance but said nothing.

'I am leaving this place. *We* are leaving, I should say. Returning to the world and – perhaps a *slightly* more suitable outfit for meeting our subjects?' He suited the action to the word and she was once more in a shimmering white dress. This time her head was ornamented with a glittering coif and the dress was covered with a long velvet cloak.'

She bit her tongue, now was not the time.

Ashtoreth himself was looking magnificent. Normally he wore pretty ordinary clothes, if a bit spiffy, but at the moment, he was tricked out like a Roman emperor, gleaming breastplate and all. Iffie wondered why? Why that particular look? Henry VIII, for example, would have been just as appropriate as Caligula. Both had been murdering egomaniacs hadn't they?'

She hid her antipathy and joined him on the dais as he indicated she should, and then …

It was as if the whole world shook on its foundations. Iffie thought at first that he was doing it, but from the look on his face, it was something else.

The sounds of screams and explosions filtered through the palace. But Ashtoreth just smiled.

It sounds as if we have visitors,' he said pleasantly. 'I'm so glad we dressed for the occasion. It wouldn't do to greet such important visitors in anything but our Sunday best, now would it?' And he gripped her arm so tightly that she wanted to scream.

'I *was* going to go out and greet the people,' he continued. 'But perhaps I *do* have time to deal with this small matter first.'

Iffie kept her face carefully blank, aware that he was watching her closely.

He smiled, satisfied. 'But wait,' he said suddenly. 'This is not quite right now, is it? This is not how I planned it. Not here. It must be in public. Before the people. A lesson to all those who would rebel.'

'Ah, well. I have no more need of this place now,' he said. And when Tamar and Co ran into the throne room to be confronted with the sight of a gently smiling Ashtoreth standing beside a disdainfully magnificent Iffie. He dissolved the dream.

There was a moment of confusion before their vision cleared, and they were back at home. Ashtoreth was standing with Iffie on the dais in front of their own house.

'But he can't *do* this,' said Cindy. 'He doesn't have the power.'

'Correction,' said Tamar. 'He *didn't* have the power.'

'Looks like he got the hang of it fairly quickly after all,' said Denny.

They were all in the same relative position to Ashtoreth and Iffie, facing the dais from about ten feet away. Tensed and waiting.

Behind them was a large crowd of people, who had certainly not been there before. Ashtoreth clicked his fingers and several of the men in the crowd detached themselves and came forward to surround the gang. 'My Nephelim brethren can be found everywhere,' said Ashtoreth in explanation. 'I estimate that at least half the world's population are descendants of the Nephelim. And they always come when I call.'

'Appropriate location don't you think?' he continued into the silence. 'Well, whether you meant to or not, you have managed to make this house, in a certain context, into the centre of the world. People are always drawn here.' He swept an arm beyond their heads. 'Look and see. *I* did not bring them here.'

They remained silent. Waiting for the punch line.

'He thrust Iffie forward. 'Have you all met my new queen?' he said mockingly.

'What's she doing with him?' hissed Stiles.

'Didn't you hear,' said Denny through gritted teeth. 'She's his queen.'

'You mean she's *joined* him?'

'Looks that way.' He looked at Jack, who hung his head.

Iffie favoured them with an icy stare. Her slicked back hair gleamed in the light. Denny shuddered. His familiar Iffie had become distant and disturbing.

'Why is her hair wet?' said Tamar. As if *that* mattered, Tamar was not facing up to the situation.

'Perhaps he's been brainwashing her,' said Cindy.

This was such a Cindy comment that, for a moment, they nearly laughed out loud.

'I've had enough of this anyway,' she added and stepped forward and called her son's name.

His eyes swivelled towards her, and he stopped dead. He looked over her head at Denny. 'It's a trick.' he shrieked. 'Do you think I am a fool? *That* is *not* my mother. You *killed* my mother and now you think to mock me with this impostor. But I know all your tricks.'

'No, Ashtoreth,' said Cindy. 'It's me. He didn't kill me. He *saved* me. Please listen to me ...'

'Cindy,' snapped Denny. 'Get back here, it's not working, he doesn't believe you. He'll kill you.'

'He's just standing there,' said Stiles. 'What's he playing at?'

'Cat and mouse, at a rough guess,' said Tamar.

Slick came forward now; he was shaking like a leaf. 'Ash, hey son, it's me,' he said. 'It's true. That *is* your mother. You believe *me,* don't you? Why else would *I* be here?'

Ashtoreth looked coldly at him. '*You*?' he queried in an icy voice. 'You abandoned me, walked away, and betrayed me. Why should I listen to *you*? You stand with my enemies now.'

And he jerked his head and blew out a great swath of flame at Cindy, and Denny ran forward and grabbed her out of the way at the last moment.

Then he stepped forward. 'Okay,' he said. 'No one else dies. 'It's me you're after, isn't it? How about we settle this one on one?'

Ashtoreth leaned forward, letting go his grip on Iffie, and extended his dragon wings. He looked down in utter contempt at Denny. 'Why not?' he said. 'And what shall be the winner's prize?' He looked at Iffie. 'Not her at least, she has made her choice. Have you not?' He turned to her.

And now her eyes were full of tears. At the mercy of this monster, was her father, her mother, her family. They who had saved the world so many times. Now it was her turn.

'Yes, I have,' she said. 'I'm sorry.' And she withdrew the Athame that she had concealed within her clothes, the same Athame that she had found in the small room in the palace, the one that had been on the dead body of Ashtoreth's warrior, as drained and empty of power as the warrior himself, the Athame that he had been afraid she was stealing from the body (although at that time she had not thought of it) and thrust it straight through the armour breast plate, which it cut through like butter, and deep into his heart.

Denny pitched forward. 'No Iffie, it won't...' Then he stopped because it clearly *was* working.

Ashtoreth was shrieking in agony and fury, and the power transfer that lit up in sparks across the blade was phenomenal. As they watched, Iffie actually began to glow and was lifted off her feet to float in the air by the sheer volume of power being taken into the Athame that she was holding onto tightly.

Ashtoreth fell to his knees, and then as the blade was removed, he fell on his face. Weak, powerless, defeated, but still alive.

The remaining Nephelim dropped their aggressive stance and looked bewilderedly around them,

It was over.

Almost.

~ Chapter Eighteen ~

IFFIE FLOATED GENTLY back to the ground, still holding the Athame. 'Whoa,' she said. 'What a rush!'

Then she looked down at Ashtoreth who raised himself onto his knees and looked up at her with bleary heartbroken eyes.

'Betrayed,' he said, and he bowed his head and folded his now once more angelic wings over his face. And Iffie looked away from him at the frozen tableau of astonished spectators, who were all staring at her in amazement and shock.

It was Tamar who moved first. She made her way up to the dais and, acknowledging her daughter with a touch of the hand and a smile, bent down to the distraught Ashtoreth. A gasp ran through the crowd as she gently turned his face towards hers and took his hands in her own. He was looking at her in bewilderment and his expression was mirrored in the faces of every person there. Only Denny was not really surprised. Tamar was unpredictable. But always, always gracious in victory. Iffie just stood as still as a statue with her mouth open in shock until Denny lifted her gently off the dais.

'Kill me,' Ashtoreth said bitterly.

'Yeah, kill him,' came a voice from the crowd. 'Kill the monster.'

The crowd took up the cry. 'KILL HIM, KILL HIM, KILL, KILL …' They all knew him. His face was all over the planet, on posters, leaflets, televison. 'KILL, KILL, KILL …'

Tamar ignored them.

'No mercy,' she said to him. And he looked into her eyes and saw the love and compassion there and saw that she could see him, right down into his tortured soul, and yet she did not hate him for it. There was no devil in her eyes, the evil that he had believed in so fervently, that had driven him for so long, was a fiction, and, at that moment, something inside him broke forever. He understood that she was saying she was not going to kill him and offer him an easy way out. But he no longer cared what became of him. He was done.

'Forgive me,' he said. And Tamar smiled and put a hand on his head like a benediction. 'Stand up, she said.

As he raised himself up slowly, the crowd surged forward with murder in their hearts. But Tamar held up a hand and everyone stopped dead, as if hitting a wall. It was not often that Tamar unleashed her power like this, but when she did she was terrifying. The crowd backed off uneasily.

She turned back to Ashtoreth, and they looked at each other for a moment then they both nodded as if they both now understood something about the other.

'I know what you want,' she said. 'Peace.'

'There is no peace for me,' he said. 'Even in death.'

But Tamar smiled at him. 'I forgive you,' she said, and as he smiled back at her, a gentle, happy smile that made him beautiful, she touched his shoulder, and he turned into stone where he stood. His final and best smile captured for eternity.

'Be at peace,' she said. 'Forever.'

'Get rid of them,' said Tamar to Denny, indicating the crowd. Denny nodded. 'Right!' he said. He turned to Stiles. 'Give me a hand?' he said, handing Iffie over to her mother's care.

'Mum?' said Iffie in a bewildered tone, as if she really was not certain that it was. 'You just forgave him, just like that?'

'Just like that,' said Tamar with a smile. 'Hey, when you've been kicking around as long as I have, you get to realise one important thing about the universe.'

'Which is?'

'Shit happens – get over it. There's no point holding a grudge.'

'Will, I?' said Iffie. 'Be kicking around as long as you now?'

Tamar glanced at the Athame. 'Looks that way, doesn't it? I knew *something* would turn up,' she added complacently.

'But ... Ash, I mean he did all those terrible things ...'

'Hmm yes well, we'll just have to see what we can do about that, won't we?' said Tamar. 'You may have Earth shattering powers now my girl, but you're about to learn that there's no substitute for experience.'

'You mean you've had a brilliant idea?' said Iffie.

Tamar just winked.

'Okay,' said Iffie, 'who are you and what have you done with my mum?' Then she turned and saw Jack heading towards her with such a strange look on his face that her heart turned over.

Tamar's brilliant idea was to place Ashtoreth's statue in the Hall Of Images, a file in mainframe which housed the marble and stone images of imaginary Beings that relied on belief to exist. Usually deities. In doing this, because Ashtoreth was both himself *and* his image, Tamar was creating a paradox and, at the same time, turning his whole reign of terror, his entire existence, in fact, into a mere legend.

She admitted that she had been toying with the idea for some time, but had been uncertain as to whether she would be able to carry it out. It depended on getting close enough to him to turn him to stone. An impossibility when they had no idea where he was, and almost as impossible when he had the power of the ancient dragons, which Tamar had known he had as soon as she had seen him, and which she admitted far superseded her own power. But Iffie had found a way around both these problems, by simply gaining his trust. Wonderful! Tamar and Denny were very proud of her. But now of course, they had another problem. Teaching her to use her new powers responsibly, when those powers were far greater than their own.

But Iffie was more than willing to learn. She had seen for herself that her mother's compassion for Ashtoreth had achieved far more than cruel vengeance could ever have done.

By forgiving him instead of hating and punishing him, she had healed the world of all that he had done. That was the power of experience, just as her mother had said.

Iffie thought this was wonderful, 'I'm not so sure *I* could have done it,' she admitted. 'I hated him so much at the end.'

'You did what *you* had to, and I did what *I* had to,' said Tamar. 'But I'll tell you this, if you hadn't, I'd probably have killed him myself to get you back.'

'I know that too, but ... you didn't have to.'

'No, and there's no point in taking revenge on a beaten opponent. It usually ends up making things worse. At least, it never makes it better anyway. I've done a few things in my time that needed forgiving.' She glanced at Denny. 'There's my own path to redemption right there,' she said. 'I wasn't always this way you know, able to forgive. I carried a lot of bitterness and vengeance around with me for a long time. And, believe me, if *I* can learn, anyone can.'

Jack had sent up a prayer of devout thanks to – no one in particular, what with him being a Faerie – but devout thanks all the same, when Iffie had turned the Athame on Ashtoreth. At that moment, he suddenly saw it all so clearly. She had not betrayed them all at all, but had been trying to save his life in the only way she knew how. He owed her more than an apology now. But it would do for a start. He considered himself a great fool for not having realised it sooner.

'There was no way you could have known,' said Iffie. 'I have to admit, I *had* been acting pretty strange.'

'There's just one thing I don't understand,' said Jack. 'There was no way that that Athame should have worked on him, unless ...'

'Unless what?'

'Unless he was still … uncorrupted.'

'Is that a euphemism for being a virgin?' said Iffie baldly.

Jack winced. 'He was part angel, with incorruptible flesh supposedly, unless he …'

There was a silence. 'Admit it Iffie, you *did* like him a lot at the beginning, didn't you?'

'Not *that* much,' she said indignantly.

'Perhaps *too* indignantly?' he wondered.

'He probably just became vulnerable when he changed into a dragon instead of a half angel.' she added. And Jack knew that he would never know.

'Besides …' she broke off, not sure whether she should continue.

'Besides what?' he asked.

'Well …' She decided to bite the bullet. If it all ended in a lifetime of awkward silences and avoiding each other then so be it. 'He's no *you*,' she said pointedly.

Jack's eyes widened. 'But you were … I mean you were always hanging round with *him*. Always going on about *him*, and you stayed in contact with him Iffie, I *know* you did.'

'Were you jealous?' she asked slyly.

'Insanely,' he admitted.

'Well, that's all right then,' she said.

* * *

Iffie was not the only one to have been impressed by the power of forgiveness as demonstrated by Tamar. Jack remembered now, Erasmus's final words to him as he had left heaven.

'M- Mother?'

Cindy turned a look of complete shock on her face. 'J- Jacky… Jack?'

Jack hung his head; suddenly this did not seem like such a good idea. He had no idea what to say.

Cindy bit her lip and pulled nervously at her hair. 'I don't expect you to forgive me,' she said. 'But … I am so sorry for all that I have done.' A flash of understanding came to her as she said these words. 'And it *was* me,' she said. '*Only* me. It was never ... I closed my heart off because it hurt too much to feel,' she said. 'I loved you as if you were my own son. I left you behind because ... Well you see I told myself I only wanted Ashtoreth for his power, but that wasn't true you see, not really. He was my son, but you ... you were more a son to me than he was, I couldn't help that. You were my baby, the one I had raised. I left you behind for the same reason I left here in the first place. To leave love behind me. It was cruel and wrong and selfish, and I was a monster to do it. But I *did* love you. I just didn't want to.'

Jack stared at her. 'That can't have been easy to say,' he said. 'I remember you were always so proud and touchy. And then you just ... you take all the blame to make me feel better?'

'The blame *is* mine.'

'Well, *yes*, but ... it's got to be a hard thing to admit to. 'Specially to me. Do you ... still ... I mean ...?'

'I love you still,' said Cindy. 'But I know that I have forfeited any chance that you ...'

'I *do* forgive you,' said Jack and was amazed to feel a surge of relief and happiness swell through him as he said it. 'You were – *are* the only mother I've ever known. I want you back.'

* * *

Soon after Ashtoreth was laid to rest so to speak, Cindy sought out Tamar. 'We'll be going away for a bit,' she said. 'Slick and I. It may not have been real to the rest of the world. But I'll always know.'

'Look I'm sorry it ...'

Cindy held up a hand and shook her head. '*I* corrupted and ruined him,' she said, 'and then *you* saved him – as far as you could after all I had done. Thank you.'

Tamar bowed her head. 'Where will you go?' she said.

'Oh, here and there, I'm not sure. We'll be back sometime. In the meantime.' she held her arms out tentatively and Tamar grabbed her in a sudden hug. 'Don't stop saving the world,' said Cindy.

* * *

A night out was called for it was agreed, and Iffie graciously suggested Griff's, as long as they did not embarrass her in front of her friends.

'It's like an open mic' night on Thursday,' she said. 'Dad could sing. He hasn't sung for like an age and a half, and he's not bad for an old guy,' she teased. 'They have a band and everything.'

They went, and Denny did sing too.

Ali, Iffie's best friend since like forever, was in mourning to hear that Jack was off the market, but when Denny took to the stage she seemed to perk right up. 'Ooh, she nudged her friend. He's lovely isn't he?' (Ali was also a witch)

'Eeeuw!' said Iffie, 'that's my *dad*. Don't be *gross*.'

'*Is* it? But *look* at him. He has the body of a teenager.'

'That's the rumour,' said Iffie acidly. 'But no one knows where he keeps it.'

'Now who's being gross?' said Ali, as Jack snorted into his drink with sudden laughter. And she marched off in mortification.

'That was … weird,' said Jack.

'Oh, anything in trousers that one,' said Iffie dismissively. But in reality she was a little disturbed. The fact was, it was just coming home to her that her family were not like other people. Her dad, up on that stage, and her mum, fending off admirers with an icy glare, hardy looked any older than herself. And what was more, they never would. Pretty soon, they would be like contemporaries. The incident with Ali proved it. It was already happening.

She shrugged. Well if you can't beat them … or something similar but more relevant. In any case, might as well get with the program.

She had a pretty mean singing voice herself, and she could play the guitar like a maestro – something her dad had never mastered, despite years of effort.

She jumped up on the stage to cheers and catcalls, swung her guitar – which she had had to call for, because manifested ones were always out of tune – and struck up a beat.

'Come on dad,' she said. 'Let's rock this joint.'

* * *

'Peace at last,' said Denny later at home, referring to both the state of the world and the fact that the moment it had all never happened all the Agency people and magic folk who had hijacked their living space had mysteriously never been there at all.

'For now at least,' said Tamar. 'You know it never lasts long.'

'Killjoy,' said Denny lazily. 'Thank "us" for the paradox file,' he added. 'Ever since we thought of shoving old Askphrit into one it's been invaluable – 'specially this time. Have I told you you're a genius lately?'

'Not lately,' she said, preening in the mirror.

'Well you are,' he said.

'It was you *who* thought up the whole idea of a paradox file,' she said generously. 'Of course, it was also you who crashed the mainframe and fractured reality. That could have been really nasty I suppose. What if someone had slipped through the cracks?'

'Hey, it was *your* idea to crash it, not mine,' said Denny half sitting up on the bed – where he had been lounging – in his indignation. 'I'm just the technical support around here.'

'You're a lot more than that and you know it,' she said fondly.

'It was still *your* idea,' he said mulishly. 'And stop trying to get round me.'

'Well, they didn't anyway,' she said. 'We'd have heard about it by now if they had. And yes okay, it *was* my idea, I admit it. But you pulled it off beautifully,' she added snaking up the bed towards him.

'Forget it woman,' he said turning over on to his face in a mock sulk. 'You aren't getting around me that easily.'

She pulled him round to face her. 'Like you said,' she told him. 'Peace at last. 'Let's make the most of it while it lasts. Who knows what tomorrow will bring.'

~ Epilogue ~

WHEN THE BOTTLE washed up on shore, the castaway thought about the irony for a little while – he was supposed to *send* a message in a bottle, not receive one. But still, it *was* the most interesting thing that had happened in *years*. That's how boring it was here. It was a shame that it was obviously not the kind of bottle likely to contain spirits, particularly considering that it was still tightly sealed.

He sat and looked at it for a very long time – well there was no point in rushing it. It might be years again before anything else happened. That's the problem with a desert island. It's not all swimming in the lagoon and falling in love with your sister.

He had never had a bottle before (well, he had never had *anything* except coconuts and sand). It gave him an idea. He *could* send a message in a bottle now. Well, he could if he had something to write with. And something to write on.

Eventually he opened the bottle.

When he regained consciousness, the Djinn was still there – a touch of the sun? After all these years, it seemed unlikely.

It was grinning at him, apparently enjoying the joke immensely.

'Wish I could see what's so damn funny,' thought the castaway. 'I could do with a good laugh.' Then he realised that *he* was the joke.

'Nice place,' said the Djinn. 'And I like the hair. What is that look called, shabby chic?'

This was a bit rich coming from this overdressed buffoon, thought the castaway.

'This is a desert island,' he said. 'I was *shipwrecked*.'

'I'm talking to a figment of my imagination,' he thought. He was not in the least distressed by this idea. He had done it before. But they were usually women, and they were not usually so convincingly real. They did not usually talk back to him either, although he had often wished they would.

'Sorry.' said the Djinn. 'I didn't realise. I thought you were some sort of a hippy or rock star or something and talking of that …'

'Who are you? What do you *want*?'

'Straight down to business eh?' said the Djinn. 'Do excuse me, I just thought we could socialise a bit first, you know, get to know each other, but have it your own way – you are the master after all. And speaking of that, it's really more a question of what *you* want.'

'Well, getting off this island would be favourite,' said the castaway.

'We-ell yes, I can see that,' said the Djinn. 'But is *that* really the limit of your ambitions? I can give you so much more you see. Three wishes. Anything you want, anything at all. Three wishes,' he repeated, to emphasise his point.

'Three eh?' said the castaway. 'So if you get me out of here – and that really is *wishful* thinking,' he punned atrociously. 'I'd still have two left like?'

'But if you make the *right* three wishes, you see, you could get yourself off this island and have everything in the universe that you can dream of,' said the Djinn helpfully. 'Supposing you had the same powers that I have for instance.'

'Why, what powers do you have?' asked the castaway interestedly.

The Djinn drew himself up importantly. 'I am omnipotent, omniscient *and* immortal,' he said.

'I wish *I* was,' said the castaway gloomily.

'Well, that was easy,' thought Askphrit, carefully burying the bottle deep in the sand. 'That should hold him for a few thousand years at least,' he thought. 'I don't want this one coming after me. No mercy this time.

'Speaking of which, I wonder what ever happened to Tamar Black?'

THE FINALE!

TAMAR BLACK TAKES HER LAST BOW

<u>Tamar Black – Pantheon</u>

Denny should never have crashed the mainframe!

Rebooting was the easy bit, making sure all the deleted files *did not* reboot was a little harder. He should have been more careful.

Now the mythological age is back, in fact, it never went away. The Greek gods are still on Mount Olympus, and the clerks in mainframe are furious and insisting that Tamar and Denny fix it. Right now!

The only problem is, they have to go back to when the age of myths was supposed to have ended and make sure that it does.

Well, that's not the *only* problem …

Also by Nicola Rhodes

SCI 'ON The Shadow Worlds

The first book in the SCI 'ON Trilogy

Whenever a decision is taken that is of significance to the world, the world divides and two alternate futures are created. In the beginning, there was only one world. That world we name SCI 'ON. All other worlds that sprang from it, we name the shadow worlds. Some believe SCI 'ON is the only real world and that all others are mere reflections, hence the name. Others believe that all the alternate worlds are equally real and important – however they may have come into being.

Whatever the case, one thing is certain. If SCI 'ON itself – the cradle of creation– were to be destroyed, all other worlds would cease to exist. For SCI'ON is the mainspring and without it, the shadow worlds would have no point of origin.

Johnny Hammond is not your ordinary computer nerd. He has the makings of a hero. When a mysterious man shows him the way To SCI 'ON, Johnny becomes obsessed. And only he can find a way to get there through the myriad shadow worlds that stand in his way. But someone doesn't want him to get there.

From earliest childhood, Ryan and Kai have been best friends. The fact that they come from separate universes is not allowed to stand in their way.

As they grow up, they realise that this ability to travel between the worlds is no mere coincidence, as their ultimate destiny unfolds.

SCI 'ON II - Legacies

Even his own mother, from the moment he was born, was afraid of Talvas, for she knew whence he had come and wondered what his power would be.

Talvas Firebrand, later known as Talvas de Bellême and "The Destroyer of Worlds" was the son of Toros the fire god. His story and that of the other Undying begins on SCI 'ON back at the beginning.

Watching him from his citadel beyond time is Johnny Hammond, the only man in all creation capable of defeating Talvas and stopping the slaughter of millions.

What will happen when these adversaries finally meet again in a new cycle of time?

About the Author

Nicola Rhodes often can't remember where she lives so she lives inside her own head most of the time, where even if you do get lost, it's still okay.

She has met many interesting people inside her own head and eventually decided to introduce the rest of the world to them, in the hopes that they would stop bothering her and let her sleep.

She has been doing this for ten years now, but they still won't leave her alone.

She wrote this book for fun and does not care if you take away a moral lesson from it or not.

You have her full permission to read whatever you wish into this work of fiction. As she says herself:

"Just because I wrote this book, doesn't mean I know anything about it."

www.ingramcontent.com/pod-product-compliance
Lightning Source LLC
Chambersburg PA
CBHW050425260626
47156CB00003B/1152